TRUTH OF THE SHADOWS

SLADE TEMPLETON

Los Angeles, California, USA

Truth of the Shadows
Copyright © 2020 Slade Templeton

Published by:
New Galleon, an imprint of Genius Book Publishing
31858 Castaic Road, #154
Castaic, CA 91384
https://NewGalleonBooks.com

All Rights Reserved. No part of this manuscript may be reproduced by any means without the written permission of the publisher, except for short passages used in critical reviews.

This novel is a work of fiction. Any resemblance to actual places, events, or persons living or dead is completely coincidental.

ISBN: 978-1-947521-41-4

200808

Praise for TRUTH OF THE SHADOWS

"A dark and spiraling journey into the abyss, TRUTH OF THE SHADOWS is a brave and unflinching supernatural thriller that manages to defy expectations."

—John Palisano,
President, Horror Writers Association

"The author's rich and dark psychological landscape shows a suspenseful tale of evil iconography, while providing room to create a mysterious world. The decisive intensity of the characters comes from the narrative's beyond world experiences. A book well worth picking up!"

—Brian Perera,
Cleopatra Entertainment/Records

"Enthusiasts of mysterious and suspenseful psychological horror will be keenly intrigued by Slade Templeton's new novel TRUTH OF THE SHADOWS. The book, which explores secrets of the past and the frisson of the unknown, is augmented by audio/visual components for a truly immersive and otherworldly experience in altered reality and perception."

—Jen Dan,
The Big Takeover

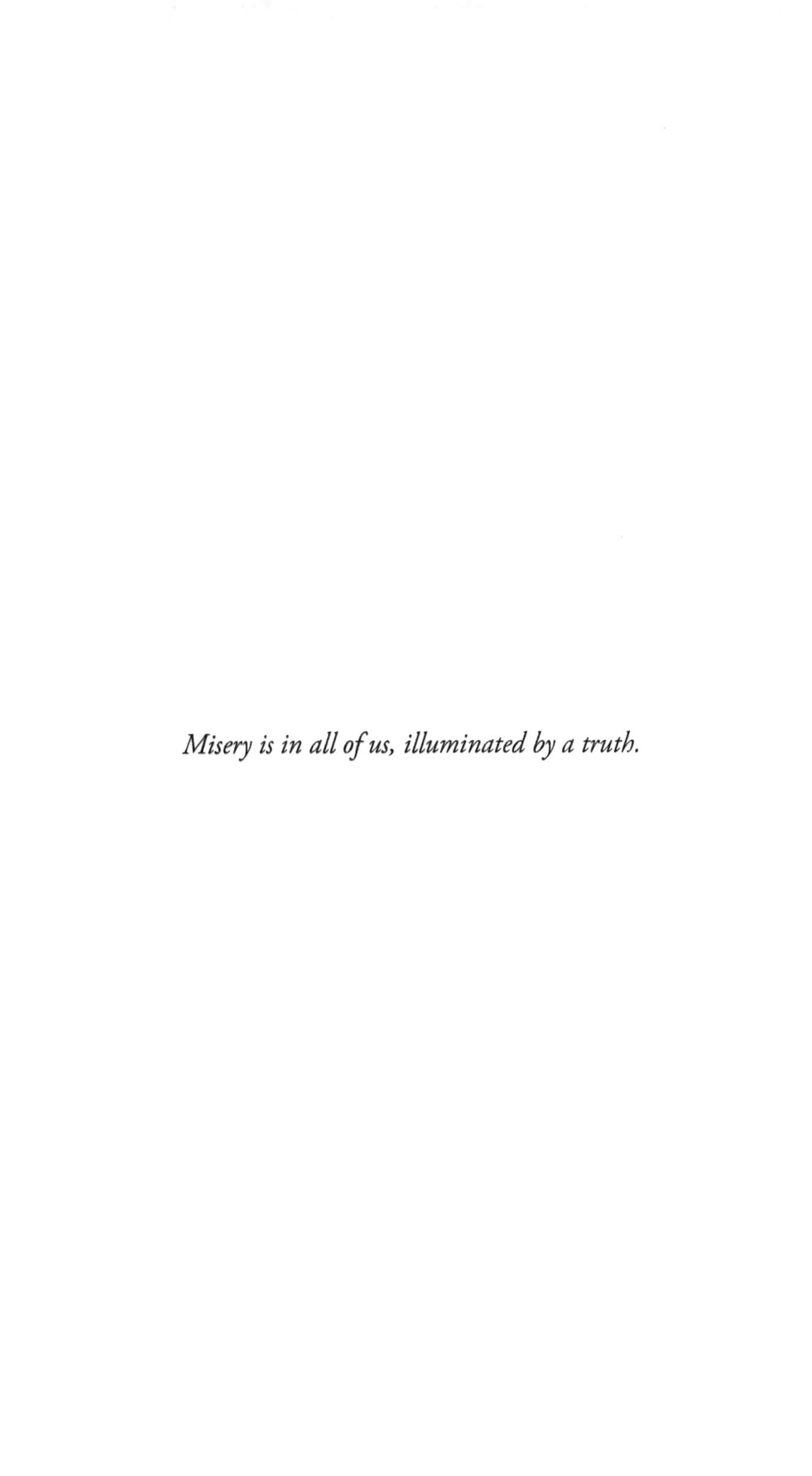

Misery is in all of us, illuminated by a truth.

A Note from the Author

I wrote *Truth of the Shadows* after having a burnout from overworking when I was on the way back from a German tour with my band Crying Vessel. I was looking through the window of the bus at the rolling hills somewhere outside of Berlin, and at that moment, I concluded I had lost my way, my passion. Wanting to dive into something "outside of music" for a bit, to give myself some peace of mind, I chose to do something I have always wanted to do; write a novel. Much of *Truth of the Shadows'* storyline is based on actual events that took place in my life years ago. My past is a very dark place, as it is for many others. I had a wonderful childhood, yet it was surrounded by a darkness deep inside, and many bad decisions stacked up over time. As successful as I appeared outwardly, inside I was ripping apart. Many of my decisions were made to numb this inner pain, leading me to arrive at death's doorstep in April 2013, and subsequently arriving in a mental ward for evaluation. After many years of battling drug addiction, which stemmed from a life spent in the music industry and touring the world, I was brought to my knees once and for all. One of the strangest things that can happen to a person is waking up in a mental ward from a decision they made while high on drugs, only to realize they are sober now and have no mental illness of their own. I was inspired by this, by what I had witnessed in the hospital, and by those healing on their own terms. Later, while getting my life straightened out, I spoke at mental wards and drug rehabilitation centers to help others battling their own turmoil and restless thoughts. This was the start of my healing process. As of 2020, I am 7 years clean. I have completed a novel inspired by the experiences from those dark times and I have made it into paranormal horror fiction for the world to enjoy. *Truth of the Shadows* is that novel.

Making lemonade out of lemons is an understatement in my case. In *Truth of the Shadows*, I attempt to make entertainment out of agony. I did not write this book to glorify mental illness, as I and others around me have suffered throughout our lives. If anything, my goal is to showcase the horrors that one must face and to show that we are all not that much different from one another, and should never pass judgement. Absolution can be one step away at any given time, no matter which side of the glass you are on. Sometimes, you just have to look inside.

With hope and love,
Slade Templeton
Bern, Switzerland
July, 2020

*This book is dedicated to
those who knew me in my darkest moments
and those who know me now.
And to all those who lost themselves to the hardest battle,
one of introspection—a wicked prowl.*

TRUTH OF THE SHADOWS

Prologue

The frost melted into the air above the damp ground, creating a shimmering fog that seeped into the moonlight. At the edge of the forest's dark fringe stood a meadow with mud huts sprinkled throughout, covered in blackened sod. The howls of the wolves seemed to hold longer than usual into the night.

The smell of burning wood cut through the cold air, and a thick plume of smoke rose over the treetops near the deep ravine. Hidden behind the tree line was a tall, thin man with toughened, leathery skin. Ash covered his hands, which hung from his arms like pendulums of soot and flesh. Fatigued and on the cusp of death, he wore nothing but a long dirty loincloth held to his fragile body with frayed twine. A glimmer of firelight touched his painted cheek, the reflection of flames danced in his dark eyes.

His head filled with pain and suffering, he gazed toward the fire pit in the small clearing while his tribe chanted ancient songs. As the drums grew louder, so did their voices, and they circled the fire with stomping feet. The man quietly worked his way deeper into the forest and along the path, hanging his head low, regret haunting his face. In the distance, the chanting rose to crescendo, then fell into a low-level hum before tapering off into silence. He knew the sacrifice had been made.

The muddy path stretched out before him. As weary as he was, he continued. At once, the forest became eerily silent. His path took him from light to darkness, then back to light again, as the moon peered from the branches of the trees above.

"Father," a voice whispered from the dense forest next to the path. Instantly he recognized it, and he recoiled. For the first time in his long experience, the trees were motionless. "You knew they would do this to me."

Listening for the voice, he parted the branches of a tree, peering deeper into the darkness to find where it was coming from. Yet no one was there. The voice was that of a young girl, but he couldn't see her. The voice echoed back and forth through the obscurity of the forest. The sound of screams and moans began to coalesce back into the child's voice.

"What do you want from me?" he whispered, anxiously hoping for a reply.

Abruptly, a chilling wind blew through the trees, and with it something circled around him before moving farther back into the woods. The man remained motionless on the muddy path and looked around in despair. Struck with terror, he stood in place, uncertain of what to do next.

"Tell me what you want from me!" he cried, again receiving no response.

The cold wind became heavy gusts, blowing through the trees. The branches swayed, and dead leaves swirled around him in the crisp air. Branches and twigs crackled and snapped as some unseen entity approached.

"*What do you want?*" he pleaded. "There was nothing I could do!"

"Be silent," the voice commanded sharply.

Whispers surrounded him, leaving him no escape. Agony and an overwhelming regret overtook his mind. The wind blasted him with a deafening voice, shattering the whispers: "You never believed!"

The man was lifted high off the ground, then pulled from side to side, dancing violently with the winds themselves. His arms twisted and lacerations crossed his face, with no explainable cause. His body was held higher and higher above the path before being turned over and hurled back to the ground, a mangled piece of flesh and bones the winds had decided not to keep. Unable to move, fading thoughts ran through his head. The man lay with his mouth wide open, his eyes fixed on the stars.

As he took his last breath, he heard her voice one final time:

"Now you will believe."

Chapter 1

"A self-aware shadow is something to fear. It will always be part of
you, without ever realizing it is of its own mind."
—Greek engraving (circa 180–220 BC)

Noise filled the halls that night. Whimpers and cries coming from the rooms. Footsteps resonated down the hallways from the direction of room 207. This was where the Bible-clenching Matthew liked to pace in circles at night. Whenever he wasn't in the hospital's chapel, he was preaching his way through the hallways. Quick, frantic skin-to-tile slapping struck the floor as he vigorously read the words of God.

"Behold, the Lord came with many thousands of His holy ones! He will come to execute judgment upon all and to convict all the ungodly of all their ungodly deeds, which they have done in an ungodly way!"

In his mind, he stood before a thousand worshippers at some kind of twisted religious rally. He then held his Bible in the air with both hands.

"The angels! I see them! They come to me in my dreams, and I see them in my waking life! I see them everywhere around me! Don't you see them too? The beautiful angels walking the earth to protect us! With the fire in their eyes! It must stop! They must stop taking us from our loved ones! They hunt for the weak, and only God will prevail! Am I the only one with this gift to see? You will believe me when it happens and—"

The slam of a metal door coming from another hall halted Matthew in midsentence. The door slammed so loudly that the entire C Ward went dead silent. The crying ceased. No more laughter. "Reverend Matthew's" words of God froze in his throat. Running boots replaced the sounds of Matthew's footsteps.

They wheeled an old restraint chair down the hall toward Matthew's room. On C Ward, the sounds of boots meant one thing: the nurses were coming. With one thing in mind, they came to shut Matthew up and give him a good dose. Scrambling back toward his room, Matthew almost made it, but they grabbed him and forced him into the harness of the restraint chair.

"You can't blind me from seeing any of this!" Matthew shouted. "You must obey! This truth is the only truth! You… musst… underrrrrr…" His preaching drifted off like a vinyl record slowly coming to a stop.

They knew the drugs had begun to work, kicking in heavily. The patients around the ward called it the "Thorazine shuffle"— and for good reason. When the nurses gave them just enough, they'd walk around the ward like the half-dead, searching for their next foggy-headed thought. With a full dose, they'd enter a world of nothingness, a comatose state. Out cold, they were placed back in their bed as a mother does when her child falls asleep in front of the TV. But the nurses didn't care for bedtime stories. There was no counting sheep, no fairy tales for the patients. All they desired when they pushed that plunger down was the sweet sound of silence on the ward.

Knocked out, Matthew was taken to his room. Several male nurses hunched over him, waiting for another sound to fall from his mouth. They followed protocol and took his vitals to make sure he was still alive under the medicated haze of the drugs. The heart monitor beeped like a metronome, and the whirr of an air pump could be heard as the blood pressure cuff closed the circulation to one arm. Satisfied, they disconnected him from the machines and left the room. Heading to their offices, they laughed amongst themselves about the latest gospel Matthew had shared.

The silence set in, and C Ward fell asleep, like Matthew. The only noise left in the building came from the security station, the low volume of the guard's small TV presenting his favorite late-night talk show. They were interviewing yet another celebrity, asking what they'd had at their last meal and other useless information. In the middle of the night, the selection of thrilling TV was limited. Instead of settling for infomercials, celebrity gossip helped pass the time. The security guard, a man named Adam who'd started at Cottage Grove only a few months earlier, sat mindlessly watching the screen. Numb to the world, as though he were also in a trance, he hung on to every word coming from the television. Adam had the ghastly pallor of a basement-dwelling gamer, which wasn't too far from the truth. A little overweight and innocent as could be, he wore his brown hair in a crew cut, obviously trying to portray the "cop look." His haircut was the toughest thing about him.

"Oh, my—that is, like, totally my favorite drink too! Wow! We're twins!" said the senseless TV host.

"So, Tanya, you were amazing in your role in *Last Night's Standoff.* How did it feel to play such a heroic character?" asked the host.

The clock ticked slower and slower into the night as Adam continued watching, munching away on his sour cream and chives potato chips. He had the oversize bag of chips in his lap and his cell phone in his hand, searching for reviews of *Last Night's Standoff* on popfilmcharts.com. A door down the hall cracked open. It was room 206, the room across the hall from Matthew's.

Sscccrrrrcchhh…

The door creaked open, hesitantly, as if the person opening it was fearful about what might lay on the other side. It was pulled back just enough to let in some light from the hallway.

"Hey, Shane," someone said. "You awake?"

Everything remained silent, except for soft snoring coming from inside the room.

"Shane, you in there? They did it to me this time. I think they finally gave me the red dose. I can feel it. I know this'll be the last time we talk and I can spread the truth. I want you to know they'll come soon for you. Stay away from the angels with the fire in their eyes. They'll hunt you down if you aren't careful."

Matthew shut the door and tiptoed back to his room.

Despite their best efforts, the nurses gave Matthew only enough Thorazine to put him in a medicated stupor for a short time. They were lucky they didn't simply kill him. But this loose regard for medical protocols was nothing new at C Ward. Just another night at Cottage Grove Hospital. Dr. Hoffmann would be arriving in a few hours for his morning rounds. By then, Matthew would be deeply asleep and dreaming of the angels.

❧

Dr. Joseph Hoffmann was always on time. Always. He was careful and precise with everything he did. At 7:30 a.m. on the dot, Joseph arrived at work every weekday—and often, on the weekends, when he was on call. At Cottage Grove Hospital, the small town's psychiatric hospital, Joseph held the position of head psychiatrist in the high-security unit.

Cottage Grove was a small town nestled near the foothills of the Cascade Mountains of Oregon. Like most small-town hospitals, Cottage Grove Hospital had a small but tightly knit staff keeping it all afloat. Joseph was captain of his ship. Though in his late fifties, he had maintained an air of youth. He was tall and fit, his salt-and-pepper hair styled fashionably. His strong good looks matched his demeanor and personality. He was proud of his reputation and enjoyed the respect that it brought him. Many of his colleagues and staff at the hospital knew him to be a wise mentor and earnest doctor, but he could also be closed off to the world around him. From the outside looking in, it seemed like everything was going his way. But those who knew him best understood the burden he carried with him everywhere.

Joseph's office was located at the far end of Hall 1, the first of four halls that formed a cross. Each of the three wards were low buildings set apart from each other, with their own staff of nurses and security personnel. Surrounded by a wide-open pasture before a thick forest, the buildings at Cottage Grove Hospital were as isolated as the patients inside. Each morning, Adam greeted Joseph at the hospital entrance before he clocked out for the day. Adam and Joseph had a certain type of mutual understanding. Adam would keep Joseph briefed about the goings-on around the ward, while Joseph would give him a bit of respect and attention, which was welcome in Adam's boring front desk security job.

"Good morning, Adam. How are you today?"

"Fine, Dr. Hoffmann. You sleep well?"

"Yes, yes, thank you. Anything new on the ward?"

"Yeah," Adam said eagerly. "Diane's back on suicide watch. She's still asking for her son and says if she doesn't get to see him soon, she'll off herself."

Joseph heaved a sigh. "Again? Lovely. Looks like another typical day on C Ward."

Adam smiled knowingly. Even though he was merely a security guard, Adam knew more about the cases on the ward than the doctors or nurses would suspect.

"Thanks for the update, Adam. Keep up the good work."

Joseph continued on his way toward his office, but Adam stopped him before he was more than a few steps away.

"Oh! Dr. Hoffmann, I almost forgot. Matthew was preaching again. I mean *really* preaching. It was the same story about the angels this and the Bible that. They hit him up with a shot of Thorazine. Later, I saw on the monitor that Matthew had slipped into 206 and talked to Shane. Something about how he was going to die from the 'red dose' the nurses had given him. His disruptions have been getting worse—and now he's going around telling other patients the nurses are dosing him with lethal medicine. It's upsetting the other patients. We can't have that happen, can we?"

Joseph shook his head. "No. Don't worry. This will be all handled. I'll talk with him. Whatever is said about the doctors or guards being threatening to the patients here—well, that happens. I'm sure it's just run-of-the-mill paranoia. The patients are going to feel that way about us no matter what. After all, we're a threat to their worlds. You'll get used it. We all do. Their mental illness, which can seem so peculiar to us, is their reality. I'm sure your reality seems just as strange to them as theirs does to us." Joseph paused and smiled. "You're doing fine, Adam."

"Thanks, Doc. See you in the morning! I pulled my eight hours, so I'll be heading home soon."

"Get some rest, Adam. See you tomorrow."

Joseph turned back around toward his office and continued with a slight wave of his right hand, his briefcase in the left, and his eyeglasses resting on top of his head. His daily journey through the main lobby took him past the recreation room where the patients spent most of their time. The nurses had categorized the patients, and though Joseph publicly disapproved, he had adopted some of the terms, which could be quite descriptive and colorful. There were the "hall walkers," patients who paced the halls or walked in circles. There were the "gamers," who always had a rivaling competition of checkers or Battleship going on. Then there was the resident "piano player," who could be found playing a non-existent piano on the edge of a table in the corner. It was a bit like an adult daycare, but with psychotropic medication. Their activities director did her level best to keep the active patients engaged, but it was a losing battle. Too many of them didn't even realize they were in a hospital, let alone have the awareness to notice if they were bored or getting into trouble.

Joseph always made it a point to glance into the activities room on the way to his office to see if there were any new faces. Seeing none, he gave a nod and a smile to everyone as he walked by. Once to the end of the hall opposite the main lobby, he slid his key into his office door, and with a quick jiggle of the knob, the door opened.

He set his briefcase on the floor next to his neatly kept desk. Thus began his morning ritual.

Flip on the coffee machine.

Turn on the computer.

Wait for the load screen.

Pour coffee.

Before the computer fully turned on, he looked up toward the black screen and caught his reflection staring back at him.

What if she were here? What would be different?

He spun his wedding ring on his finger and asked himself those same questions every morning. Was it really twenty-five years gone? What if it had never happened?

There had been a time when he woke up to Helen's smiling face. His morning routine then was to give his new bride a kiss on the cheek and say "I love you" before taking his morning shower and getting dressed. Then he would grab his belongings and head out the door to Cottage Grove. It was his first year as a resident psychiatrist there, and his marriage was perfect. His life had finally fallen into place. He had worked very hard on his education and wanted the best life for Helen and himself. But Joseph never grasped how to relax or how to balance his professional drive with the other parts of his life. Helen had repeatedly warned him that he would die of a heart attack if he kept working as hard as he did.

On that fateful day, Joseph had promised to meet Helen for lunch, but then work got away from him. Joseph could be so stubborn when it came to his work, so rather than argue with him, she went for a run.

✌

12:30 p.m., Cottage Grove, Oregon; Twenty-Five Years Earlier

A three-tone chime resonated over the hospital's overhead intercom.

"Dr. Hoffmann, report to the front desk. Dr. Hoffman to the front desk, please."

"Yes, Jocelyn?"

"Dr. Hoffmann, these police officers are here to see you."

Joseph brightened. He came around the front desk and clasped the first man's hand. "How are you, Jeff?"

"Fine, fine," Jeff said absently. "May we speak with you privately?" Joseph led the men down Hall 1 to his office.

"To what do I owe the honor of a visit of three of Cottage Grove's finest?"

Jeff didn't return Joseph's jovial smile. "Let's sit down and talk, Joseph."

Up to this point, Joseph had thought little of the police wanting to speak to him. It wasn't the first time the police needed his help. But something of Jeff's demeanor made him uncomfortable. He had only ever come to deliver another patient from the local lockup. There was no prisoner with him this time, only the two other officers.

As he turned the knob to his door, he said, "Have a seat, gentlemen. Would you like something to drink?"

"No, thank you."

Sergeant Wilson and Joseph sat on opposite sides of his long wooden desk. The other two officers stood behind the sergeant, hanging over each of his shoulders like wings.

Jeff looked down, then up to make eye contact with Joseph. "We've known each other for a while now, right?" He hesitated, but cut off Joseph's response. "There's no easy way to tell you this. Helen was hit by a car around eleven this morning. When we arrived on the scene, she was already gone. The EMTs did all they could to revive her. I'm sorry, Joseph. I know…" But he couldn't complete the thought. It didn't matter if he did. Jeff could see Joseph had gone entirely blank.

Joseph's heart shattered into a million pieces. His face was white as snow. He was staring at an empty space on the wall above the door between the two standing officers' heads. His eyes welled, and then he broke into tears, each drop filled with a different emotion.

Pain.

Anger.

Agony.

Regret.

Disbelief.

It was all there, flooding in his head. The news pierced his heart like a dagger—and he placed the blame on himself.

"If I'd met her for lunch…" Joseph murmured.

"Joseph," Jeff said, sitting forward in his chair. "You can't blame yourself. Would you like me to arrange for a professional to talk to you? They're—"

"Professionals?" he asked, coming out of his stupor. "You have people who can help?" Joseph shouted. "This is a psychiatric hospital, for heaven's sake. What are they going to do, make none of this happen? How would you respond to news like this? I just… I … I can't…"

Joseph kept mumbling, slipping from anger into deep sadness and regret. With each rapid breath, he knew his world would never be the same. He felt like his wedding band was turning into lava around his finger, burning through to his soul.

☙

Ever since that day, Joseph spun the ring as part of his morning routine. It was a tic, a comforting mechanism he didn't even realize he was doing. With the coffee turning cold next to him, the ring felt tighter around his finger as each second passed and he waited for the computer to boot up. The darkness of the screen mirrored the obscurity that lay deep within Joseph's heart.

Joseph continued to stare at the black screen, his reflection still glaring back at him. Then the screen flickered and turned on. The flash blindly brought him back to the present.

"Dr. Hoffmann, there's a call for you on line one."

Chapter 2

"Fears that are dormant in the heart stay awake in the mind."
—stone tablet (Qin Dynasty, circa 221–206 BC)

A flashing light next to line one blinked, and Joseph picked up the phone.

"This is Dr. Hoffmann."

"Joseph! Hey, ya booger! How are you?"

"Anna!" Joseph had moved from Wiesbaden, Germany to the United States for college when he was eighteen, but he and his younger sister Anna had remained close. Anna was someone Joseph could confide in without reservation. She was one of the only people who accepted and understood him for who he was. And she never judged him for his past or the darkness he often lived with.

"I'm good. Just arriving to work. Same ol' same ol'. What about you? How are things with Mark? I hope things are better for you both."

"It's very much back and forth," Anna said. "I think the stress of Mom's health gets to us at times. I know it's hard on him to see me have to take care of Mom. He knows how much it affects me and he hates to see me hurting. He is supportive, but the stress I bring home makes things hard on both of us. I know I spend a lot of time at the old folks' home, but it's what I have to do."

"I'm so sorry. I truly wish I were there to be able to help more. I think about being there a lot. How's Mom doing?"

Anna sighed. "She's getting worse, Joseph. She seems to always get worse right when I think she might be getting better. Lately it's been a nonstop effort to make sure she's comfortable. It's exhausting. I think she's ready to be with dad. I mean, she's been ready ever since he passed away ten years ago."

"She must be… It's always such a struggle to hold on when you've lost so much. I'll try to come for a visit as soon as possible."

"That would be great," Anna replied. "So look, I also was calling about what we should do with all of Mom and Dad's belongings. I know you're thousands of miles away, but I'm certain Mom would love for you to have some of these boxes of things she held on to for us."

Joseph leaned back in his seat and smiled. "Of course, I'll take some of the stuff. Thanks so much. I'm sure some of those boxes will bring back good memories. Remember all the times we went up north to the sea? And how Dad always looked so much like he was from Netherlands—since he was so tall, with blond hair and blue eyes—that people would speak to him in Dutch the second they met him?" Joseph laughed merrily.

Anna giggled. "I remember! Dad used to stand there wondering what the hell they were saying to him!"

There was a mutual silence between them. These were good memories. Something they both needed.

"Oh, I miss you, Anna, and I hope to see you again soon. Work is just… Well, it's work."

"Miss you too! Oh! Forgot to tell you too—Mom keeps telling me to give you a specific box. Something from Grandpa that was meant for you that she never got around to giving you."

"Grandpa Hoffman?"

"No, Grandpa Franz," said Anna. "Mom said it's in the basement somewhere. She wants you to have it, but that's all I know."

Joseph and his grandpa were always close. Joseph had warm memories of all the stories his grandfather would tell. Although Joseph loved those stories, they became more and more bizarre as Grandpa Franz got older. The rest of the family assumed his stories were silly and never believed any of them. As he lost his mind to dementia, the stories lost even a semblance of credibility. But for reasons he couldn't explain, Joseph always remained intrigued and believed everything Grandpa Franz said. He found truth in all of it—the strange legends, peculiar myths, and long-forgotten folklore fascinated Joseph. He'd go to school and tell his friends about the latest history lesson his grandfather had given him, only to have the other kids laugh at him. What made perfect sense to Joseph and Grandpa Franz were seen as tall tales. As Joseph got older, the people around him lost interest in the stories and thought Joseph was becoming as crazy as his grandpa for believing them. Eventually, these grandiose stories would become distant memories, and Joseph would stop talking about them to anyone.

"Oh, Grandpa Franz! Sure, I'll take it. It'll be nice to have some of his stuff."

"Great! Okay, Joseph. *Ich hab' dich lieb.*"

"*Ich hab' dich lieb*, Anna!"

Joseph put the handset back in its cradle. His ancient computer had finally booted up, and he opened his daily task list and printed it.

June 26

Morning Patient Sessions
    Travis Ratcliffe (room 405)
    Diane Lynch (room 302)
    Matthew Quinn (room 207)
~~Lunch~~ (He scratched it out and wrote "gym" instead.)
Meeting with Ward Supervisory Group
Mr. and Mrs. Macklin (new patient urgent call-in)

Joseph had mastered the trick of keeping his eyes slightly adjusted to his task list as he walked toward the door of the office and out into the main halls of C Ward, all without glancing up to make sure he didn't run into a wall. As he approached room 405, he folded the schedule and slipped it into his top pocket.

Joseph knocked lightly before opening the door. "Good morning, Travis. How are you feeling today?"

Travis sat on his bed facing away from the door. Joseph could see Travis's reflection peering back at him in the window. Travis was looking outside with a deep mindfulness in his eyes. "I can't believe I am here again. I belong out there, Doctor. Out in the real world," he said quietly and carefully. "I know I can do it, be out there again. I know I can handle it. I just need all of you to know that I'm ready. That's all."

Standing in the doorway, leaning against the doorframe, Joseph gently responded, "I know you feel that way, Travis. But we both also know this won't be possible anytime soon. You keep getting in trouble every time you go back out there. What you did this last time was…" Joseph paused, searching for the right word. He finally settled on "bad. You know that, though, don't you?"

He looked over the young man, who still stared at the barred window. Travis's red hair and freckles made him look like a boy, not a man who'd found himself in an armed standoff with the police. This wasn't his first time in Cottage Grove Hospital, but if he didn't get himself figured out, it may be his last, if only because he'd wind up in prison or dead.

Travis slumped in his bed. "I know it was bad. Things just got out of hand. It's just… no one would listen to me. I tried to talk to them. I really did. My grandma never listens to me. She just nods and smiles, but I know she's not listening. And it wasn't my fault that the cops showed up. I just needed to get some time by myself, and everyone freaked out." Travis turned to look at Joseph for the first time. "I have to prove I'm just as powerful as they are. All the cops worshiped me for a moment," he said, breathlessly. Something in the way the doctor looked at him made Travis start to hide his emotions again. "I wouldn't do it again, though. I promise you. Not unless I had time to board up the second floor too."

"Well, that wouldn't be wise either, Travis. Not wise at all. So tell me, what is this I'm hearing about you hiding cell phones in your room?"

"They're all lying!" Travis said. "All people do here is lie 'n' die at Cottage Grove. I mean, come on! They have nothing better to do, do they? They get dosed up and make up stories to create drama." Joseph watched as Travis's demeanor changed in an instant. He smiled, shark-like. "The suspense sure is fun though, isn't it?"

Joseph knew all about Travis's cell phones, of course. He had somehow managed to sneak them in during each time he came to C Ward over the years. He had a strange obsession with stashing things as if he needed them to survive. He put phones, water containers, plastic bags, and other objects behind shelves and wall fixtures in the hallways. Anywhere that he could wedge something in for use at a later time, he did. Of course, he always denied it, even when confronted with evidence from the hospital's security cameras.

"You know how this works, Travis. If we can't trust you to follow the rules in here, how can you expect us to let you out in the world? Society has rules to keep people safe. The same goes for our hospital. There are reasons those objects aren't allowed here."

"Name six." Travis said flippantly.

"You wouldn't give a plastic bag to a suicidal person. Or a ball of yarn in the hands of someone who will swallow anything they can fit in their mouth. Or," he said, making eye contact with Travis, "a lighter in the hands of a person who threatens to burn down houses. Does any of this sound familiar, Travis?"

"Oh, now I get it. I'm the bad guy and you're the know-it-all doctor who thinks he's helping us by keeping everyone on lockdown all day. Keeping us thinking we're wrong when we just want to be heard. Keeping us locked in our own minds."

"I *hear* you, Travis. I understand your concerns and your frustrations. I'm here to help you get your thoughts out. You have my full and undivided attention."

"You're no different than my grandma," Travis scoffed. "She never listens to me. I won't ever shut up until someone listens to me."

"Okay, Travis. As I said, it's my job to listen to you and hear what you say, and I'll listen any time you need me to. Let me know when you're ready to talk again. My office is right down the hall. Just tap your button, and I'll come here and talk to you at any time. Do you need anything else? Is there anything I can do to help you for now?"

"No. Nothing. No one can help me. It's me against the world, Doc."

"Well, count me in as part of your team. It's *us* while you are here. Us together, helping you feel better."

"Thanks. I will believe it when I see it. See you soon, Dr. Hoffmann. I need to rest." Travis replied as he laid his head back down on his pillow and looked up at the tile ceiling.

"I'll see you again soon, Travis. I am here for you."

Joseph stepped out of Travis's room and locked the door behind him. He often pondered how horrible it felt locking the patients' rooms as if they were in cages. It never got easier for him over the years, either. He unfolded the schedule from his pocket and checked off Travis from the list. Time to move on to room 302.

Joseph left Hall 4 and made his way toward Hall 3, saying "hello" and "good morning" to some of the patients along the way. Hall 3's patient rooms sat across from the medical examination rooms and personal-safety rooms—known to the patients as the "padded rooms"—used only for suicidal or violent patients. When Joseph walked up to room 302, he heard a nursery rhyme sung in a thick French accent.

"There was an old lady who swallowed a spider
that wriggled and wiggled and tiggled inside her.
She swallowed the spider to catch the fly.
I don't know why she swallowed a fly. Perhaps she'll die!
There was an—"

The song was cut off when Joseph opened the door. "Well, then. Good morning, Diane. What a beautiful song you're singing. A good way to start the day, I suppose."

"It brings him back," she responded firmly.

"Brings who back?" Joseph replied as he pulled up a chair across from her.

"Jean-Paul, *bien sur*." Her French accent resonated throughout the small room. "My son comes back to me if I sing his favorite song. He left me. I raised him and cared for him, and he left me." Diane's calm demeanor flashed to rage. "But when he comes to visit me, none of you bastards will let me see him!"

Joseph ignored the accusation. He knew better than to be drawn into *that* conversation again. "So why did Jean-Paul leave this time?"

"He did what anyone would do when they grow up. Left the nest and moved on. I knew the day would come when my lil' leapfrog would become a full-grown man. I had no idea it would be so soon. The last thing he said to me was that he would be back in a hurry. I hear him knock on my window at night to be let in. But no one lets him in. *No one*! I've asked all of you over and over, but no one helps him!" Diane wrung her hands.

"Perhaps I can ask if anyone has met him or seen him. What does he look like?"

He would ask about her son's appearance each session, because her description changed each time. Jean-Paul's appearance directly reflected her thoughts and feelings for the day. Recently, however, he had noticed the description was starting to become more consistent each time he asked.

Joseph found Diane to be an interesting case. She claimed to be a gypsy from France. Her French accent was convincing enough, even if sometimes over the top, but the hospital records showed she was born and raised in Iowa. Her once thick black hair sat atop her head like an unruly mop that had been dipped in silver.

Heavyset and nearing seventy years old, she had suffered from hallucinations for most of her life. She had hitchhiked from the

Midwest to the West Coast in the 1970s, an authentic hippie. What she had been doing for the intervening 50 years was anyone's guess. Diane had been brought to Cottage Grove the previous month after wandering the streets, going door to door, asking for the father of her son.

"Jean-Paul is so handsome. Tall with dark hair. He takes after his father," she said with a sideways grin and wink.

Joseph smiled. "How old is Jean-Paul?"

"30. Or maybe he's 20. It's hard to say. But I finally feel like he has grown to the man I remember most." She paused, lost in thought. A light came into her eyes, and she seemed almost lucid for a moment. She looked up at Joseph and said, "He is old… old like me."

"Jean-Paul is your age now?"

"No. Not yet. He will be soon, I think. When he comes back each night, it reminds me of better times! I remember the pregnancy like it was yesterday. So much pain, for so much worth!"

Diane sat straight up in her chair. "Do you know, I was pregnant for nine years. Nine long grueling years. It took a long time for me to even realize Jean-Paul wanted out. But once the time came, I let him go."

"And what made you realize it was time?" Joseph asked, leaning forward.

"He wasn't eating anymore. He said he needed to find more food or he'd die. I had to let him go. It was time. He wasn't inside me anymore." Her tone grew angrier. "He said he'd be back home after he was done eating! Out there in the wild! All alone! But like I've told you a million times, no one will let him in!"

Diane was known to ask other patients for food in hopes that her son could be fed. Everyone assumed she was eating the food herself. Eventually, a stench took over the halls and a stockpile of rotten food was found in her closet next to a coloring book.

Joseph tapped his temple with his pen. "I have an idea. Why don't you tell me when he wants in, okay? Then I can come to see him and let him in for you. Does that sound like a plan?"

"But he only comes at night, Doctor! You're only here during the day. Like I told you, he knocks on my window at night to be let back in. It's hard to sleep while I worry about my son. It eats up my thoughts every single day."

"I can imagine," Joseph replied in a comforting voice. "Let's do this then: I'll let our overnight security guard and nurses know you're having these issues with Jean-Paul. That way, when I am not here on the ward, they can be sure to help you. You can let the nurses know when he's here, and they can come let Jean-Paul in. Doctor's order. That way we'll know he's safe, and so are you. I want the best for you, Diane."

Diane nodded. "Good, because Jean-Paul is getting cold. He misses his mother. He misses his warm place here at home."

"At least we can rest easy knowing that it's summer. It's warm outside, even at night," Joseph said, trying to ease her mind.

"Outside those doors is no place for the warmth. He needs the strength to continue. He's tired and growing old. *I* am his strength. Home is wherever his mother is."

"Okay, Diane. We'll help Jean-Paul find his strength and his way home." Joseph cleared his throat. "I did want to speak with you about something else. I was informed you've been threatening suicide if we don't let your son in."

Diane took a deep breath while looking into Joseph's eyes, then turned and stared at the corner of the room behind Joseph. "I can't kill myself, or Jean-Paul won't find his way back home. Why would I take that away from him? Would you like your only path back home taken away?"

"No, I wouldn't, Diane. I don't think anyone would."

"So then why do you keep him from me? Warmth is all my son needs. He'll come back again tonight, and it'll be the whole thing all over again."

"We'll keep an eye out for Jean-Paul, I promise you. Doctor's order."

Joseph turned toward the door and put his pen into his clipboard.

"Sure you will," Diane muttered. When Joseph went to pull the door shut, he heard her say one last thing. "If you heard knocks from your child at night, you'd want to let him in too. I promise you. You could never say no."

"Well, sadly, I don't have a child. I agree that would be a hard thing to say no to."

After leaving Diane's room in Hall 3, Joseph looked at his agenda: next psychotherapy checkup, room 207. He walked past the lobby and the security offices before opening the big swinging doors into Hall 2. Walking the halls of a mental hospital was an experience unto itself. Banging coming from one room, crying from the next. Every type of emotion from a different patient, all of them trapped like caged animals—caged in their own minds, locked up with their own thoughts.

Joseph knocked on the door to room 207.

"Go away!" exclaimed a voice from the other side, but Joseph walked in anyway.

"Hello, Matthew. How's everything going today?"

"What do you think?" said Matthew.

"I don't know. You tell me."

"It's going the same as any other day. Same blind people around me. Same crappy excuses that I'm crazy. Same shit, different day. What about you, Doctor?" Matthew pointed toward the lobby. "Still blind and wandering aimlessly through the crowd of dreamers out there?"

Joseph pulled a chair next to Matthew's bed and sat down. "Dreaming isn't always a bad thing, Matthew. Dreams are what make people accomplish great things. They show a person they can have endless possibilities, even if some of those possibilities only can happen while they sleep."

Matthew shook his head vigorously. "You don't get it. I'm not talking about dreaming when you're asleep. I'm talking about the dreams that are in your waking life. *Right now.* You're dreaming, Dr. Hoffmann. You're in a dream right now. But me? Nope. I'm awake more than ever." He put his hand in the air and pointed to the ceiling as though he were praising a god above him. "I see the angels right in front of me. They're here to save us all from the evil that no one else cares to see."

"I understand you were talking about this to the whole ward in the middle of the night. They had to give you a sedative and—"

Matthew cut Joseph off. "Pah! Sedatives? They aren't sedatives. They're spiritual blockers. You're all trying to keep me from seeing the truth. Keep me blind, just like you. You can't keep me from seeing, no matter what you do. I get fogged up for a bit, sure—but only until I meet the angels again and start seeing the truth for what it is. You'll see too, Dr. Hoffmann. You'll see when the time comes."

Matthew was in his early twenties, with pale skin and shaggy brown hair. He had grown up on the outskirts of Cottage Grove, where his family was involved in an alternative religious movement called the Fifth Day of Genesis. Matthew didn't fall far from the tree. His father had been in and out of Cottage Grove Hospital for many years before passing away several years ago. And now, Matthew followed in his footsteps, on and off for a few years consecutively. Most recently, he had walked into another church, telling everyone they could never see the light with their false beliefs. He wouldn't leave, even after the cops were called.

Matthew was then arrested and brought into Cottage Grove for further evaluation since he seemed to be in a psychotic state of mind. It was obvious to Joseph and his staff that Matthew couldn't accept reality for what it was, even as hard as the doctors had tried to convince him of his illness. He experienced visual and auditory hallucinations of angels and paranoid delusions of heaven and hell daily. A clear diagnosis of schizophrenia. Schizoaffective delusions often revolved around religious content, and with Matthew's upbringing, this was amplified tenfold. He was neck-deep in his illness and wouldn't find a way out anytime soon.

"We don't like to sedate you." Joseph said, scooting his chair a bit closer to Matthew. "Let's talk about this. I want to make something clear. We aren't here to hurt you. We don't want to keep you from anything. We're here to help you find balance and peace. But it's a problem when you're preaching in the hallway at night while the rest of the patients are trying to sleep. We're trying to help them too. Can you imagine if the whole ward couldn't sleep? How much of a problem would that be for everyone?"

"Ha! I know what no sleep feels like. I feel that way all the time. I can't *ever* sleep. The angels won't let me. I must make sure everyone believes me, believes in *them*. Every single night. They come to me at night. That's the only time they're even allowed to."

"Okay, Matthew," Joseph said with a quick nod. "I see in my notes that you've been refusing your Aripiprazole. You need to keep taking your medication. It's very important. It's not healthy to keep having these hallucinations. You can fall deeper into your illness. We need you to take the medication we give you with your dinner, so you can sleep and have a bit of peace from the angels keeping you awake at night."

"But I'm the chosen one, Doc," Matthew protested. "You gotta believe me. If I don't tell everyone the truth, no one will. Those drugs take the angels away from me. I'm the chosen one," he repeated.

"I understand. Delusions can be unsettling, but we want to bring you back to the real world. A world without angels and people talking to you in your sleep." Joseph put his hand to his chin in deep thought, trying to come up with a strategy that could help Matthew. Then it dawned on him, "I have an idea. How about we bring a tape recorder for you? You can recite your religious lessons for the day into it, and then we can decide if it's something we should play at Sunday services. In exchange, you take the medication we give you. We can play the recordings for anyone who needs to know about your teachings. Deal?"

"I don't know. I mean… I guess. Sure, we have a deal. But no funny stuff, Doc. I have to tell *everyone*—or else."

This made Joseph pause. "Or else what?"

"Or else we might all lose ourselves forever to this evil inside us that keeps eating at us, day and night. All of us have it inside of us. That means you too, Doc. You too."

"Okay, Matthew. We don't want that to happen. Thanks for understanding and agreeing to this. Our plan can really help everyone. I'll have the nurses bring your tape recorder each day after lunch—starting today. Be sure to let me or the staff know if you need anything else."

Joseph stood up and left, closing and locking the door behind him.

Chapter 3

"If you keep your eyes closed long enough,
darkness becomes the only truth you know."
—engraving in the Kanheri Caves
(Mumbai, India, 2nd century AD)

"How was the gym, Dr. Hoffman?"

"Fine, Jocelyn, just fine," Joseph said as he passed the front desk on the way to his office.

"Skipping lunch isn't good for you, you know," Jocelyn admonished him.

"So you've been telling me about a decade."

"Two," she said. "Two decades."

Going to the gym gave Joseph respite from his innermost anxieties. There, he could release his inner darkness, transferring the weight of his anger into the machines, where it could be used for constructive purposes and not eat away at his soul.

"I left an apple on your desk," Jocelyn called as he headed back to his office.

He smiled and nodded.

Pulling his schedule from his top pocket, he perused the rest of his day.

Meeting with Ward Supervisory Group
Mr. and Mrs. Macklin (new patient urgent call-in)

He refolded the paper back into a perfectly creased square and replaced it in his coat pocket. He stopped by the staff lounge to grab a bottle of water before continuing to his office.

The phone was ringing as he entered.

"Yes, Jocelyn."

"I'm sorry to bother you, Doctor. But your three o'clock is here."

Joseph checked the clock. It was barely after noon.

"Aren't they a little early?"

"I know, Doctor, but they're insisting on seeing you now. Should I ask them to come back?"

Joseph paused for a moment. The supervisory meeting could wait a bit.

"No, send them back."

"Yes, Doctor."

A moment later, there was a knock on the door. Joseph let Mr. and Mrs. Macklin in.

Mr. Macklin was a big, burly man, with a dirty trucker cap and a striped button-down shirt. His wife was a petite woman who seemed a bit more fashionable and dainty. Her polka-dot skirt and neatly tied-up hair gave her a childish, doll-like look. They didn't seem like they belonged together, and if it weren't for their matching expressions of concern, Joseph would have presumed they were there for two entirely different reasons.

"Hello, you must be Mr. and Mrs. Macklin. I'm Dr. Hoffman. Please, take a seat."

The couple sat across from Joseph's sturdy oak desk with concerned looks and glossed over eyes.

"Hello, Doctor," Mrs. Macklin began. "Thanks, so much for squeezing us in today. I know it might have been a bit of a schedule conflict for you and a little last minute."

Joseph smiled kindly. "Not at all. Never a problem, especially when someone is in need. What can I help you with today?"

"We need… um… some professional help. Our daughter has been acting strange lately, and we aren't sure what to do. We kept waiting for it to get better. After weeks of this, we decided it's best for us to see someone. Dr. Fredrickson suggested we bring her here, as she felt it was something needing full observation."

Mr. Macklin sat to her left, his index finger and thumb pinching the ridge of his nose. He looked down, slightly shaking his head in a moment of sadness that they even had to sit here talking about this at all.

"How is she acting strangely?" asked Joseph.

"When she wakes up every morning, she keeps saying her room is switched around. She says, 'Who keeps moving my bed and my stuff?' But of course, we aren't moving anything. We don't understand any of this."

"Can you tell me a little bit about your daughter? How old she is? Her background or interests? Please tell me anything that might help." Joseph pulled out his desk drawer and placed a piece of paper on top of his desk before grabbing a pen from a wooden jar.

"Her name's Jennifer, and she's nineteen years old," Mrs. Macklin replied. "She was a straight-A student and even got a full-ride softball scholarship last year to Oregon State. She went to her first year of college. That's when this all started. It began with her getting confused when she was driving home from school to visit us. She'd get lost and call us, asking where she was or where she needed to go. I mean, it's only an hour drive from here to Corvallis. We assumed something was wrong with her GPS, or she was just studying too hard and was tired. Then things got weirder. Her dormmates at school said she had stopped eating. She was suspicious that they had put something in her food. She also started sleeping for long periods. Like twelve hours or more. So we brought her back home with us here in Cottage Grove. But then she only got worse."

She paused, tears welling up in her eyes. Mr. Macklin picked up where she left off. "She said she didn't want to live anymore. We thought she was just seeking attention, but it started to seem very real when she would lock herself in her room and not come out. Sometimes she doesn't even make sense. Her eyes change when she looks at us. Flat and expressionless. She's paranoid, suspicious of everything everyone is doing. Sometimes… sometimes she can become so angry that we are scared she will hurt us." The shame in the big man's voice was palpable.

"I fully understand your concerns. And you said you had taken her to Dr. Fredrickson. But I don't see her name in the system here," Joseph said, glancing over the hospital database.

"No, no we haven't taken her anywhere. She just stays in her room talking to herself. We would have to force her outside. This is why she isn't even here with us right now. We spoke to Dr. Fredrickson briefly on a telephone call after scheduling an appointment. When she heard the situation, she suggested that we come straight here, saying it was probably for the best since it was an urgent matter."

Joseph looked the Macklins over. This meeting was out of place, but Joseph couldn't put his finger on it. Most of the patients were court appointed. Others had episodes that had led them here, some more urgent than others. Joseph couldn't help but question why Jennifer wasn't already being seen by a psychiatrist. Something else had to be going on.

"May I ask if she's ever had a history of drug use?" Joseph said.

"What? No!" Mrs. Macklin exclaimed. "Absolutely not. She's a good girl. She'd never do that. Plus, they gave her drug tests for sports. We would have known."

Joseph nodded. "I'm sorry, but I always have to ask. You'd be surprised by the number of patients we have coming in here who we thought were mentally ill, only to find out they were high on drugs when they had their episode. Then, two or three days later, after getting it all out of their system, they're ready to head back home. The problem with that is that we have to keep patients here for no less than five weeks for observation, so this can cause great distress to the patient and their family if it was a short-lived, drug induced psychosis. Some of our patients end up in the prison system, and some are threats to society, or even to themselves. We feel it is best if they are seen for this standard length of time so we can know the full picture. We can see their relationship and interactions with our staff and other patients. This gives us the diagnosis we need in order to make the right decisions for their next step."

"It's definitely not drugs!" Mr. Macklin insisted before continuing. "And, yes that *is* a long time, but I understand it takes time."

Mrs. Macklin put her hand on his knee, and he took a deep breath.

"Sorry, Doctor. It's just that we're very worried," Mr. Macklin said. Joseph saw desperation in the man's eyes. "Jennifer is like a whole different girl now. My wife and I have talked about it, and we think we should bring her in. She needs professional help and needs to be examined by someone like yourself."

"Of course," Joseph said. "If you feel it makes the most sense, then by all means please bring her in. Based on what you've told me, I think she'd belong here at the crisis unit, where she'd be under full supervision. Then we can make sure she's okay and get to the bottom of this."

Mrs. Macklin looked at her husband, who nodded, almost as if they had telepathically made an agreement, then turned back towards Joseph.

"Thank you, Dr. Hoffman. We'll go home and pack her things and tell her we're going to visit her grandparents for a surprise trip. I think that's the only way she'll come. She's already so paranoid and suspicious about everything we do. We need to somehow bring her in without her knowing we are. She would never come in here on her own. Can you be sure you have your security here to help when we arrive, in case she resists? I can only imagine how she'll act."

"Yes, I'll inform security, and we'll be sure everything is as easy as possible on you and on her. What time are you planning to bring her in?"

Mr. and Mrs. Macklin exchanged glances again, then turned back to Joseph. Holding back her tears, Mrs. Macklin continued, "First thing tomorrow morning. Her grandparents live in Idaho. When we visit them, we always leave early. We can bring her then. Let's say around six a.m.?"

Joseph turned toward his computer screen and started typing while talking at the same time, "I have her in the system for expected arrival tomorrow morning at six. I won't be here then, but the overnight nursing team will be there to admit her. I'll see her when I arrive, during my rounds. I promise, she'll be in good hands." Joseph stopped typing with a smile and nodding gesture before reaching into his drawer.

"I have here the forms for you to sign and fill out." Joseph said while handing them the admittance forms. After a couple minutes of pen-to-paper scribbles, Mr. and Mrs. Macklin handed the signed papers back to Joseph.

"We can't thank you enough for taking in our little angel," Mrs. Macklin said. "She means everything to us. We just hope she's okay, and you can handle whatever happens."

"She'll be taken care of. Please try not to worry."

Joseph stood up and walked Mr. and Mrs. Macklin to the door, "Down the hall back the way you came, through the double doors, turn right at the lobby, then through the security checkpoint and out the main doors. They'll buzz you out. I'll inform reception and security now about Jennifer's arrival tomorrow."

As the couple walked toward the big swinging doors of Hall 1, Joseph returned to his desk to call reception about their daughter's arrival. After he hung up the phone, he paused. He couldn't help but think about Jennifer's parents. It felt... off. They felt off. Something was rubbing him the wrong way about the whole meeting. A feeling deep in his gut. After mulling it over in his head for a little while, he decided to make a note and attach it to her record.

Before he knew it, the windows were dark. 7:00 p.m. had come up fast. Deciding he had done enough for the day, he shut down his computer.

Sitting back in his chair, he stretched his arms and yawned. Then he stood up and walked to the coat rack and hung up his white coat before reaching for his keys in his pocket. He closed the door and locked it behind him, then headed to the lobby.

Adam met him at the door. "Hey, Dr. Hoffmann. Looks like I beat you to my desk again." He smiled triumphantly.

"Hi, Adam. Why are you here so early? Doesn't your shift start at ten?"

"I had to cover the end of Tyler's shift. He went home sick, so I'm picking up a few extra hours. Time and a half!"

Joseph grinned. "You're a hard worker, Adam. We need more people like you. Hey, since I have you here, you will want to know that we're trying a new strategy with Matthew, and I also spoke with Diane to put her mind at ease. We're working toward a better understanding regarding what to do to take care of them both. It shouldn't be too noisy for you tonight. I hope," he added as an afterthought.

"Always working that magic, Doc! I'm sure they're happy to have someone like you taking care of them. You and the rest of the staff really do great work with the patients."

Joseph responded with a tinge of doubt in his voice. "Ah, if it were only that easy."

Adam pushed the button that disengaged the lock and buzzed Joseph out.

Despite himself, Joseph was finally on his way home.

ℰℐ

Joseph lived thirty-minutes from the hospital.

Both Cottage Grove Hospital and his house were situated on the outskirts of the city in dark forested areas, almost directly opposite from each other. He hadn't chosen the place for its physical distance from the hospital, but he wasn't unaware of its psychological distance from his patients and the stresses they represented. He brought enough stress to the table without needing to take his job home with him.

Joseph drove on the Loop, part of the highway that circled the city. In the morning he'd take the forested side roads to help relax before his job ran away with him on his long shifts, but at night, the Loop was always faster to get him home so he could relax from a hard day of work. As Joseph neared his house, his roof came into view when he ascended the hill near the edge of the forest.

Joseph pulled his BMW into the gravel driveway of his ornate Victorian home. Helen and Joseph both fell in love with the place for different reasons. She enjoyed the fairytale gingerbread look of the thick towering walls supporting the gabled roof, all tied together by white trim, moving from corner to corner like wooden veins. Large cigar-shaped windows filled the empty voids of the gray bricks, all hung with gold plating around the frames. It was as if the house had its own soul. The historic stories of bygone years pulsed away from it, deep into the surrounding forest. If someone were to crack a wall, Joseph was ready to believe that blood might trickle from its wound.

But it wasn't merely the house itself that appealed to Joseph. He didn't need a real estate agent to tell him that the most important feature of the house was its location. The trees provided both beauty and protection. Not from intruders, but from the weight he carried with him. Like the house, he put on a friendly, good-looking mask and smiled at the passersby. But something about being surrounded by beautiful things, in a fortress-like house, on the edge of a dark wood that went on for miles mirrored the layers of armor he used to keep his darkness in, and his pain out.

Joseph grabbed his key from the ignition and stepped out, admiring the home. Joseph would be the first to describe his neighborhood as safe. Nevertheless, he locked the car before walking up the short flight of moist concrete stairs that led to the front door. He unlocked the deadbolt and headed inside.

The house felt deserted. It was deserted. Each time he entered the front door, the cold air made him shiver to the bone. If he wasn't clinging to the painful memories that had haunted him, he would have moved on a long time ago. But this home reminded him of Helen, her joy whenever she would come through that door, and he couldn't let go of that.

As he moved through the house, the memories of her pelted him like moths to a light. He had managed to get the scent of her out of a few of the rooms—his office, the bedroom, the master bath, the kitchen—but the rest of the house belonged to her. Helen's presence could be felt throughout the house, her belongings littering the rooms, left exactly how they were since that awful morning. She had decorated this place to suit her tastes, to match the house's grace and gravity. Massive Baroque artwork hung on the walls in the main parlor. Pillars supporting Renaissance busts and sculptures lined the dim hallways, their shadows casting eerie images whenever the vintage lights were turned on.

His life was a series of rituals. Every evening upon arriving home, Joseph made himself a ham sandwich with extra mustard and ate it while putting away his belongings. He then got into his robe and headed into his office, where he poured himself a glass of whiskey and lit a cigar to pair it with. He sat down in an old, comfortable chair—one of the few things from his life before Helen—and read a book until his eyes became too heavy. Looking at the words on the page, unsure if the wine or exhaustion were to blame for his blurred vision, was his signal to check in for the night. At that point, he'd make his way up to his room and fall fast asleep.

But tonight, something was different.

While reading Into the Past: The Fall of Rome and Odoacer's Rise, he came to a line where the author spoke about barbarian raids in Rome and the mystery of why the Pantheon, the old temple of the gods, had remained to this day.

Joseph looked up and away from the book. In his eyes were the reflections of candles and, in his mind, the reflections of the past. His heart felt heavier than his eyes, and he dropped deeply into a memory of better times.

cɔ

Rome, Italy; Twenty-Eight Years Earlier

Sunlight shot down from the oculus in the middle of the Pantheon's dome, lighting up the space and making it feel like a vault to the heavens. Joseph's eyes were fixed on the curls of Helen's hair, which gleamed in the light shining through, leaving a golden halo around her. She was staring at the top of the dome, smiling, the dimples in her cheeks as noticeable as the deep-blue eyes above them. Joseph fell more and more in love with her each day; he could hardly contain the emotion swelling inside him, and he began to wonder if his heart would burst from the enormity of it all. He watched Helen while she admired the magnificent dome. Each moment was like the first moment he had ever seen her.

A large group walked by, an English-speaking tour guide leading the pack. Helen turned to Joseph and grabbed his hand. "Joe! Let's sneak in the back and follow the tour! Come on!"

Hesitating, Joseph smiled then shook his head, but he was no match for Helen's firm grip as she pulled him into the back of the group. They crouched slightly in a vain attempt to avoid being detected while they listened to the tour guide.

"The dome you see above you is roughly one hundred forty-two feet tall. This is the same as the diameter. Even two thousand years later, we're impressed by how harmonious and perfect the proportion of this room is. To the left here, this aedicula or shrine is actually a tomb. Located at the base is the resting place of Raffaello Sanzio, the well-known painter from the Renaissance, better known as 'Raphael.' The bronze bust you see to the left is of Raphael. This was bust was created in 1833 by Giuseppe Fabris.

To the right and on the top is the epitaph marking the tomb of Maria Bibbiena, Raphael's fiancée, who's buried to the right of his sarcophagus; she died before they could marry.

"The inscription you see here says 'Here lies Raphael, by whom Nature feared to be outdone while he lived and, when he died, feared that she would die with him.' It's so sad to know you never can marry the love of your life. Raphael made sure they would be buried next to each other for eternity, so their love would live on forever. Next let's head over to—"

The group moved on while Joseph and Helen locked gazes. "Can you imagine losing each other?" Helen asked. "Could you imagine if I died before we could marry?"

"No, I can't—and I don't think it's good idea to think about that kind of thing while we're on a peaceful holiday together. Right now, today, we're both standing here breathing and living, right in front of each other."

"But either one of us could die tomorrow, or today. Don't you think about that sort of thing?"

Joseph hesitated. He didn't like where this was going. Perhaps if he humored her, she would let it drop. He reached out and took her hand. "God forbid you died before we were married, I would never let you go. I couldn't live with myself knowing you weren't with me anymore."

Helen cut Joseph off by putting her hand over his mouth. "Oh dear, I forgot how seriously you take things! It was just a question. You're right, today we're alive and together. Let's enjoy ourselves," she said, extracting them from the tour. "I want something sweet. Shall we find some gelato? Maybe strawberry, or pistachio!"

✆

The chiming of the clock brought Joseph back to the present. He looked up, expecting the hour to still be early. Midnight. As quickly as it had come, the memory of Helen retreated back into Joseph's subconscious.

He shook himself awake and looked down to see his book half closed over his index finger, holding it in as if it were a bookmark. He reached to the small table to his right for his last drop of whiskey and took a sip. It was time for bed, and then another long day at the ward. Perhaps sleep would relieve him from the burden of his memories, but he knew it would never be that easy.

Chapter 4

"Stillness of skies shall lead the way,
for in the night, we rid the day.
In the moonlight the angels call,
until we meet the shadows, thin and tall."
—anonymous (fifth century AD)

Through the driving summer rain punctuated with spears of lightning, Joseph arrived at work at 8:45 a.m., as late as he had ever been in his twenty-five years at Cottage Grove. He looked up at the security camera, expecting the doors to magically open before him as the morning entrance guard buzzed him through. But the doors remained closed. He waved, but still no response. Finally, drenched with rain and frustrated as much with himself as with the slow response from the front door, he made his way in as quickly as possible.

The front entrance guard station was abandoned. Another first at Cottage Grove. He considered going straight to the hospital's guard captain and putting in a complaint, but that was in B Ward across the quad, which would mean braving the rain once more.

He had had his fill of rain for the day, so he headed back to his office to see if he could still resurrect the remains of his schedule.

Joseph arrived in his office and hung his soaking wet jacket and umbrella on the coat rack to dry, then sat at his desk. Due to his late arrival, he would have to skip his morning routine, which was irritating him in ways he didn't have time to contemplate. This was not the way he wanted to start the day, or any other day for that matter. He turned on the computer to print his day's agenda so he could start his daily rounds.

With a roar of thunder and snap of lightning, the computer screen flickered as it booted up. Black then white. Then black and white again. Something was wrong. His computer wouldn't turn on. Joseph watched the screen flash a couple more times. He reached behind the monitor and checked to see if the monitor cable was seated in its socket, but to his surprise, it was. He was no tech wizard, but he knew his way around computer hardware. And besides, calling maintenance would be both time consuming and embarrassing. Left with no alternatives, he decided to crawl underneath the desk to check the monitor cable's connection to the computer. He firmly held on to his desk and braced himself to crawl under, then put his hand behind the computer and searched for the cable. It was just out of reach.

Out of nowhere came a scream that was so earsplitting he jolted straight up and hit his head on the underside of the desk. It wasn't close, but it was *loud!*

Who the hell was that? he thought, rubbing his head.

Screams weren't uncommon on the ward. Noises like these sprinkled the halls every day. But this scream was different; it *felt* different. It was a scream that could shatter glass. A chill of fear surged through him, turning his stomach sour and causing his brow to sweat.

A deafening silence followed the scream. Joseph took a moment under the desk to collect himself. Before he could extract himself from the footwell of the desk, the door to his office slowly cracked open. Something made him hesitate, the unknown locking him in place, and he decided to stay beneath his desk for a moment longer. He cautiously peeked under the bottom of the front desk panel, hoping to get a look at who was on the other side. With his face firmly against the tile floor, he smelled the sweet aroma of floor wax and pine-scented degreaser. Slowly, the door swung fully open. A shadow formed in the hallway, but he couldn't make out who it was. Joseph found himself frozen with fear. He took a slow, steady breath, trying to break the spell. He pulled his head back up from the floor, hoping he wouldn't be seen or heard. Shallow sliding footsteps moved toward him in an odd pattern. Not being able to see much, he sensed the approach of whoever it was coming closer.

Scufff... scuffff... scuff...

The footsteps approached the desk, and then two feet slid under the front desk panel, one by one, right below his face. Mud covered the soles of bare feet. The light scent of floor wax somewhat masked the strong smell of rain and earth.

"Doctor, I can see you under there."

Joseph recognized the voice. It was Susan from room 202, a longtime patient in C Ward. The tension that had been building left him all at once. Nevertheless, he was puzzled why she was there and especially why she had mud on her feet.

"Oh, is that you, Susan?" Joseph said, clearing the fear from his throat. He moved back out from underneath his desk. "I was just... I was fixing my computer. Quite a storm we have. Is everything okay? I heard a scream and was coming out to see what had happened."

"I heard 'em scream too, doc. It came from down my hall somewhere. But when no one came to check on 'em, I decided to find help. When I couldn't find anyone, I came to your office."

"Well, thank you," Joseph said, brushing himself off. "Have you been outside? How did you get mud on your feet?"

Susan cocked her head like a curious dog. "No," she said slowly, "I haven't been outside. My feet are clean." She looked him up and down. "You okay, Doctor?"

He looked down at Susan's feet. They weren't muddy at all.

Maybe I hit my head a little too hard, Joseph thought. *Or perhaps it was simply shadows on the floor.*

"Did you call the nurse? Or ask the security guard?"

"What security guard?" Susan asked, sounding confused. "There was no security guard. The only person I could find in the hospital was you."

That made him pause. "Everything is fine, Susan. Let me get everything sorted out. Please go back to your room and stay put, all right?"

Joseph led Susan out of his office then closed and locked the door behind him. He escorted her back toward Hall 2. As he approached the main lobby, he could see Adam and a nurse facing away from him, deep in conversation. From their tone, it was some kind of argument, but he couldn't make out what was being said. Something was odd about their words, as if they were speaking in a language he couldn't understand. A language he couldn't even recognize. Their voices drifted past him like clouds through the window of a fast-moving airplane, indistinct and diffused.

Susan said there was no one else in the hospital. Why would she tell me that if Adam and the nurse are right here?

Joseph walked up to Adam and the nurse, but no matter which angle he tried, their heads remained facing away from him. The strange voices flowed in and out of white noise and radio chatter, and it felt like they were circling his head.

Another frightening wail came from the direction of Hall 2, breaking Joseph out of his confusion. He ran as fast as he could to the doors and, with a vigorous charge, pushed them open. Everything went completely silent, then the doors shut behind him and the hall became as dark as night in the forest. No more strange chatter, and the only light was the exit sign at the end of the hallway, which glowed neon red. The hospital was vacant, and Joseph felt very alone.

Knock. Knock. Knock.

The knocks echoed from down the hall, reverberating as though they originated in a deep, faraway canyon. He headed toward the exit sign and the knocking sound.

Knock. Knock.

Another pair of knocks came from the left side of the hall.

I think they're coming from Matthew's room.

With a feeling of terror growing inside him, Joseph moved carefully down the hall. He heard something like static or white noise originating from Matthew's room. The sound grew louder as he approached the exit sign's hazy glow. He turned left toward Matthew's door, then heard a click and someone talking from inside. It was the same strange language the nurse and Adam had spoken, but it was in Matthew's voice this time. When Joseph opened the door, the room exhaled loudly, as if it were the mouth of someone holding their breath for a long time that had just opened. Inside Matthew's room was ice cold.

Matthew continued speaking in that strange language, weaving in and out of noise that sounded like a broken radio stuck between stations. Joseph couldn't see him through the fog that filled the room.

"Ohanzee... Wayo... Kapi... Kokipa..."

Joseph's breath hung in the air like frost during a winter's night. He exhaled a cloud of mist as he scanned the room for Matthew and the source of the sound. Rain pounded on the window, blending in with the hissing radio sound.

"Ohanzee… Wayo… Kapi… Kokipa…"

"Matthew? *Matthew?* Is that you? Where *are* you?" Joseph's voice trembled. A knot in his throat grew tighter, making it hard for him to speak.

"Ohanzee… Wayo… Kapi… Kokipa…"

The voice grew louder while the storm became more violent outside the windows. Day had turned to night, and Joseph wondered if the ward had turned into Hell. Flashes of lightning painted the sky white, while rumbles of heavy thunder lingered outside the hospital.

"Ohanzee… Wayo… Kapi… Kokipa…"

The voice pitched down and became more aggressive. The strobing of the flickering lights became Joseph's searchlight; each time lightning flashed outside, his eyes caught a different part of the room. When he walked toward where the voice seemed to come from, he noticed a chair facing the corner of the room.

"Ohanzee… Wayo… Kapi… Kokipa…"

The voice became raspier, deeper, and more abstract. Joseph continued walking cautiously toward the voice.

"Matthew?"

"Ohanzee… Wayo… Kapi… Kokipa…"

Sitting in the chair facing away from Joseph was a shirtless figure. The flash and strike of lightning from outside the window revealed someone with long, black, dirt-crusted hair.

That isn't Matthew…

Very slowly, Joseph made his way to the side of the person in the chair. He tried to see the face, but it was caught in the shadows. He could barely make out what seemed to be someone who was stuck in time, frozen in a moment of dread. The mouth hung wide open as though it were in a continual silent scream, and the eyes were glossed over white, with no life left in them. On its lap, near soot-covered hands, was a cassette player, playing back a haunting pitching loop of the strange language. It was the same tape player and recorder that Joseph had given Matthew the morning before.

"*Ohanzee… Wayo… Kapi… Kokipa… Ohanzee… Wayo… Kapi… Kokipa…*"

Knock. Knock. Knock.

The knocking sound was now even louder than before, and it came from the other side of the room, outside Matthew's window. Joseph turned around. The window's curtains were flapping as though they were hanging outside in a breeze, and frost had begun to take shape on the corners of the glass. Joseph walked slowly, step by step, toward the window.

Knock. Knock. Knock.

The knocks became even more rapid. Joseph could still hear the eerie voice on the recorder behind him playing out.

"*Ohanzee… Wayo… Kapi… Kokipa…*"

Knock. Knock.

Knock. Knock. Knock. Knock.

The window began to crack, hairline fractures spreading out toward the edges of the glass. Then the knocks became so loud that Joseph felt them hitting him deep in his chest next to his pounding heart.

Knock. Knock. Knock. Knock. Knock.

"*Ohanzee… Wayo… Kapi… Kokipa…*"

The glass bulged inward, on the verge of shattering.

Joseph opened his eyes.

A storm was raging outside, and a tree branch near his bedroom window was tapping on the glass.

Relief flooded into his chest as he realized he was at home, safe.

Shaken to the bone, he tried to get his senses back. This nightmare had felt so real. Trying to transition back into reality, he sat up in bed and looked around the room, expecting to see

Matthew or Susan looking back at him. His eyes latched on to the alarm clock's bright-red glow next to his bed: 6:00 a.m.

I'd better get ready for work.

⌘

The storm was still going strong when Joseph arrived at the hospital. Adam greeted him at the entrance, just like any other day. This time, Joseph could see his face.

See, it was only a bad dream, Joseph thought while exhaling a sigh of relief.

"Hey, Doc!"

"Good to see you this morning, Adam," Joseph said, chuckling at the irony.

"You too! Ready for the morning briefing?"

"Hit me," Joseph said.

"The new patient, Jennifer Macklin, is in room 407. She came in this morning around six a.m. Her parents seemed okay but sad, and she was compliant. The typical 'No, I don't need help!' debates were had, but overall, she seemed okay to be here." Joseph stuck on this thought for a moment. Jennifer's parents had told him she was paranoid and would never be okay with coming there. Adam didn't notice Joseph's brief preoccupied expression and continued on. "Other than the new patient, Diane had a bad dream or something and screamed out for help in the middle of the night. She was fine when they checked on her. No security measures were needed at least. The nurses said every time they switch her meds she does this."

"Yeah… that medication can make for some strange dreams. So Adam, let's circle back to Jennifer. Let me get this straight. Jennifer was completely compliant? No issues whatsoever?" Joseph asked.

"Well, I mean, compared to some of the patients that come through admissions. She didn't put up a fight, physically or verbally. She just seemed… okay, I guess. Kind of like she was expecting all of this."

Joseph decided he would address that with her when he did his rounds. Talking with her should be revealing. He continued on after burying the thought, "Any more outbursts from Diane about knocks on the window? The nurses were instructed to check with you if Diane asked about someone outside."

"Nope, nothing about that. Other than the bad dream, she didn't say much. Come to think of it, she was pretty quiet all night otherwise."

"That's good to hear."

Joseph tapped his fingers a couple times on the security desk, still trying to shake the thought of Adam and the nurse in his nightmare. It still felt far too real.

"Well, then, so long, Adam. I have to get to work, and I'm sure you have to get off the clock soon."

"Right you are, Doc! It was a long night since I worked those extra hours. Definitely going to sleep like a baby when I get home."

"How do you do it?" Joseph said.

"Do what?"

"Go home when the sun is up and still be able to sleep? I could never do that."

"You get used to it," Adam said, standing up and stretching. "I guess I now know what it feels like to be a vampire." He smirked and winked at Joseph.

"All right, Vladimir, have a good sleep."

"Thanks, Doc! Have a good one."

Joseph continued through the doors and into Hall 1 while Adam went back to the security office to switch shifts with the day guard.

Time to get my morning cup of coffee.

A few minutes later, with a cup of coffee in his left hand, Joseph's right index finger hit the green "print" button on the industrial-size printer, and the pages rolled through. The first page to come out was his daily agenda, followed by intake documents for Jennifer, and the other patients' updated statuses for his files.

June 27

Morning Patient Sessions
    ~~Travis Ratcliffe~~ (room 405) — *at group therapy*
    Diane Lynch (room 302) — *new medication*
    Matthew Quinn (room 207) — *tape recorder*
    Jennifer Macklin (room 407) — *new admission*
Lunch
Meeting with Ward Supervisory Group

The sound of printed pages slapping the plastic printer tray were echoed by a scrape on the window behind him.

"You've got to be kidding me," Joseph said, hesitant to look, fearing he was deep in another layer of a nightmare and hadn't woken up yet. Pinching himself, he slowly turned around. A raven flew off toward the dark forest as soon as it laid eyes on Joseph through the glass.

Just a bird. I really need to pull myself together.

Chapter 5

"Fear feeds off the restraints of our own solitude."
—tombstone in Arizona (1872)

A black block-lettered "Room 302" sign hung on the white concrete wall to the right of Diane's door. Joseph needed to catch up with her and make sure the new medication was helping. Adam and the nurses had told Joseph she had been on her best behavior lately. In most cases, it was usually the meds talking. Clipboard in hand, Joseph walked into the room while flipping through Diane's file. He arrived at a page with her new medication listed: fluphenazine, 10mg.

"Good morning, Diane. How are we today? How are the new meds treating you?"

Diane sat up in bed, trying to gather her words and thoughts. "I'm… I… I am. I can't… see him."

"Who can't you see?"

"I can't see him. He is… gone. *Disparu.* He was just here, but now he is gone."

Joseph knew she was referring to Jean-Paul so the new medication must have been working. Diane slowly turned her head toward Joseph. Then her lips twitched as though she were trying to say something. She made eye contact with him then mumbled, "B-b-b… I… c-ca… fe… him."

Joseph couldn't make out what she was saying. He walked over and sat next to her on the bed. Diane's gaze fixed on the wall ahead of her, a blank stare in her eyes.

"Diane, what are you trying to say?"

"B-but… I f-feel him."

"You feel him? You mean Jean-Paul? How do you feel him?"

"I f-f-feel him but… I c-c-can't see him. He isn't here anymore."

The medication definitely must be working.

"Well, Diane, it's a good thing you can't see him anymore. That's the first step toward making you better. Jean-Paul isn't real. And since he was part of you in your imagination, you might still *feel* like he's with you. This too will disappear with time and more therapy. You'll get through this. I'll come back to check in on you soon and see how everything's moving along, okay?"

"Doctor… I-I want feel b-b-better. I need *him* to be b-b-better."

"That's what we're doing here. That's what we all work toward. Making you better."

Joseph stood up and walked out of the room while jotting down notes about their conversation and confirmation that the new medication was doing its job. He took a right out the door before heading to Hall 2.

As he passed through the double swinging doors to Hall 2, a shock of anxiety hit him. A combination of déjà vu and dread, he flashed back to the nightmare of the previous night. In the space of a few seconds, he relived the screams. He heard the knocks. He saw the red glow of the exit sign and felt the dark shadows surround him. Quickly, he looked up and realigned his senses. He was relieved to see that the hallway was well lit, and there was no chanting or screaming, or at least, no more than usual. The exit sign was indeed red, but not surrounded by a strange haze or accompanied by an ice-cold breeze. Just a pair of patients playing cards, and a nurse pushing an empty wheelchair down the hall. He continued toward Matthew's room before stopping and turning his head to the right and looking at room 202. Deep in thought, he hesitated for a second.

Susan's room… She felt so real last night in that dream. But why Susan? And why do I remember it all in so much detail?

He moved forward, trying to forget it.

It was only a dream, he reassured himself. *No need to let it bother me all day.*

He opened the door to Matthew's room. With a piece of him still expecting to see a chair in the corner and Matthew nowhere in sight, he walked in to find Matthew sitting at his desk, writing, the tape player next to him.

"Hello, Matthew. What are you working on?"

"What does it look like?" he scoffed. "My sermon."

"Oh, perfect! Have you been recording your sermons for us to hear? And have you been taking your meds?"

Matthew waved a hand. "Yeah, yeah… You know what, Doctor? These tape machines can take your soul from you." He pointed his pencil to the microphone on the tape recorder. "You throw your words out and they land in there, that little black hole. They get all jumbled around inside and put back in order whatever way they need to be. Whatever way helps them be heard. Sometimes it doesn't even sound like me—I swear."

"I think it's unlikely that the tape player is taking your soul, Matthew. It just makes a recording of your voice."

"My voice? Yeah. My voice all right… That's because I'm the only sensible voice in this place."

"Does that mean you've made your first recording?" Joseph asked, a little more eagerly than he intended.

Matthew shrugged.

"Care if I take a listen?" Joseph said, moving toward the desk and the tape recorder.

"Go ahead. I mean, you *have* to listen anyhow, don't you?"

Joseph picked up the tape recorder and pushed the "rewind" button until it ran back to the start of the tape. The "play" button clicked into place and the tape began to play.

"Okay… is this thing on? I'll start this whole recording thing with saying how stupid everyone is for not listening to me. If they wanted to, they could be saved. The dark day is coming, and when it happens, no one will see anything but their own self-consumed worlds. Their own grief. Their own issues. They'll all surface and build their own realities without ever recalling what had happened, returning into the darkness forever. My reality is the only truth, and they talk through me to warn others. I don't care if this thing takes my soul. These words aren't mine anyway… What? What do you mean? Of course I can tell them that! They should know about all this. Okay, then that's what I'll do… No, he needs to, but he won't wake up enough to see it… Okay, so anyhow, like I was saying, these words I deliver can save you from your own misery. But you must listen! The dark day will come. All will be shown from the past, present, and future for all that is bad at once. We'll need to embrace the words and lessons because they're the only hope we have. She will lead us away from God. But an angel on earth will give us strength through the longest night. She will—"

Joseph stopped the tape player. "Sounds like you're doing very well getting this all out. Do you mind if I take this tape with me? That way we can learn from these daily teachings you're providing. You have enough cassettes, right?"

"Yeah, sure. I've got a whole drawer full. Do whatever you want with it. It was your idea, anyway. You probably just think I'm crazy anyhow and you'll just write in your little handy-dandy doctor book how many crazy things I'm saying, and you won't believe any of it."

Joseph shook his head thoughtfully. "I assure you, Matthew, we only have your best interests in mind. You tried this experiment, and so far it seems to be working out well." He paused thoughtfully. "Which reminds me, have you been taking your meds at night to help you sleep?"

"Yeah. I sleep hard from those. Sometimes too deep, though. She can't reach me when I'm in that deep of a sleep."

Joseph considered for a moment. "You keep talking about a *she*. Will you tell me who *she* is?"

For the first time, Matthew seemed uncertain. "To tell you the truth, I don't know. She just tells me these things. And then I say these things. I don't know her. But she seems to really know me."

"Okay, Matthew. Thanks again for the recording. I'll be back for the next one soon. Thanks to you, the halls have been quiet late at night and the patients are able to sleep. So this really does help us all. This and your teachings of course," Joseph added quickly.

"Yeah, whatever. She'll find her way in whether or not it's through me."

Joseph stood up and put the cassette with Matthew's recording into his coat pocket. He exited the room and pulled his schedule from his pocket, unfolded it, and looked to see where the new patient, Jennifer, had been placed: room 407.

Nestled at the end of the long corridor of Hall 4 was room 407. According to the notes from Adam and the nurses, Jennifer's admission had gone more smoothly than most.

He had seen it a hundred times. Usually there was plenty of kicking and screaming, but Jennifer was compliant, and even was noted to have been "understanding" as to why she needed to be in the crisis ward. This didn't match her parents' assessment that she was paranoid and would resist coming here. Joseph still was curious how Jennifer would act once he met her. Every patient's case was like a new puzzle, and it was time for him to find where the illness hid in the labyrinth of Jennifer's mind.

When Joseph walked up to her room, he saw Travis walking toward his room, which was next to Jennifer's. Joseph gave him a friendly nod, and Travis returned the nod gesture, but with far less of a smile than the doctor had shown. As a nurse closed and locked the door to Travis's room, Joseph turned back around and knocked lightly on Jennifer's door before unlocking it and walking in. Jennifer was sitting on her bed, looking out the window toward the forest. Jet-black hair with slight waves made the ends twist along the back of her standard-issue sweatsuit like ribbons hanging down from her head. Almost in a meditative state, she wore a slight smirk while watching the raindrops' tails bead down the window. In the reflection, a white doctor's coat vaguely appeared.

"You must be Dr. Hoffmann," she said, turning toward Joseph. She smiled cheerfully.

"That's me. And you must be Jennifer. The rain's really coming down, isn't it?"

"Yes. An ocean of thoughts comes to mind when someone looks out into a blanket of rain like that." She pointed toward the window. "Each drop is suspended like another emotion, as they pour through us. Isn't it great?"

This was not the response he was expecting. She was apparently intelligent and also talkative. Being that social wasn't something Joseph was used to with most of his patients. If he hadn't heard the stories from her parents, in any other context he wouldn't believe she was anything other than a poet.

"Do you like poetry, Jennifer?"

Her face lit up. "Wow. Yes, I do! English and writing were always my favorite subjects in school. Well, that and drawing. I like words and I love stories. I like how they can mean so much but so little at the same time. Words can do great harm or great good, depending on the slight variations in the way they're laid out in a sentence. It's like a wonderland to me... built from fragments of a person's imagination and memories."

Joseph started to wonder why she seemed so... sane. He knew the importance of getting to know her. She was being open with him, which made his job easier. Something about her demeanor, however, was off. Joseph knew that confirmation bias could harm his relationship with his patients, so he was careful not to assume he knew her troubles better than she did. He also knew that deeply set, in between her words, he would find her illness. He could already hear notes of it in the way she spoke, her attitude towards this place.

"... Fragments of a person's imagination and memories," he repeated, as if tasting the words. "I've never thought about it that way. Very astute observation." He pulled a chair up to her bed and sat down. "I would imagine you're a bit curious about what's happening and how things work around here. Let's go over some rules and procedures here at Cottage Grove, and then we can get to know each other. First off, let me hand you this."

Joseph gave Jennifer several sheets of paper with the Cottage Grove Hospital guidelines and her legal rights, among other things.

"Your parents also have these papers, but because you're an adult, you're entitled to them as well. This way you can look at them at any time to figure out how things work around here."

Jennifer stood up from her perch on the bed and headed to her desk. She sat down in the desk chair and began to look over the documents. The entrance forms explained voluntary and involuntary admissions and their differences. Information about the Mental Health Act of 1973 was listed on another page. Some patients pored over every word, every nuance, whereas there were others who never gave the laws a second thought. The next document was the most important. It explained that at Cottage Grove each patient was under twenty-four-hour observation with a minimum of five weeks of treatment before an evaluation and decision for release could be made. Jennifer looked everything over then placed the papers on her desk.

Joseph noted that she didn't seem particularly interested in the laws section. She glanced over it as if it had no purpose at all. He filed that away.

"Okay, so there's that," Joseph said. "And here's the daily schedule of what's expected from our patients, including meal times and rules." Joseph stood and handed her another sheet of paper with the calendar for the months of June and July. Listed were wake-up times, meal times, free time allowed outside of the room, and other details she might need for her daily routine at the hospital.

"Okay, Dr. Hoffmann. Thanks for these. I'll look them over probably another hundred times because I'll be so bored sitting here all freaking day."

Joseph gave her a comforting smile. "Oh, no, it's not that bad. We have a library here. You're allowed to check out one book at a time. It's at the end of Hall 2. You'll have plenty to read. And our Activities Director will make sure you're not tearing your hair out with boredom." He watched her reaction to this. Quiet acceptance matched with a smile. "So now that we have all the paperwork handed over, let's talk a little bit about you." He pulled his chair up to Jennifer's desk and sat down. "Your parents have informed me about certain… episodes. Times when you get lost or think the furniture in your room has been switched around while you sleep. I'd like to hear more, if you're willing to share."

Jennifer sighed. "It all started a couple years ago, when I was a freshman at college. I started to have strange thoughts that were distracting me from doing my homework or normal things. Sound, emotions, images… they all started flooding in. I held it together well enough, though, and didn't tell anyone because I was scared they'd all think I was crazy for believing these things were real. Really, I was afraid that if I admitted it, they would *know* I was crazy. It wasn't until the fear of what was happening in my head got stronger than the fear I had of what people would think of me that I finally decided to tell my parents. They weren't very concerned. When I brought it up again, they just assumed I was on drugs. I told them I never touched drugs and never would."

Jennifer slumped in her chair and paused for a long moment, seemingly lost. "I became confused about life. This got worse when I started having dreams about my room switching around. They weren't really dreams, though. I was certain it *was* switching around. I would wake up in the morning and my bed would be in a different place. I'd ask my parents but they insisted no one had! It was though! I was certain all of this was happening, Doctor. I am certain it still *is* happening. That's the thing… It is happening, right?"

There it was. The illness between the words. Joseph started to see the first signs of schizophrenia. Jennifer was at the age when it begins to invade a person's sanity. Like a ravenous leech on one's mind, it hangs on, and takes the person's world down with it.

"You see, Jennifer, for someone like yourself, these things definitely could seem real. To those around you, though, they might not be something they can see, feel, or hear like you do."

"Like magic powers?" Jennifer said with a playful grin.

Joseph smiled kindly. "I wouldn't go that far. It could be something much more innocuous. What you're experiencing is likely hallucinations. You can *see* and *hear* things others can't, but that doesn't make them real in the world around us."

Jennifer straightened up. "Doctor, do you ever wake up from a dream and know you had a dream, but you can't remember what it was?"

This made Joseph pause. He covered quickly. "Of course. We all do."

"But do you ever wake up from a dream knowing exactly everything that happened and wonder *why* you can remember? Why it was put in front of you?"

"I mean… I sometimes wake up from dreams that were very vivid. I remember what happened, but I have never come to the point where I wonder why I remember some dreams and not others. From what I know in the literature I've read, it's something about waking up in the middle of REM slee—"

Jennifer cut him off. "No! See! That's exactly what you *lead* yourself to believe. We know very little about sleep, don't we? When I sleep, I feel more awake than when I'm actually awake. When I'm awake, I feel like I'm observing life through someone else's eyes. When I'm awake, I crave for the night so I can return to reality again. *Real* reality." She looked at him with a stern, unhappy-teacher expression on her face. "I would be a little more cautious in attempting to use science to explain what is unseen or unheard if I were you, Dr. Hoffmann."

Joseph leaned back and crossed his arms. "That's just it, though. I'm a doctor. Science plays a large role in my job. Science and psychiatry go hand in hand. I don't believe what I can't hear or see unless I have proof in some other form. Science helps provide that proof for me, and it lets me understand what is otherwise incomprehensible. That's also how we treat illnesses—with science and reliable medication and with proof of their results."

"Doesn't this make you feel like you're isolated and restricted in your beliefs, Doctor? Don't you feel like there's so much more to know beyond science?"

Joseph shook his head. He wasn't happy about where the conversation was going. "The world doesn't accept stories or beliefs like these. It can't. The world accepts what's proven or shown. Not seeing what is there can make a person feel misunderstood, but it is also what keeps an illness in someone's mind. Without science, we don't know what to treat, or how, to rid us of these elusive thoughts." Joseph felt himself tensing up. For some reason, Jennifer was able to push a button with him. With every ounce of effort, he pulled himself back to his professional role, his position as the authority. "Don't worry. We'll get you back to normal soon enough." he said with great assurance.

Jennifer sat with her legs crossed, looking at him and giving him a knowing smile. Then she looked to the window and continued. "Not viewing the world for what it really is makes a person a loner. They live in the blindness they've created themselves. They live in their past filled with too many truths. Too many facts." With the words smoothly rolling off her lips like a poetic avalanche, she turned back to her desk and looked at the daily patient's schedule.

"It says here that lunch is soon. They say lunch is the most important meal of the day! So, what's on the menu today?"

The abrupt change of subject was not lost on him. He cleared his throat. "I think you mean breakfast. Breakfast is the most important meal of the day."

"Not to me. I prefer lunch. Lunchtime is when we're able to reflect on what's behind us and also on what's in front of us for the day. With breakfast we can only look forward. But the past is just as important, isn't it? The past can be *everything*."

Joseph sat motionless with his index finger curled over the bottom of his chin, mulling over what Jennifer had said. "Once again, very poetic, Jennifer. I think we'll have some great talks with a mind like yours."

"And also with a mind like yours! You're the smart doctor, after all. But we both know that."

"You're right. It's almost lunch. I won't keep you any longer. You must be hungry."

Joseph walked to the door with unease, wondering what had just happened. The whole conversation felt very mature for a nineteen-year-old girl with the signs of schizophrenia. The entire conversation felt sane, but also out of control. He was well aware there was always a thin line between brilliance and insanity, but Jennifer might be living right on that edge. He turned around before leaving the room to look back at what she was doing, expecting her to be watching him leave. But she remained seated, looking down at her schedule and tapping her foot on the floor.

"So long, Dr. Hoffmann! It was good to meet you. Let's talk again soon."

"You too, Jennifer. Your treatment here is my highest priority. I will be visiting with you every day. I'll do my best to keep up with you," he smiled. "If you need anything at all, let a nurse know or push the button on the wall there." Joseph pointed to a red "call" button on the wall next to the bed. "That's not a toy, though. No games are to be played with that, or we'll turn it off. If you push it, it'll let the nurses' station know you need them for something important."

"Something important like you or some medication?" Jennifer asked.

"Yes, sure. If I'm here, I'll come to talk with you as quickly as I can. The nurses and I will help get you on the right medications to help with everything. You should be fine once we get you squared away."

As Joseph left the room, their conversation ran through his head. He felt a sense of disorientation. He began to wonder if they had actually been having two different conversations. That wasn't too terribly uncommon, but this time he felt like he had failed to communicate something important. Or failed to understand something equally essential. He knew all too well about everything she'd said, though, along with his feelings being bottled up, stuck in the past. It was like Jennifer already had all the answers he could possibly give her with his professional care. For a short time, he had felt like he had become her patient, and she, the doctor.

She's a really smart girl, he thought. *I'd better keep my eye on this one.*

Chapter 6

"Into the hidden forest I go, to find myself and lose my soul."
—anonymous (London, 1748)

At lunchtime, Joseph decided to eat in the hospital cafeteria, which was located in a separate building. To get there, he had to walk along a small roofed path from C Ward that passed through the fenced-in yard. Even though it only took a couple of minutes to get from his office to the cafeteria, this stretch was never favorable in the winter or in the muggy summer months, but it did give the patients who were allowed to eat in the cafeteria some fresh air for a short period, even on a stormy day like today. The nurses and security would walk side by side, both in front and in back of a line of patients. Dylan, a longtime patient of C Ward, had a fascination with birds, and as soon as he'd step foot outside, he'd make the most fabulous bird calls for every type of bird he heard. It was uncanny, almost identical to the real thing. Another patient, Stefanie, occasionally tried to run. She would earn her cafeteria privileges and stay good just long enough for them to really trust her, and then she would run again. She couldn't get too far, though, since the fences were very secure—massive structures, with a second fenced in perimeter, both topped with concertina wire, rolled up on top like a Slinky of death. No one was getting out. The likelihood of escape was much higher during patient transfers to other facilities, but the huge field surrounding the hospital made it nearly impossible to be hidden for any length of time. But even the open field had its own fenced perimeter. This served to keep would-be accomplices away from the hospital, and funneled visitors to the front security entrances instead. The forest on the edge of the field looked like a safe haven if an escape were successful, but even then, it was so thick and dense with evergreens that someone would have a hard time making their way through unless they stuck to the paths. The dogs would be on them so quickly they probably wouldn't even see them coming. The dogs wouldn't bite, but the patients didn't know that.

Much to his own surprise, Joseph actually liked the food in the cafeteria. For someone with such rich tastes, it never ceased to amaze him how enjoyable the food was there. No caviar or Camembert at Cottage Grove. Just goops of lasagna or greasy fried chicken-patty sandwiches. The cafeteria was split into two sections. One for the patients, and the other for the staff. Both sections were served by a central kitchen and buffet, placed on opposite sides of a wall. The patients' side had far less of a selection, limited to the daily menu items, and were served by the hospital's kitchen staff. The medical staff's side had some self-serve options, along with the daily menu being served.

Joseph preferred to eat alone. On the rare occasion when his favorite table wasn't open, he would grab a light snack and eat it on his way back to his office. He would never dare to eat in his office, maintaining separation of his work life from his small escapes. Much like his time at the gym, lunchtime was an emotional sanctuary from the hustle and bustle of the hospital's drama. He couldn't handle everyone talking to him while he tried to enjoy his meal. In fact, he would prefer to eat off the grounds if everything wasn't so far away.

Joseph walked across the yard shortly after the patients and nurses made their way over to the cafeteria.

He headed to the self-service area and grabbed a turkey sandwich, a Jell-O parfait, and a cup of fiesta chicken soup. He continued to the drink cooler to pick up a bottle of water before heading to a seat in the far corner facing the window at a table by himself. He sat down and dug in. The table next to him was full, with four female nurses talking among themselves. The nurses were talking so loudly he thought he might as well be sitting at their table. He kept trying to tune them out, but they were overly excited about something.

"What! Are you serious? When did he ask? How did he ask? Wow, Olivia. I am so, so happy for you!"

"Me too! That is so amazing, Oli! Congrats!"

"I couldn't believe it either!" Olivia said. "Marcos took me to this fancy-shmancy overlook area next to the park where we used to meet back in high school. You know that park over on East 35th? The one with the rocket-shaped slide? We went to the overlook area down the path from there, where we'd ended our first date with our first kiss. He was sweatier than he should have been from walking down such a short path, so I asked if he was okay. But instead of him nearly having a heart attack, it was me. *Boom!* Just like that, he reached into his pocket and knelt. 'Will you marry me?' he asked with the shakiest voice *ever*! I nearly fainted. I was like 'Oh, my God! How romantic!'"

"That's so cute!"

"Yeah, Oli! I'd better be one of your bridesmaids!"

"And I'll throw the party!"

The group of women laughed, arguing over who should be the bridesmaids and who should handle the bachelorette party. It sounded like a group of high-school girls talking about their newest crush rather than adults talking about a proposal.

"So, when is the wedding?"

Wedding. The word rang out in Joseph's ear and stuck firmly inside his head like glue on wool. He spun his ring as it tightened. Its grip on his finger began to burn, and memories began to set in. He stared at his plate and his half-eaten sandwich, with his mind fading into the past.

❧

"Come on! Let me take a peek!"

Joseph stood outside the room where Helen was getting prettied up for the wedding. Since they were having a traditional-style wedding, he wasn't allowed to see Helen before the ceremony. But that wasn't going to stop him from trying.

"No! Go away, ya creep!"

The bridesmaids all laughed. He was jokingly trying to poke his head into the room before he received a playful nudge from a woman. His groomsmen, standing behind him, were laughing too.

"Okay! Fine then! I guess I'd better go back to my room and hope I don't get cold feet!"

Joseph and his groomsmen headed back toward their side of the church to finish getting ready, all the while joking about how he was about to be hitched and locked in with one girl for the rest of his life.

"You *sure* about this man? You *really* want to do this?" one of the groomsmen teased him.

"Guys! Come on! I truly do! Helen is the love of my life!"

"We know! We still gotta have fun with you, though. You could end up divorced five times like Alex!"

"Hey guys! It's three times, thank you very much!" Alex snapped, but he was laughing too.

"We love you, man. We know you'll be a great husband… and sugar daddy!"

"Yeah, Helen's gonna love that doctor money!"

"Ha, ha, ha. Very funny, guys," Joseph said.

The guys kept messing around until there was a knock on the door.

"Come in!" Joseph called out.

The door swung open, and a lady from the church entered with a huge smile. "It's time, Joseph. Time to get this wedding going! You ready?"

"Ready as I'll ever be! Feet are still feeling warm, so let's do this!"

First the grandparents and parents moved down the aisle and took their seats. Joseph was thrilled his entire family was able to fly in from Germany for this special occasion. It was time for his cue, and he stood waiting. He walked down the aisle feeling weak in the knees and hoping he wouldn't sweat too much because there was a lot of hair gel that might fall down into his eyes, and the wedding photos would look ridiculous. Eventually he made his way to the front and took his place facing the officiant at the altar. The rest of the wedding party trickled in behind them. Joseph's friend's daughter came leaping in, dancing in circles and throwing flowers everywhere, while her three-year-old little brother, the ring bearer, stood crying at the back doors, too scared to come down the aisle. He dropped the pillow and rings, then covered his face. His dad quickly stood up to help him get his courage to make the journey to Joseph. The church resounded with an explosion of "Aw, so cute," which probably made things worse for the boy. Eventually the father and boy made their way to the altar with the rings before sitting back down. Silence took the lead for a moment while the organ player flipped to the next page of her music book.

"Please stand for the bride!" the officiant announced powerfully and boldly, as though it were huge a ceremony made for a queen's entrance.

"Here Comes the Bride" began to play on the organ, and the doors spread open.

Standing at the end of the aisle was someone made from everything beautiful and brilliant about the heavens. The golden curls of Helen's hair hung on her shoulders at the perfect length, melting into the roses of the laced sleeves that led down to her wrists. Her sparkling diamond-blue eyes looked up at Joseph and made eye contact that ignited the butterflies in his stomach and turned them into a flapping frenzy. It was a look he would never forget. Helen's smile took over her perfectly made-up face, and her unforgettable dimples took over her cheeks. This was the moment he always had dreamed of. A moment that felt like something from a fairy tale. This stunning woman was his bride-to-be. There was no doubt in his heart or mind that Helen was the woman of his life. The one he would grow old with. She was walking down the aisle into his arms for eternity, and Joseph would never let go.

When Helen arrived at the front, the officiant asked everyone to be seated. Joseph and Helen couldn't stop smiling. The words the officiant spoke didn't even matter. When it was time for the vows, Helen and Joseph were in such a dreamy fog that they both had to be prompted to even speak.

"Joseph, you are my best friend," Helen began. "You are the beacon of my life. I will love you when we're together, and I will love you when we're apart. I will forever be by your side, in sickness and health. "

"I, Joseph, choose you, Helen, to be my wife. Since the day I met you, I knew you were the one. The smiles we have shared. The tears we have shed. They're built from our love for each other. I will be with you forever, both in darkness and in light. I am yours, and you are mine. Do you take me to be your husband?"

"I do."

Joseph held Helen's hands, which were beaded with sweat, and placed the ring on her finger. Helen then placed Joseph's ring on his finger.

∾

In the cafeteria, spinning the ring obsessively around his finger, Joseph felt his world crash down on him once again. *It's my fault. It's all my fault. She was my everything*, he thought, bringing his attention back to his plate. His sandwich looked disgusting. Everything about it. He had lost his appetite and couldn't even handle the smell of the cafeteria. The nurses next to him continued talking about Olivia's wedding plans. Joseph wanted to be angry at them for being able to live a moment like that and enjoy it. To have love. To enjoy life and live it to the fullest with so much to look forward to. Right now, the only life he had to live was one of pain and regret.

It's not fair. None of it's fair. We had so much planned. So much to live for.

But he also knew, better than most, that life isn't fair. Every day he dealt with unfairness with the patients he treated, and it would be selfish of him to think only his problems mattered. He downed the last sip of his water before he walked to the trash can and threw away the rest of his food. The last words Helen had said to him echoed in his mind: Don't work too much, Joseph. You'll die of a heart attack.

But it was back to the grind for him. It was all he had. It was time to bury himself again, deep in his work and other people's problems, masking his own.

✸

The veil of night took over the ward yet again. Diane sat up in bed to catch her thoughts, which were diluted with meds. She'd felt like something or someone was trying to get her to wake up. She pulled her legs out from under the sheets in a motion to get up and move around. She then stood up and looked at the clock next to her bed. It was 2:30 a.m. The storm, which had raged throughout the day, had long since passed, and the moon was glowing brighter than usual. All the gaps between the curtains threw moonbeams out, casting geometric shapes onto the floor. Diane moved as though she were disoriented, pacing in front of the window and looking confused. She was searching for something she had lost but didn't seem to know what it was.

He's gone, you idiot. They killed him. They took him away.

The voices—something Diane hadn't heard lately—had come back. The drugs must have been wearing off.

You can't just sit there. You know Jean-Paul is out there. You have to find him. He's your son.

Diane seemed to have found the thought she was looking for. But she still couldn't find her son.

"The damn doctor put this cocktail of forgetfulness in my head," she said.

Yes. Yes, he did. But that's going away now, isn't it?

"Oh, shut up!"

Diane paced again before looking back at the clock.

"It's after 2:30 a.m. It's time for him to come home. He has to be out there somewhere."

She sat back down on her bed, took a deep breath, and shut her eyes.

Just come back home. This is your warm place. Mother misses you.

Yes... She misses you. She misses your rude knocks at night that keep her awake all the time.

"Stop it. Stop it. Please stop it," Diane whispered, holding her ears and shaking her head. It was a battle for reality. She knew the voices in her head weren't real. At least the nurses and doctor had told her that. But she was still certain Jean-Paul was outside, wanting to get in. She continued to argue with herself and beg for help.

I can't make it without him. I can't make another night wi—
Knock, knock, knock.

Three short raps came on Diane's window from behind the curtains.

"Jean-Paul! Is that you?"

A raspy, hollow voice said, "Mother, I can't get in. I'm so, so cold. Please, Mother, help me get warm again. I need you."

He isn't real, you idiot. You can't let someone in who isn't there.

"He *is* real!"

Yeah, sure. Just like I'm real and not part of your imagination.

The voices echoed in Diane's head, making her feel queasy and dazed. Black shapes appeared on the floor next to her, a shadow of a head, shoulder, and an arm came into view, cast by the moonlight.

"I'm here, Mother. Let me in."

Diane looked toward the window, between the splits of the curtains, where the figure stood. She made out what seemed to be a tall, thin body shape peering in.

"I'm here, Jean-Paul! I'm coming!"

Just as Diane moved toward the window, the door to her room opened and two nurses rushed in.

"Ms. Lynch, what are you doing up this late?"

The shadow disappeared when the fluorescent lights from the hallway took over the room.

"But m-m-my son! He's here!"

"Calm down, Ms. Lynch. Calm down and please sit back on the bed."

"He's right there!" Diane ran to the window and threw the curtains open. "See!"

Outside the window were the yard and the cafeteria, a corner of the hospital that tucked around the edge of the grounds, and two trees standing still in the night.

"Where… where did he go?"

"Diane, please sit down. Relax for us, please."

"You took him again!" she screamed. "You took him from me! You're supposed to help me. The doctor said you would."

Diane was livid. She picked up a book and threw it at the nurses, who quickly ducked out of the way. One of the nurses lifted her radio to her mouth and called for security.

"If I don't see Jean-Paul again right now, I will kill myself!" Diane screeched.

"Diane, please sit down and take a deep breath."

"He's my son! I know it was him!"

Adam rushed in with a restraint chair. Diane knew it must be time for the dose, but that didn't stop her.

"You will *never* keep him away from me!" she went on. "I'll kill myself before you take him from me!"

Adam and the nurses held her down on the bed, and one of the nurses gave her a dose of Thorazine. Diane felt the prick of the needle as it slid into her arm. She slowly drifted off, and then a nurse took her vitals. Like listening through a fog at a distant ocean, Diane continued to hear what was being said even though she couldn't move a muscle.

"You think we need to throw her in PS1?"

"No, I don't think so. She just needs to sleep, and these meds should hold her over. Let's just make sure we keep an eye on her."

"Poor Diane. She was doing so well lately."

"Meds must have worn off. We'll let her doctor know."

The two nurses looked back at Diane. Once they thought she was fast asleep, they placed her back in her bed and left the room with Adam trailing behind them. As soon the door closed, Diane opened her eyes for one last lethargic glimpse at the window. The shadow was back and looking in through the crack between the curtains, but Diane wasn't able to move. She knew the small amount of energy left in her body wouldn't be enough to bring her to her son. It would never be enough to let him in.

Chapter 7

"Goodnight to the stars. Goodnight to the moon.
Goodnight to the ghosts who play in my room."
—anonymous (Ghent, Belgium; 1775)

In the middle of the night, Joseph woke up and found it difficult to get back to sleep. The clock next to the bed shined bright: 2:35 a.m. As hard as he tried, he couldn't relax and felt on edge for no apparent reason. He was used to not sleeping deeply; some days his anxiety and obsessive mind couldn't rest. Tonight, it was different. A strange buzzing feeling coursed throughout his body, as if someone were pulsing an electric current through his muscles. He decided to go downstairs and pour himself a glass of water. In the kitchen, he still felt strange and couldn't put a finger on why that was. He looked up to the ceiling, put his hands on top of his head, and let out a deep breath.

Instead of trying to figure out if he'd be able to sleep again, he decided to call his sister. It was 11:35 a.m. in Germany, and he felt the need to check in on his mother.

After a short ring, Anna picked up. "Joe! Is everything okay? What are you doing calling at this hour? It's the middle of the night there!"

"Yeah, I know… No worries, though. I'm having a rough time sleeping. Maybe I'm getting the flu or something. Not sure what's going on."

"Well, let's hope not. When you get sick, you act like a little baby."

Joseph chuckled. "Oh, shush. I'm not *that* much of a baby! I'd say more like a toddler."

"Ha! That's about right. Either way, you'll most likely need a diaper soon enough, Grandpa."

"Very funny, sis. But yeah… so I was calling because I couldn't sleep, and well, I had this urge to check on Mom. How is she?"

"Let's say she's not getting better. She's starting to lose her mind, Joe. She's not all there most of the time."

"Wait—what? Losing her mind?"

"I think it's just old age. The doctor said this can happen due to the cancer treatments. They call it chemo-brain."

"Yes, that's true," Joseph said, switching into doctor mode. "Patients can have complications of delirium and confusion from the treatments. But I just spoke to you a couple days ago. Was this happening then too?"

"No, it's recent. Started yesterday. She keeps talking about Grandpa. And she keeps talking about that damn box you're supposed to have. It's like the only thing she talks about lately. That and some strange words that make no sense. But they come and go."

"Strange words?"

"Like mumbling. You know, like people do when they're beyond tired and can't fully get out a sentence. The only thing she can talk about that's understandable is the box and Grandpa.

Then she goes back into these memories and stories, coming up with elaborate things we never actually did. She said we went to Egypt once. When the hell did we ever go to Egypt? And what would we have gone there for? I know we didn't go for a holiday, did we? Was I too young to remember?"

"No, we definitely never went to Egypt."

When the word "Egypt" came out from his mouth, he felt himself falling back into another memory.

&

"What do you mean, a seventy-eight-foot-long scroll? Like a piece of paper? He reads a piece of paper that long?" a young Joseph asked Grandpa Franz with the utmost curiosity and excitement.

"Well, yes, but he actually uses this to pass over into heaven easier. It's a text for his own funeral. Like a guidebook for the underworld. How to navigate to make it through."

"Wow! So, they write this, and then they get made into mummies? It sounds like a really cool life!"

"Mummies in the real world are much different than the spooky ones you read about in your Halloween books," Grandpa Franz said. "They were mummified because they believed their bodies were needed in the afterlife too. Like this scroll, which helped them cross to the afterlife more easily."

Joseph sat with his legs crossed in front of his grandfather, who was sitting in a rocking chair, slowly swaying back and forth.

"So cool! Can we go see a mummy, Grandpa?"

Grandpa Franz was a stern-looking man. Almost soldier-like, he held himself straight and tall. He wore full-body jumpsuits that ranged from light blue to gray in color, and on special occasions, he'd pull out the red one. No matter which color jumpsuit he wore for the day, he placed a handkerchief of the same color in his back right pocket. White hair sat atop his head like a rug made of silky cotton. His kind eyes and even kinder smile were two of his strongest features, and everyone knew he loved Joseph with all his heart.

"I suppose we can someday. There's a museum in Wiesbaden's city center that has a mummy."

Joseph's eyes went wide. "Has he ever come alive before? What if he's cursed and now he's really angry at us for putting his body into a museum that everyone looks at and takes pictures of every day?"

"I've never heard about a mummy actually coming to life. Those are stories of fiction, Joseph! Made-up nonsense!"

"But... but what about the story of the medicine man's daughter? Mom always told me that fortunetellers and people who use magic are liars and not to be believed. But Grandpa, you have told me a lot of stories about these things. If a mummy coming to life isn't real, but a cursed medicine man's daughter is, how do I know what to believe?"

"Maybe your mother just doesn't believe in things she can't see. The cursed medicine man's daughter was not only seen, but even written about!"

"But shouldn't I believe mom?" Joseph asked. "I told mom the medicine man's daughter only tried to help the tribe and the chief! She just was doing her job. And Mom told me it's all nonsense!"

"Your mom hasn't seen the same stories that I have seen. It's not her fault for not believing. And the medicine man's daughter was trying to help. She fell victim to her own grief. Her own trust."

"So, since mummies are real, and she is real, do you think her tribe ever made mummies too?"

Grandpa Franz grinned. "There were so many rituals across the Americas that it could be possible. The Aztecs did. Most tribes would have different practices, though. They would cremate or bury bodies too."

"Cremate! Gross!" Joseph mock gagged. "Like they're made into cream?"

"Oh, God, no! To cremate means to make into ash! Geez, Joseph, where does your mind go sometimes?"

A voice came forcefully from the other room. "Okay, that's enough! Dad, stop talking so much about death to Joseph! It'll mess the kid up."

"Mom!" Joseph protested. "I'm old enough!"

Joseph's mother barged into the living room. "You're nine! You have enough to worry about without the idea of death right now. Enjoy being a kid! Go outside and play with your friends!"

"It's okay, Katrin!" Grandpa Franz said with a toothy smile. "The boy needs to learn someday. And these stories are important. Important history lessons!"

"Yeah, about death! And myths!"

❧

"Joseph... hello? You fall asleep or something?"

Joseph snapped back into the present. "Oh, oh, so sorry! I must have zoned out for a second."

"Sheesh!" Anna said. "What were you thinking about? I thought the call dropped, but the phone showed it was still connected."

"I'm here. Sorry. I just had a crazy memory about Grandpa and Mom."

"Let me guess... His stories?"

"Yeah, just some stories. Mom always looked out for us, didn't she?"

"Very much so, actually," Anna said. "She's sort of the ultimate mother, isn't she?"

"She could mother a rock if you gave her one."

Anna chuckled softly before her tone turned serious. "I don't know how much longer we have, Joseph. Can you make it here to see her?"

"I'll have to check my hospital schedule. Dr. Riley should be able to cover for me. I'll do what I can." He paused, not sure he wanted an answer. "Will Mom even recognize me? Does she even know where she is most of the time?"

"It's hard to tell lately."

"Exactly what I feared," Joseph said. "I'll make it happen. I'm so sorry."

"Don't be. Really, don't be sorry. Just do what you can to get here. There's nothing any of us can do at this point. I'm also certain she'd rather you not remember her like this."

"But she's my mother. I have plenty of memories to outweigh ones of how she is now. Listen, I need to try and get some rest before work. I'll talk to you soon. My eyes are getting heavy again."

"Rest well, Jojo. *Ich hab' dich lieb.*"

Joseph responded in a somber tone, because he was tired and also sad about the situation with his mother. "*Ich hab' dich lieb,* Anna."

❧

Early the next morning, Joseph returned to the hospital feeling more exhausted than usual. After clocking in, he turned toward the lobby, where he found Adam reading a magazine before closing it and putting it in his desk drawer.

"Mornin', Doc!"

"Good morning, Adam. How are things?"

"Good. Just prepare yourself—Travis didn't sleep much. Up all night talking to himself and screaming. The nurses gave him some meds and he slept a bit. Said they heard him at it again this morning. Diane also had an episode again. She had to be given medication to help her sleep. She was quiet the rest of the night, though. But Travis seems to still be dealing with something."

"Thanks, Adam. I'll head over there right away."

"All right. Have a good day! I'm out of here."

"Okay. Get some rest."

"Sure, Doc! Speaking of rest, you feeling okay? You look a little worn out."

"I'm fine. Just a bad night's sleep. Maybe it was a full moon or something."

Both men smirked and moved on in their own directions. Joseph dropped off his belongings at his office and grabbed his coffee, completed his other morning routines, then headed toward Travis's room.

When Joseph arrived, he heard Travis talking in his room, so he walked more slowly toward the door. He tried to hear what Travis was saying before he entered, to help him better understand what might have happened the night before.

"The end? The end of what?"

Silence.

"No, not for anyone but me. It's not like they would understand anyway."

Silence.

"Oh… okay. Then I will. Shh… hold on."

A few seconds later, after some more silence, Joseph unlocked the door and walked in.

"Good morning, Travis."

Joseph found Travis laying in his bed. He had his eyes closed, as though he were asleep the whole time. Joseph wondered if maybe he had been talking in his sleep.

"Travis?" Joseph said lightly.

Travis opened his eyes and rubbed them gently. "Good morning, Doc. Everything okay?"

"Sorry to wake you up, Travis. I just got news that you've been wandering around your room, talking to yourself throughout the night. That doesn't sound like you. Are you feeling all right?"

Travis sat up. "I feel fine. Maybe I was talking in my sleep and the nurses thought I was talking to myself. That would make sense, wouldn't it?"

"That definitely would make sense, Travis. But are you sure you weren't up walking around too? Have you ever had problems with sleepwalking or talking in your sleep?"

Travis shrugged. "I don't know. Maybe it's the meds."

Joseph frowned. Travis seemed evasive, clearly covering for something. Joseph knew his behavior couldn't be from the medication. Travis had never shown any signs of schizophrenia or hallucinations and wasn't on any medication that could cause this. He was diagnosed with a behavioral disorder. Ever since his dad had passed away and he had to move in with his grandmother, he'd been having defiant and hostile outbursts. None of which would relate to symptoms of schizophrenia.

"Yes, could be," Joseph said, knowing it wasn't true. "I'll have to check your meds and decide what to do."

"Okay. I feel fine, though. Really."

"All right then, Travis. I'll come back later and check on you."

"By the way, you doing okay, Doc? You look worn out. Rough morning chasing crazy patients around or something?"

Wow, do I really look that bad today? Joseph wondered. "I'm fine. Just didn't have a great night's sleep. I'm sure I'll sleep wonderfully tonight, though, and I hope the same for you."

"I will, Doc. This time, I won't be talking in my sleep. Promise."

Joseph left the room, but while walking back toward his office, he couldn't shake the thought of Travis lying to him—that he claimed he wasn't walking around or talking to himself. That meant Travis knew he was talking to himself.

Why in the world would he start talking to himself? That doesn't sound like him at all.

Joseph decided to stop by the security wing again and check the TV monitors from the night before. He had to know if Travis really was wandering around all night and what he was saying.

Adam already had left for the day, and the first-shift guard, Reggie, was sitting in his usual spot by the front door.

"Hey, Reggie. Do something for me," Joseph said, walking briskly to the guard.

"Sure. What can I help you with?"

"I need to see the cameras from last night in Travis Ratcliffe's room."

"Oh, yeah, that's right. I heard he was having problems last night. Looks like they had to try and get him back to bed."

"I need to see what he was doing and saying."

Reggie nodded. "Okay, boss. Come with me."

Joseph and the guard walked into the security center, and Reggie sat down at the desk in front of the hospital's camera monitors and computers.

Reggie's practiced hand went to the camera control board and he pulled up the footage on the DVRs for room 405. While Reggie scrolled back and forth on the recording, they saw Travis had gone to bed around 10:30 p.m. After moving around in his bed throughout the night, he sat up a little after 2:00 a.m. Reggie slowed the fast-forward, and the recording began to play at normal speed. There was no sound, no talking. Just Travis sitting motionless, looking toward the window with a blank stare.

"Turn it up, please," Joseph said.

Reggie reached for the volume control. "It is turned up."

Joseph watched and listened as closely as possible. Travis remained motionless at the edge of his bed, not making a sound.

"Speed it up right here. Let's see how long he sits there for."

After watching for some time at 4X speed, Travis finally stood up. The time code showed about twenty minutes had passed.

"There! Okay, let it play…"

Reggie played it at normal speed. Travis turned around and looked toward the door then turned back to the window and spoke.

"I'm right here," he said. "I have been."

Silence.

"No one has any idea. They talk to her like it's no problem."

Silence.

"They won't believe me. They never do. Even if I tried. You have to understand this."

Silence.

"Yes, they kept doing it to her too. I always listen, though. They never do… So what am I supposed to do?"

Silence.

"Okay, but that is what I do. Every single time!" Travis's voice grew louder, and he angrily stomped around the room. Joseph began to wonder if he were arguing with himself, or if his delusion was so real, he actually thought he was arguing with someone else.

"I know it's not an illness. It's *not*! They just don't know this. They can't see it. I have to stop it before it's too late. It's only going to get worse!"

Then came a longer pause than the others before it. Whoever or whatever was speaking to Travis had a lot to say this time. With a nod of agreement, Travis slowly turned around and looked directly at the camera, which was situated in the corner of the room. Joseph's stomach turned, and Reggie murmured, "What the hell?" Travis and Joseph made eye contact through the screen, and then it felt like time stood still and things were moving in slow motion around him. Joseph moved his face closer to the screen and kept his focus on Travis. He became mesmerized by the look in Travis's eyes, feeling as though he had fallen into a deep dark cave he couldn't climb out of.

"It will find you too, Doc... It always does... It... is... one... of... us."

The words came through the monitor's speakers, shattering the silence. Joseph was breathing heavily, and his mouth was open in disbelief.

"Whoa! What a *freaky* kid!" Reggie said in a giddy, nervous tone, which brought Joseph the lightheartedness he needed at that moment.

"Yeah..." Joseph could barely speak as he pulled himself away from the screen.

On the monitor, Travis went back to bed and lay down as though nothing had happened. Joseph fumbled through his files and found the comments from the nurses from the overnight shift: "4:17 a.m.: screaming came from room 405. Had to administer sleep aid to Travis Ratcliffe."

Joseph checked the timestamp on the screen: 2:40 a.m. He remembered sitting up wide awake in his bed at 2:35 a.m. the night before. With a knot in his stomach, he had Reggie rewind the video to 2:35 a.m. That was the exact moment Travis had looked into the camera and spoken. Not believing in such nonsense, Joseph wanted to place the blame on coincidence and shrug it off, but he was finding that increasingly difficult.

"Okay, Reggie, now move forward to when the nurses said the screams came," Joseph said.

Reggie cued the video to the timestamp. Travis remained motionless on the edge of the bed until a little before 4:17 a.m.

"How is this kid sleeping sitting up? Is that even possible?" Reggie asked while rewinding the video to where Travis began to move again. Travis cautiously walked to the window, his hand in front of him, reaching for something... or someone. Static noise came from the monitor. A low rumbling voice swirled around the security room, seeping out from the monitor's speakers.

"*Ohanzee... Wayo... Kapi... Kokipa...*"

"*Ohanzee... Wayo... Kapi... Kokipa...*"

"*Ohanzee... Wayo... Kapi... Kokipa...*"

Chills overtook Joseph's body. He quickly regained his composure, hoping Reggie hadn't noticed.

The video's time display clicked down, and then, at the very second it struck 4:17 a.m., Travis screamed loudly and the other voice stopped. On the screen they saw him run back to his bed and get under the covers, screaming until the nurses came in. The nurses then gave Travis medication to put him to sleep. Joseph had Reggie fast-forward the video until shortly after 5:00 a.m., when Travis started to talk to himself again. After speeding up the playback, they watched him continue to talk, walking around the room right up until Joseph arrived that morning. He watched Travis get into his bed right before Joseph unlocked the door and came in, as if he knew that Joseph was on the other side listening.

"Damn, Dr. Hoffmann. You have your hands full with this one."

Joseph wondered what he had just witnessed. *Is this another dream of mine?*

Hoping he could pinch himself awake, he tried but couldn't.

It sounded like the same language I heard in my dream... It couldn't be, could it? And why does this all sound so familiar?

"Doc, you okay? You look really tired."

The voice that had just spoken didn't feel like it was right next to him. It sounded like it was coming from down the hall instead.

"You really do look tired. You been working too hard again?"

"What did you just say?" Joseph responded fearfully as he turned toward Reggie.

"Nothing—I didn't say anything, Doc. You okay?"

Joseph trembled. *If that wasn't Reggie, who the hell was it? Where is this all coming from? I must be so tired that I'm hearing things.*

He focused his eyes back on the security monitors and looked over all the other rooms to see what was currently happening. Everything seemed to be as it should until he got to the Hall 4 camera. Jennifer was allowed out of her room during her free time. She was watching Travis talk to himself. Joseph decided he needed to have a chat with her.

Chapter 8

"Even from the depths of the darkest oceans,
I can see my reflection looking back at me."
—anonymous (Vääksy, Finland; 813 AD)

"All right, Jennifer." Joseph walked toward her while shaking his head. "You shouldn't be looking into other patients' rooms, even during your free time. That isn't allowed. If this continues, we're going to have to lock you in your room. This isn't a punishment. It's for your own safety."

Jennifer sighed. "I'm sorry, Doctor," she said. "I was just seeing who he's talking to. I heard it all night long into the morning. The screams. The rambling and pacing around. It never stopped. It made it really hard to sleep. Once my free time started this morning, instead of going to the rec room, I wanted to see what was going on with him."

"We already know," Joseph said. "We're assessing the situation now. Travis will be better soon. No need to worry. Please stay in your room or hang out in the recreation room."

She nodded slightly. "But I enjoy walking the halls. When I am allowed, at least. It's like looking into dioramas at a museum. You can see what torments them or what makes them tick, just by taking a look into their rooms. It's like a gallery of lost souls. There's something hidden away in each of them, only to be found out and admired. Isn't that right?"

"We've been doing this a lot lately then, have we?" Joseph responded, raising his eyebrows.

"We? Not *we*. But I'm certain *you* have. You do this every day. You realize that, though, don't you? You're writing and rewriting your own story every day through all the patients' problems and their little twisted displays you have set up. Memories scattered throughout all of it."

"I… I really don't know what you're trying to say Jennifer, but I suggest—"

Her demeanor shifted abruptly. "You suggest *what* exactly? More medicine? More notes written down? More lost people reaching out, prying through their turmoil-filled minds in search of a saving grace? And then *you* come rushing in thinking you're some unwritten hero, here to save us all? When's it all going to end, Dr. Hoffmann? When are you going to say you've had enough?"

"Stop right there, Jennifer. I'm just asking you not to look into any patients' rooms. Please be respectful of everyone at this hospital, and that includes me and my staff."

"I'm sorry. Did you think I was being disrespectful? I would never do that to you. Not at all. I was just explaining why I like the halls, remember?"

Joseph crossed his arms over his chest. "The bottom line is as much as you like the halls, they aren't the best place to spend your time. Especially when you're observing other patients in their rooms. They don't need stalkers. They already have enough to deal with."

"You don't need to stand in the halls to observe them," Jennifer said. "Come on, you know that. And let's be honest—you get to truly see what they're made of when you watch through those cameras you have hanging around. But you have to be careful. There won't be much left of these patients when you strip down their dignity and privacy this much. Just empty shells walking around, wondering what's left for them. Why do you have cameras in our rooms anyway? Is that even legal?"

Joseph couldn't help glance up at all the cameras glaring down at them while Jennifer talked about their existence. He felt very exposed.

"These cameras are for security and for when we need to figure something out that might have gone wrong," he said matter-of-factly. "We didn't always have them. But we've had far too many mishaps and needed documentation of what went wrong, such as suicide attempts and outbursts that have hurt staff. We don't have staff constantly watching our patients, if that's what you're getting at. We aren't Big Brother. We're a hospital helping people feel better. Sometimes we have to take extra measures to ensure this happens, and we also must enforce safety precautions."

"Helping people feel like caged animals is more like it."

"That is uncalled for, Jennifer. No one is an animal here." He paused, collected himself. He resumed his role as doctor, something he was more comfortable with. "Why are you so angry?"

A smirk took over her face, ignoring the question he had asked.

Joseph looked up to the cameras, then back at Jennifer. He reminded himself he didn't believe in coincidence.

"What's wrong, Doc? Cat got your tongue?"

That old line. Joseph had heard that before…

☙

"H-how… how can I help you?"

The girl stood at the bar, waiting for Joseph to speak. "Cat got your tongue?"

Admiring her beautiful golden hair and her dimples, he was instantly knocked off his feet. Joseph felt overwhelmed and at a loss for words. She looked at him from across the bar. He was afraid she might pick on him for his German accent, so he took it slow and easy.

"Oh… uh… how can you help me today?" Helen said. "Well, asking what I'd like to drink would be good for starters!" She giggled in a teasing tone. She and her friends found Joseph's loss of words rather charming.

"Yes, that's it… What drink would…?" Joseph's mouth hung open again like he was choking on his words, and they felt far too large to swallow and try again.

"Wow, what kind of accent is that? Where are you from?"

He felt embarrassed that he couldn't hide his accent from her. "Deutschland… I mean, Germany. A town called Wiesbaden." Nervously he fired back with his own question. "And where do you come from?"

"America." Helen and her friends laughed playfully again. "Nothing as American as sitting here at this loud, smoky bowling alley ordering a Coke on a Saturday night is there? So what's your name? Is it something super German and hard to say?"

"Joseph."

"Well, that's not too hard! Hello, Joseph. My name's Helen. Good to meet you."

It felt like he had known her his whole life, yet they had only just met.

"Good to meet you too, Helen."

"How long have you been working here? I haven't seen you before. We tend to come here often."

"Only a couple of weeks."

"Oh, that's why! So, Joseph, what brought you to America?"

Helen's friends informed her they'd be at their table at lane six. They could tell she was interested in this handsome foreigner.

"I came here for school. I go to college here. And you?"

"Well, you see my great-great-great grandparents came over on the *Mayflower*—"

After Helen's joke, Joseph felt the ice break between them, and he let out a laugh, much louder than needed.

"What are you studying?" she asked.

"Psychiatry."

"Oh, wow! That must be super interesting! Do you, like, work at insane asylums and stuff?"

"No, no, no. I mean… at least not yet. That will come, but for now I'm only learning about psychiatry and how it all works. All the technicalities and studies behind it. All the details of the human mind."

"That sounds like really *crazy* stuff to study."

"Yes. *Crazy* stuff indeed."

They both stood still for a second, looking at each other, then smiled. They realized they both had the same cheesy sense of humor.

"So what about you, Helen? Why are you here in Oregon?"

She leaned closer toward him. "I'm originally from upstate New York, but I moved here for college too. I run track and field, so I guess they thought I was good enough that they wanted to put me through school. Not sure how far running will take me in life, but at least it gives me a chance to get an education."

"Wow, so you must train a lot for that kind of athleticism."

"Athleticism?" Helen laughed. "Is that even a word? I mean, yeah, I guess I do train a lot. It eats up a lot of my time. Between studying and running, it's about all I have time for. Except once in a while on a Saturday night like tonight, I come out with my friends to do something fun. For instance, tonight it's whooping their asses at bowling!"

"I've never actually bowled," Joseph blurted, unsure why he even needed to mention this.

"You *what*? Joseph, you're working here now. It's about time you give it a chance! How about you come join us in our game?"

"Oh, I'd love to, but I'm working, and well… they definitely won't let me bowl while I'm on the clock."

"Then how about we make a plan for another time?" Helen suggested. "Let's say Wednesday at five? We were supposed to have a track meet that day, but the other school's field got flooded or something, and they had to reschedule the thing for next week. So I have time for whatever!"

"I… I do get half-price games since I work here."

"Well, there we go then! It's a win-win. You get us cheaper games, and I get you bowling like a pro!"

Joseph grinned. "Sounds like a funny time."

"A funny time? Like ha-ha laughing funny time? It'll definitely be funny since it'll be your first time bowling, but I mean—"

"No, no! I mean a fun time! In German the word '*lustig*' translates to 'funny.' My roommate teases me about that too."

"Well, Joseph, we'll have a *lustig* time! Promise you that!"

"Thanks, Helen. See you Wednesday at five."

༃

The memory faded away, and the fog of Joseph's past eased its way out of his mind.

"Really, though, Doc. You okay? You have a blank look on your face."

Joseph rushed back into the present. Jennifer was standing across from him.

These memories of Helen are getting stronger and more intense lately, he thought. *Not sure what's going on.*

"Sorry, yes, I'm fine. Just remembered someone saying that 'Cat got your tongue?' line before. No big deal. Just a memory."

Jennifer nodded. "You look tired, Doc. You really should get some rest."

"I've heard that about twenty times today. I'll finish my rounds and head home this evening when I can. I must look like death for everyone to be saying that so often. But anyway, please try and follow the rules and keep to your room or the rec room. Or you could go to the library. Will that work?"

"You got it."

"Thank you, Jennifer."

Chapter 9

"Lost and alone, I felt the darkness take over.
I saw the eyes looking back at me,
but I freed myself from their gaze by sticking to the path."
—anonymous (Gordes, France; 1744)

Joseph took a deep breath of the crisp air and inhaled the pine that perfumed the wind. After leaving the parking lot, he stepped onto the rocky trail and headed into the forest. Although the trail looked muddy, Joseph was prepared to walk around any puddles he found along the way. Scattered with thoughts from this morning's events, he tried to process everything he had seen, heard, and felt. It was all too bizarre to be real. Every time a feeling of panic bubbled up, he'd take a deep breath and keep walking.

Maybe I've been working too much, he thought. *Maybe I'm making my patients' problems my own. There's no way any of that could have been real. And why is Travis hearing voices?*

Between thoughts, he took a few steps, soaking in the beauty of the forest's dark-green and brown hues.

I do this job to help these patients, and it used to comfort me. Mom is sick. The patients are sick. I'm starting to think I'm sick. I'm not sure I can do anything for them anymore. I'm not even sure I can do anything for myself.

Joseph walked deeper into the woods, then searched for a place to sit and rest. A large rock looked like the perfect place to sit down, but it was a little ways off the main path. He noticed a long log he could step on to make his way across the underbrush and bracken. He stepped on it cautiously, then balanced himself. Walking along the fractured log, he stepped on a patch of slippery moss, and his foot slipped into the sticky mud on the forest floor.

"Oh, great. Of course. Exactly what I'd expect from a day like today."

He bent over, trying to pull himself up from the mud without losing his expensive leather shoe. Something caught his eye.

Footprints? Why are there fresh footprints everywhere? And barefoot? Who would be walking around the forest without shoes?

The storm had just ended that morning, and would have washed away any evidence of the strangers' passing. They couldn't have come through long before Joseph had. He tried to count the number of different pairs of feet, but some of the prints were a little more worn than others. It looked like there were three or four different trails to follow. It was clear that they came from deep in the woods and made a path to the edge of the forest, where they stopped before entering the field across from the hospital. Joseph walked back onto the trail and decided to head deeper into the woods to follow the footprints as best as he could from the dry path.

Joseph followed the trail for quite some time, delving deeper into the dark forest. The prints seemed to be heading towards a large, unnaturally shaped tree. As he approached, haze and fog drifted in like arms reaching in to embrace the forest, and everything within. Something about the tree made him pause.

He made his way, stepping from log to stone, to get a closer look without falling into the mud again.

The footprints. They're coming from this direction.

When Joseph got close enough to the tree, he could see that this tree wasn't straight and tall like its neighbors. Something about this tree was familiar.

It took him a moment, but then he put his finger on it. It was a prayer tree. Grandpa Franz had told him about this sort of thing.

ᔆ

Grandpa Franz and a young Joseph walked through a forest in southern Germany.

"Now, Joseph, not all funny-looking bent trees are prayer trees."

"What about that one?" Joseph pointed to a gnarled tree in front of them.

"No, no, no," the old man snickered. "We've never had prayer trees in Germany."

"Why not?"

"Well, the early people of Europe likely marked their trails in different ways."

"Wait a second. So prayer trees don't have anything to do with praying?"

"They're trail markers, my boy! Native Americans would bend young trees to give directions for trails to their tribe. Then the trees would grow bigger as time went by, and they formed into the strange L-shape I've told you about."

Joseph rubbed his head in confusion. "Then why are they called prayer trees? Did they lead to places where people prayed?"

"They could have! But that isn't why they were called prayer trees. They're bent over, so it almost looks like they're praying. But people would use them to mark trails to food or water and other important places they needed to visit for survival."

"That's so cool! I want to see a prayer tree someday."

"I would love to see one myself. You know what else? They're also very sacred to the Native Americans who made them. They're living artifacts filled with history and stories of their ancestors."

"If I ever see one," Joseph said, "I'll make sure no one ever hurts it."

"That is good of you, Grandson. Very kind. I'm sure the spirits of the forest will thank you for that too."

Young Joseph walked up to a tree and felt the texture of the moist bark before picking at a piece of moss hanging off it. "Are those prayer trees the same ones that followed the medicine man's daughter and pointed to her?"

"Yes, exactly the same ones."

"Why did they follow her?"

"The forest left markers leading the path for the people to find her after she—"

A loud snap of a branch stopped Grandpa Franz in midsentence. A branch fell directly onto Joseph's shoulder. His grandfather ran to him.

"Oh, no! Are you all right, Joseph?"

"I'm fine! It barely scraped me! But wow, that was scary!"

"I'd say!"

☙

Joseph caught himself touching the tree's moist wet bark just as he had as a kid. The memory of his grandpa's story lingered but started to fade. He looked back down toward the footprints on the forest floor then back up at the prayer tree. The footprints followed in the direction the tree was pointing, directly toward the hospital at the edge of the forest. He examined the tree to see if it was naturally a strange shape.

Wow, this really is a prayer tree, he realized. *And to think it's been right here by the hospital this whole time. I wonder if anyone else knows about this. How could I never have seen this tree after years of walking in these woods? I can even see my office window from here.*

Joseph continued to examine the bark and the tree before looking back at the footprints in the mud.

Fresh footprints… and they lead from the tree to the edge of the forest and directly toward the hospital.

Looking toward the edge of the forest, Joseph saw the road he always drove to get home, then wondered how long it would be before he would be able to leave for the day. He looked at his watch and realized he had to get back to the hospital. If he didn't hurry, he'd be late for his next appointment. He quickly stepped from rock to log, then made his way to the path before jogging through the forest and across the field. He knocked the mud off his shoes, then looked back at the fog weaving around the trees of the forest and couldn't help feel gravitated to it.

Why does this all feel so connected?

☙

Following what seemed like an eternity, Joseph finally made it home. After his nightly routine of whiskey and a cigar to calm his nerves, he tucked away in bed. It wasn't long until the calm of the night took hold of him, and soon after his dreams did too.

"Joseph. Sit back down *right now!*"

"But the bike, Mother."

A young Joseph stood up from the sofa and walked toward the front door. Beyond the porch, standing upright on a perfectly trimmed green lawn, was a red bike. The morning dew crystallized every blade of grass, giving them a sparkle through the haze. The bike had yellow streamers hanging off each handle, and a heavy fog hung over the yard. The rest of the neighborhood was lost to a white blanket so thick you'd think the world had lost its color... except for the bike. Small but bold, shiny and red, it stood out as though it had been painted on a blank canvas.

"I just want to go for a ride!"

"You'll surely get lost in that fog, and no car will be able to see you, Joseph! You will *not* walk out that door! Stop right where you are!"

Entranced, Joseph steadily walked to the door. Even though he heard his mother speaking to him, he couldn't see her. The rooms melted away behind him, deeper and deeper into the darkness of the shadows.

"You don't know what's out there, Joseph! You won't find your way back home!"

The bike was all too tempting, and he kept moving forward before he stopped at the edge of the porch. Joseph didn't recognize the house, but that didn't matter to him. All that mattered was the red bike.

"Ya know what, little partner? You have to do what you have to do to make your dreams come true... Follow the path."

A voice from behind him cut through, and Joseph turned around to find Grandpa Franz sitting on a rocking chair, moving forward and back gracefully, his cane between his legs tapping the wooden porch. He held a straight-eyed gaze on the front yard, as if he was seeing something Joseph couldn't.

"With every memory is a story, Joseph. Some are harder to find. Some are harder to remember. You have to know what to do once you find the memories that mean the most."

"But Grandpa, Mom said—"

"Your mom will forgive you. I'll talk to her when she gets out here."

Joseph returned his attention to the yard. The bike had vanished. In its place was a little girl, crying, her hands over her eyes.

"Hello?" Joseph called out.

The girl didn't respond.

"I said hello. Are you okay?"

He tried to get a response from the girl, but she continued crying and holding her face. Joseph felt like he had known her all his life.

"They… they took my bike. Have you seen it?" the girl finally said.

"The little red bike? Yes… yes, I did see it! Was that yours?"

"It *was* mine. But they took it."

"Who?"

Joseph turned his head to the left then to the right, looking around the yard for the bike and whoever might have taken it. The fog was still far too thick and made seeing much of anything impossible. With the cloud of haze surrounding him and the girl, he lost sight of the house and Grandpa Franz.

Isolated in a world of nothingness, Joseph looked at the girl, who pulled her hands away from her face. "I have to go now," she said. "Please don't be scared. The truth will show its face."

Slowly the fog consumed her. As she was being pulled into the white void, they made eye contact for a split second.

Joseph knew those eyes. "Mother?"

෬

The sound of phone vibrating on the nightstand pulled Joseph out of his deep slumber.

He tried to pull his head from his pillow, but it felt like it weighed a million pounds. His hand seemed more awake than the rest of his body, so he felt around, searching for the buzzing phone on the nightstand. Once he found it and got enough energy to pick it up, he sat up in bed and looked at the screen: "Anna— Incoming Call." The call had shattered the silence of the night, and his heart beat fast and heavy. His anxiety took over because he knew why she was calling. It must be the call he had been dreading for so long.

"Hello? Anna? What's the matter?"

"Joseph... I'm sorry to wake you—"

"It's fine. Just tell me what's going on. Is Mom okay?"

"Mom..."

"Mom *what*, Anna? Just tell me!"

"She... she passed away in her sleep. She went peacefully."

Joseph was silent. He could only think about the fact that he was never there. He had always stayed away, and was far too focused on his own life—his own self-consumed career. He knew this guilt would build inside of his mind for years to come.

"Joseph? Are you okay?"

"It's... I mean, I knew it would be soon. I knew it would happen. But it doesn't make it any easier. It makes me think about all the years I've been away from her, and you, and our family. I could have been there more. My work was everything, and it's hard to realize I could have spent more time with her. I should have been there for her. I should have been there for you. I always make the same mistakes over and over."

"It's okay," Anna said. "She went peacefully, and she wouldn't have wanted you back here anyway. She knew you were finally living your dream of being a psychiatrist... And after everything that happened... you... you needed to be there. You needed to do what you had to do to get by. You've dealt with enough death and grief. You know how this feels the most. I am certain Mom realized this and supported you in the best way she knew that she could; letting you live life and stay happy. To continue moving forward."

Joseph sighed. "You're right. Her way to support us was always letting us be. Letting us learn the way we needed to learn and believing in our decisions. I'll book a flight as soon as I get off the phone. What do we do now?"

"You just make it back home. That's all you need to worry about. I'll handle everything here. Most of it is already taken care of because we knew this day was coming. She wanted to be cremated. Nothing special or fancy. We were the only family she had left, and she just wanted all the pain to end. She's finally at rest, and now she can be with Dad."

"I'll take the soonest flight out."

"Joe... are you *really* okay?"

"I'm fine. I can handle it."

"If you need anything," Anna said, "call me. And let me know once you have your flight booked so I'll know when to pick you up from the airport."

"I'll text you after I get my ticket. And Anna..."

"Yeah?"

"You'll think I'm absolutely nuts, but I had a dream just now. I can't fully remember all of it, but I do remember most of it."

"About Mom?" Anna asked.

"No, well, not exactly. It was like we were at this house, but it wasn't our house. It was an American home but before I ever lived in America. I must have been seven or eight. I saw a bike in the front yard and felt like I should go ride it and that it belonged to me. I also saw Grandpa. And I heard mom tell me not to go outside. There was so much fog and then..."

"And then *what?*"

After a couple more seconds of silent contemplation, Joseph continued, "There was this girl. She was dressed in clothes from the fifties. And... I think it was mom. But it was her as a kid."

"So, you both were kids?" Anna asked. "At the same age?"

"I guess. I know it sounds crazy. The girl said, 'Please don't be scared,' then vanished. Then I woke up to this call from you. You know I don't believe in all that superstitious nonsense, psychic powers and all. But something's starting to grab me lately. I've been feeling things and sensing a lot going on around me that seems a bit… odd. Things in my dreams and things at work. Then Mom telling me not to be scared, and lately I've felt overwhelmed. And Grandpa… Grandpa's stories are starting to come back to me."

"It makes sense that you feel overwhelmed," she said in a motherly tone. "It's probably the stress with Mom and everything going on."

Anna was talking with her supportive tone that Joseph knew well. But even as understanding as she was of him, he assumed this would have been too far gone, too crazy, even for Anna to comprehend. So he continued, knowing he could go even deeper into the truth.

"No, it doesn't feel like stress. It feels like something else. It feels like something changed and something has been following me home from work at night. And now this… this dream was so vivid in certain parts that I remember it fully and like I was actually there. And Mom, Mom was there. I need to figure out what's going on with my head. I'd say I think it's good I come home, but this isn't the circumstance I was hoping for."

"We'll talk more when you're here, but for now please just find out when you're coming home and let me know, okay?"

Joseph didn't reply.

"Are you there?"

"… Yes. Okay. I really hope Mom is finally at peace."

"She is, Joseph. And she's not in pain anymore. That's the most important thing to remember."

"You're right. I'll be there as soon as possible."

"Okay, Jojo. *Ich hab' dich lieb.*"

"*Ich hab' dich lieb*, Anna."

Joseph booked the soonest flight he could to Germany. This would be the first time he had taken time off from the hospital for a family emergency since Helen's death. As much as he knew he had to do it, it wasn't easy for someone with such a fierce work ethic as his to take time off. He felt as though he were betraying his patients and his colleagues. Although Joseph knew this was irrational, he still felt the hospital wouldn't hold up without him there. Even so, deep in his gut he trusted it would be fine while he was away.

Chapter 10

"Nothing will teach us, change us, move us,
and shape us more than Death itself."
—anonymous (Corsica, Italy; 290 BC)

During the nights following Joseph's departure, the ward seemed more erratic than ever. One would assume the lack of his presence was the culprit, but this was far from the truth. Something much bigger than Joseph seemed to be watching over Cottage Grove. Something that knew exactly why it was there.

The sky broke and a single drop of water fell.

Isolated, the raindrop was pushed side to side by the stormy winds. After a couple of trembling moments, the desolate drop came to rest on the window of room 302. Diane was wide awake, looking out, when the small splatter of water hit the glass. The raindrop broke into pieces, and smaller droplets rolled down, leaving long thin trails behind them. As Diane looked up at the dark and gloomy sky, the rain began to fall. The moment the sky began to cry, so did Diane.

"Why do you keep telling me to do this? Please leave me alone!"

Diane was talking half out loud and half behind a shaky breath.

"Why would you take my son? And now you want me too?"

The storm was building and the rain was getting heavier, and so was Diane's conversation with whatever was outside the window. She paced nervously, every so often looking up at the window in hopes that whatever was out there was leaving her alone.

"Stop looking at me. Stop looking at me! Just *stop*!" she snapped.

Diane turned her back to the window and wrapped her arms tightly around her body, hugging herself, then rocked back and forth. She could feel whoever was at the window, and they didn't want to leave anytime soon.

"Leave me alone!"

After a short moment of silence, she inhaled deeply, then sighed with relief.

"Finally…"

Just as she felt satisfied that whatever was outside the window had left, long, terrifying scrapes moved across the glass behind her. Between each scrape was the sound of a low rumbling voice that was unintelligible.

"I won't do it! I won't kill myself just because *you* want me to!"

Diane gathered the courage to face whatever it was and tell it to leave again.

"Go away!" she screamed, her eyes closed tightly. The noise stopped, and she stood with her eyes closed, frozen with fear to open them.

A moment later, a voice came. "Mother, it's me."

"Jean-Paul?"

Diane pried apart her eyelids, in hopes of seeing her son standing there. It took every bit of her courage for her to do so, and once she got one eye open, a figure came into view: a tall handsome young man standing outside the window. His sleek black hair was pulled back, and his hand was held out in a caring gesture.

"Jean-Paul, it's really you. You've finally come back to me!"

Diane ran to the window and put her hands on the glass. The man walked toward her with both arms out. Step by step, he moved closer to Diane. The rain was pouring down, yet he was bone dry.

"Something isn't right…" Diane began to question what she was seeing.

"Mother. It's me, Jean-Paul. I found my way back home. I found my way back to you! I told you I'd never leave you. Come be with me, Mother!"

The young man was only a short distance from the window when Diane noticed something below him—a reflection staring up from a puddle on the ground. But it wasn't Jean-Paul looking back at her. It was someone else.

"Mother…"

"Stop! Stop right there! Who are you? And what did you do with my son?"

The man stopped, and then, with an expression of disbelief, looked terrified. Diane glanced down again at the reflection of the puddle and noticed a shape taking form. It was an old man, with black weathered animal fur draped around his shoulders. He carried a long crooked walking stick made from branches, and thin bone beads hung down his chest. In his right hand was a bundle of broken, muddied eagle feathers and small bones. Before Diane could make out in detail the full features of whoever was in the reflection, the door to her room sprang open, and the light from the hallway erased the apparition from outside the window.

"Diane, we need you to lie back down. We need you to go back to bed."

Loud noises were coming from every direction in the hallway, and the nurses were extremely on edge. Behind the nurse in Diane's room, other nurses were frantically racing up and down the halls in both directions. One of them ran up and tapped the nurse on the shoulder.

"We... we," said the nurse, who was having a hard time catching his breath. "We need to go on lockdown *now*! Not a single patient is asleep, and they're all walking around their rooms and the halls, talking to themselves and having some kind of hallucinations!"

The nurse holding the door open turned to Diane. Realizing Diane might be the least of her worries, she quickly left the room.

"But... but I saw something. Someone's here with me. And it's not my son," Diane said, shaking, and a little too late for the nurse to catch a word of what she said. "The handprint... The handprint on the window." The door was already shut, and Diane once again was alone with herself, her thoughts, and whoever was outside her window staring back in.

∽

It was a long trip and an even longer couple of days since Joseph's arrival at Wiesbaden. The funeral was small and intimate. Their mother's wish to be cremated made for an even less monumental ceremony, with no casket in sight. It was only a minister, Joseph, his sister, her husband Mark, and a huge bouquet of lilacs sitting on each side of the urn. Although it was what their mother wanted, it felt a little lackluster for celebrating someone's life. Joseph couldn't help wonder if their mother's choice to be cremated had to do with Joseph working and living so far away. She must have worried whether he could make it home in time or make it home at all. Either way, he was there now, and Anna had encouraged him to stay a bit longer to clear his head before returning to the States and the ward.

Joseph looked up an old childhood friend, Patrick. They decided to meet at a local bar to catch up. It had been many years since Joseph had been home, but they'd remained in touch. Patrick was a small, witty guy who always had been much different than Joseph. Joseph avoided dirt, and Patrick became an automotive technician covered in oil and grease. Joseph always liked to stay inside and read, while Patrick had urged him out to go to dance parties and be more extroverted.

Patrick and Joseph planned to meet at the Towny Irish Pub. It was a quiet bar until the nightlife took over, and then it turned into a college hangout. The same college hangout where Patrick and Joseph used to sneak in and drink underage. They would sit at an older friend's table and take a few swigs between each pass from the waitress, somehow avoiding getting caught. Patrick swung open the door with a huge smile on his face. Joseph stood up to greet him with a hug and pat on the back.

"Joe! My man! It's been *so* long! Seems like forever!"

"It sure has! Over ten years!"

Patrick was short and stocky but well defined. His black hair and dark skin made him the opposite of Joseph in appearance as well.

"Hot damn! Ten years? Really? Wow."

"Well, let's face it," Joseph said, "I don't have much reason to make it back here."

"I'm not enough of a reason?" Patrick said. "I'm just poking fun, Joe! So why you here? What's the big reason that brought you all the back across the pond? You find out you got a girl pregnant back in our heyday and have a long-lost son to catch up with?"

"No, actually my mom died."

There was silence, and Patrick's demeanor changed. "I'm so sorry, Joe. I had no idea. Are you okay?"

"I'm fine. I mean… we saw it coming for a few years. She was sick for a long time. It doesn't make it easier, though. It just makes it… different, I guess."

"I remember Anna was taking care of her, wasn't she? I ran into her five or six years ago at the Christmas market. She seemed happy but a little worn out."

Joseph nodded. "Yeah, she was—or rather, still is. But I think this will help alleviate some of her exhaustion and time restraints."

"Yeah, it's bittersweet. Death is always hard. You know this, though. You've been through hell and back. But you're the strongest man I know because of it."

"Well, I have you fooled then, haven't I?"

They both had a good chuckle, and then they ordered a couple of beers from the waitress before returning to their conversation.

"So how's work and life?" Patrick said. "You still a quack for those crazies?"

"Psychiatrist for the mentally ill, yes. But sometimes I feel like I'm the one going crazy."

"Don't we all, though? Last week my boss was driving me nuts. I literally thought I could put my hand through the wall. I'm not even an angry guy, but sometimes things just drive us mad."

"It's hard to explain. Something's been going on with me lately." Joseph said with a troubled voice. "I've probably just been working too much."

"Whoa! That's not the Joe I remember. You never would have said you work too much. Every time we've caught up, you've been doing seventy-hour weeks at the hospital. And after Helen… I mean… after, you know…"

"Her death?"

"Yes, sorry. I'm just saying, after that, you seemed to immerse yourself in work even more. We'd talk once in a while on the phone, and then I wouldn't hear from you. And when I'd email you, I wouldn't hear back. I was wondering what happened to you off and on for years, what happened to our friendship. We were so tight. But your sister said you just buried yourself in your work after everything. And that was years ago."

The waitress returned to their table with two pints of beer. Joseph and Patrick both took long sips.

"I'm sorry, Patrick. It's true. I do work too much. I did and I *still* do. I seem to be making all my patients' problems my own lately. I get too involved."

"You can't save them all. You know that, right?"

"I'm not trying to be a hero or anything. I guess I lost my reason for why I do this job in the first place."

"I totally understand that. I do."

Wearing a haggard expression, Joseph sighed. "I wasn't always like this…"

"Oh, I know! Well, you were always a bit of a nerd and homebody though!" Patrick chuckled.

"Hey, that's probably true. I never exactly understood why you hung out with a nerd like me anyway. You always had cool cars and cool girls and cool everything."

Patrick leaned his head back and let out a boisterous laugh. "Come on! All that stuff is nothing. Look how far any of that got me. You always had something I never had. You had drive and passion. Ambition. That's something many people lack. That's why you got the hell out of here. You were meant for something so much bigger!"

"Maybe…" Joseph paused, then added, "But sometimes I wonder what if I'd never left."

Patrick took a long draw of his beer then placed the glass down. "You'd be doing a whole lot of nothing, just like the rest of us."

"No, I mean all of it. What would be different? What if I never met Helen? She would be alive and living a happy life with someone else somewhere."

"Okay, stop right there!" Patrick said. "This is life, man. Every moment we decide to make a small little decision it will forever impact everything else that plays out. You have to take the punches life throws at you. Take them head on. You've always done that, and that's why you're such a strong person."

"Maybe so." Joseph sighed again. "But I feel like it's all caught up to me now. I feel weak and a bit lost and confused. It feels like something is eating me alive from the inside out."

"That sounds horrible. It'll get better, though. It has to."

Joseph leaned back in his seat and placed his hands on the table in a matter-of-fact gesture. "Sorry. Enough of this pity party I'm throwing."

"No, really its fine. Clearly you need to get it all out. And you've always been one for emotions."

Joseph laughed while taking a last drink of his beer.

"So, Joe. How long are you here? When are you heading back?"

"Well, I would have gone back tomorrow, but Anna thinks it's best that I stay a few more days."

"From the sound of it, she's more than right. What are your plans while you're here? You surely can't coop yourself up there at your mom's. You need a place to stay?"

"Oh, no. It's all good thanks. I'm actually at a hotel downtown. The Edelweiss Inn."

Patrick's eyes went wide. "No way! Have you seen any ghosts yet?"

"None that I know of. Why would I see ghosts?"

"Man! You don't remember, do you? When we were kids, everyone thought that place was haunted. We'd all go there and ghost hunt, remember? It's the same building—used to be an old hospital, but they turned it into a hotel. St. Elizabeth's Hospital. It was long shut down when we went in there. Spooky as hell."

"Well, great! Now I won't sleep a wink tonight!" Joseph said jokingly, trying to hide his failed attempts to remember the building.

"You still got that book?" Patrick asked.

"Which book?"

"*The* book, man! The book you always took with us to do our witchy stuff! We took it with us on our ghost hunts at the old factory too. The book your grandpa gave you."

Finally, it started to come back to Joseph. The book. His grandpa. The witch stories and ghost hunts. Some of his childhood seemed like it had happened yesterday.

"Oh, that book. My grandpa never actually gave me it—I just kind of borrowed it back then."

"Woo-wee. Those were some crazy stories in there. Handwritten things in the margins too. Weird notes and stuff. Where the hell did he even get that thing?"

"I don't know. I don't even know what happened to it," Joseph said, his mind consumed by nostalgia.

"That one about the Native American girl gave me nightmares!"

Joseph began to remember all the times he'd taken his grandpa's book and shown his friends. He always was so proud to show everyone that creepy book. It had a strange black leather casing and, like Patrick had said, handwritten notes in the margins. It was almost like his grandpa was doing some sort of research while reading the stories in that book.

Weren't they simply just stories? Made-up fairy tales like Mom always said they were? Joseph was deep in thought, looking toward another direction of the bar while Patrick kept talking.

"You definitely believed all that stuff! You even made me a believer back then. You still think all those weird oogie-boogie black magic stories your grandpa told you were real?"

Joseph laughed. "No! Definitely not! You think I'd carry all those stories with me all these years? I mean, hell, if I did, I'd be dead from fright by now. Those stories were downright creepy."

"I always wondered what happened to those stories as we got older," Patrick said. "Did we just forget them? And if so, how? They were all we talked about back then. Man, life is funny sometimes."

"You're telling me! Those stories were my obsession when I was a kid. I guess I just got sick of everyone making fun of me for believing them once I got older. As everyone grew up, I felt like I needed to grow up too. Move past those stories and become a man."

Patrick ran a hand over his face. "Kind of sad when you think about it, isn't it? We were all so innocent and believed everything we were told. But it made life a lot more entertaining—that's for sure."

Chapter 11

"Don't fear the darkness when it is a part of you.
Because then you will fear yourself."
—anonymous (Cuenca, Ecuador; 1532)

Joseph finished his last beer and said his farewells to Patrick, promising he'd stay in touch much more often than he had over recent years. After he left the bar and headed to his hotel, questions filled his head. A flood gate had opened inside Joseph's mind. His memories began to pour in one by one, until they were all overshadowed by the memory of the book.

What was with that strange book and what happened to it? Why was Grandpa taking notes? How could I have forgotten so many of my childhood memories? And why are they all coming back now?

All this raised a curiosity in Joseph that was so strong it consumed his thoughts.

I must find that book.

He wanted to hurry to his mother's house to look for the box right then, but Anna had the key to the house and it was far too late. He would have to wait until the morning before he could get to it.

Joseph finally made his way back to the hotel, and now that he remembered it used to be St. Elizabeth's Hospital, he felt a little spooked as he walked in. Most of the lobby was exactly as it was when he was a kid, and he couldn't believe he hadn't remembered that when he first had arrived. Of course, it wasn't broken down or abandoned, but it still had the same red and white tiles that outlined the walls and doorframes. The big gold front desk where people checked in was where the hospital admittance desk had been located. The same vintage-style lanterns hung off the wall with Victorian light bulbs in them. When he moved past the front lobby he looked down the hallway to see if the door by the old cafeteria was still there. He remembered now—that used to be the only way for him and his friends to get in when they snuck in from the back alley at night.

When he approached the elevator, he looked to his right and saw the big doors still swinging from the bellhop who had just walked through them. They reminded him of Cottage Grove— and any other hospital for that matter. The big swinging doors were a surefire giveaway that this was a hospital at one time. After Joseph got into the elevator and looked at the number panel for the building floors, he saw the button for the fourth floor.

That's it. That's the floor we always broke into from the stairwell.

He remembered it was the creepiest floor. One end was the old children's play area, and the other end was the surgery department. They could tell because the room had white tiled walls with a drain in the middle of the room. It was similar to a butcher's killing room. Joseph and his friends would do their Ouija board readings there. It also was where he and his friends had smoked their first cigarette. Patrick had stolen it from his grandmother and brought it to one of their hunts. They'd had so many experiences in the old hospital—both exhilarating and scary.

Joseph stepped onto the fifth floor where his room was located. As he walked into the hallway, he recalled the time he and his friends could have sworn they'd seen a headless nurse walking the halls. She was slightly transparent, with her hand up, as if she were snapping a latex glove on. She had stopped, and her torso turned toward them, as though she were making the effort to look at them with her nonexistent head. The boys were frozen with fear that she could sense their presence as much as they could sense hers. The nurse then turned around and continued on her way before disappearing into the darkness at the end of the hall. All the boys screamed and ran down the stairs as fast as they could. The grownup Dr. Hoffmann knew this memory couldn't have been real. Kids like to feed off each other's fears and make them into their own reality. Basic Psychiatry 101. But he remembered the feeling young Joseph Hoffmann had of each of his hairs standing up when the decapitated nurse walked directly in front of him.

Joseph eventually arrived at his room. He got his bed ready and plugged in his phone. He noticed he had three missed calls from Cottage Grove Hospital. Any other time and any other day, he would have called back and make sure everything was okay. But not today. Joseph was locked into nostalgia. Work had taken him away from his childhood and his memories all these years. He had promised Anna he would take a few more days off before going back. And Patrick was hurt that he never had time to reply to his calls or emails… It was all because of work. Work caused nearly everything wrong in his life. Even Helen's death.

But maybe they need me?

After battling with himself to respond to the calls for a good ten minutes, he decided that his bed, his memories, and his promises to his sister and Patrick were the most important things at that moment.

They have other doctors there. I'm sure everything's fine.

ᆼ

Back at C Ward, things only got worse. It had been days since the nurses could recall any of the patients getting a full night's rest. The staff couldn't get a handle on it. They had already increased to a ratio of one to every six patients, and with none of them sleeping, it was nearly impossible to keep up with any of it. They racked their brains trying to figure out why this was happening, and after many failed attempts to reach Dr. Hoffmann, the nightshift nurses had to take all the problems into their own hands.

Amid the chaos was Matthew, who was wandering the halls with his tape recorder in hand, interviewing each of the patients. Meanwhile, Travis was crouched in a corner of his room, afraid to open his eyes and look up at anyone who tried to talk to him. The ward had been moved to lockdown, and all patients were forced to remain in their rooms until they could get the proper medication to each of them. Both of the personal safety units were occupied, and the other patients were forced to strip down and wear thick quilt-like garments called suicide gowns. These would keep them from hanging themselves with their clothes by tying them together or tearing them apart to make a noose.

After everyone was locked up, the noise grew louder. Now the loud banging and talking came from each of the rooms instead of the hallways. The patients were caged up like vicious lions, each calling out their demands. "You can't keep me here forever, you pieces of shit!" came from one room, while "It wasn't me! I swear I didn't eat the last cookie!" came from another—all surrounded by laughter and the sounds of crying, screaming, and cursing. The patients were in total disarray, and the ward had become a circus of insanity. And Joseph was none the wiser that any of this was going on.

In room 207, however, it wasn't the same commotion coming from the rest of the units. Instead of bursts of nonsense, it was a tape player, playing back Matthew's interviews from the day. In something like a demented talk show, Matthew was asking each of the other patients how much they believed in God and what their favorite food was from the cafeteria. Between the questioning, Matthew was talking to himself, agreeing or disagreeing with whatever was said. Once the tape came to a stop, he picked up the recorder, carried it to the corner of the room, and placed it on the desk. He then went to sit back down on his bed, but before he could, the tape started to play on its own. Static noise took over the room, and Matthew looked toward the darkly lit corner, where the tape recorder was partially hidden. After a few short moments of loud static, Matthew walked over and picked up the recorder and shook it. The static stopped. With a feeling of relief, he began to walk back toward his bed, but then the tape player clicked twice, and the small red light blinked on.

"I get it, okay? You want to interview me now. So what! I have nothing to hide from you!"

The sound of static grew louder.

"Come on! You out of anyone know I'm a soldier for God! I talk about him all the time. Isn't that good enough for you?"

The red light on the recorder flickered, and the static grew even louder. When the static swelled in volume, the rest of the ward seemed to get louder too. The red light flickered again, and the static noise became deafening, as did the screams from the other rooms. The power and volume of the recorder seemed to reflect and relate to the rest of the ward's intensity.

Matthew held his ears and crouched. "Stop! I can't take it anymore!"

After another moment of deafening sound, the recorder stopped. The entire ward became silent for the first time in forty-eight hours. Matthew slowly peeked out from his tightly sealed eyes and removed his hands from his ears. The shadow in the corner of the room where the tape recorder sat was growing larger and darker. As its dark cast became even more defined, Matthew looked up in horror. He could barely get the words out from his constricted throat.

"It's not… you. Who are you?"

The shadow in the corner started to swallow the room, leaving Matthew crawling backward toward the door in a panic. Choked with fear, he crawled faster and faster, his hands grabbing and reaching for something to hold on to and to help him fight off whatever was coming at him.

"Help me! Somebody help!"

Matthew turned around and banged on the door as hard and loudly as he could. As the sounds of footsteps thundered down the hall toward his room, he continued banging as loudly as possible. Then he stopped. The ward once again went silent except for the sound of jingling guard keys and footsteps, while the ward's night team raced toward Matthew's room.

"Come on! Hurry up!" said one of the nurses anxiously as they ran down Hall 2.

"*Matthew?* Matthew, are you okay?"

The nurses eagerly waited to enter the room while Adam fumbled with his keys, trying to find the right one.

"Come on already!"

"I'm trying!"

Adam found the key he was looking for and went to put it in the keyhole, but the key wouldn't go in. The hole seemed to be sealed by something from the other side. Adam pulled the key out and examined it. "What the hell is this?"

Both the key and lock were wet and dripping with muddy water. Adam rubbed his finger onto the dirty wet liquid coming from the hole, then rubbed his fingers together before bringing them to his nose.

His brow furrowed. "It's mud… and it's ice cold."

The keyhole began to weep even more, the muddy water streaming in a steady line until it rested at the bottom of the door, where it pooled on the floor. Adam and the nurses backed up from the door and put their backs to the wall behind them. Then there was a click and a bump before the door unlocked and slightly opened. It was as though someone had jiggled the doorknob, but only enough to barely open it.

"Adam, you go first," one of the nurses said.

Adam stepped carefully toward the door with all the nurses hunched behind him, nudging him along.

"This is so messed up," he muttered. Once he arrived at the door, he cautiously pushed it open. "Matthew… is that… is that you?"

Adam peered around the door to find Matthew sitting on a chair in the corner of the room, holding the recorder. He was half in the shadow, half out. He pressed the "record" button, and the red light went on.

"Tell me, Adam… How much do *you* love God?"

"What the hell, Matthew! You scared the shit out of us! Please bring me the recorder and come sit down on your bed."

"But I've seen it now. It showed me what it really is. It's right here with us."

"Okay, Matthew. Go to your bed and give me the stupid recorder."

"But you won't believe me. You won't believe any of us. You think you're doing your job, but you're actually helping it take control."

Deciding that discussing this wouldn't work, Adam rushed Matthew instead. He and the nurses held Matthew down and gave him Thorazine.

Before Matthew could be put into a deep slumber, he yelled out one last warning: "This might keep me broken down, but it will only make it stronger!"

Adam and the nurses put Matthew back into bed and tucked him in for the night. They searched the room for anything he could use to hurt himself, then took the tape recorder with them. On the way out, Adam looked at the keyhole from the inside and found a chunk of mud in the lock. Having no idea where Matthew could have gotten the mud from, they left the room and made their way back down the hall. Adam jiggled the handles to all the other patients' doors to make certain they were still locked.

Adam and the nurses talked among themselves as they made their way to their offices.

"They all seem to be locked. No idea how that happened with Matthew's room."

"Dr. Hoffmann won't believe any of this when he gets back."

"Let's be frank. None of this makes sense. I mean, why did everyone go silent at the same time? It's not like we medicated them all. Maybe they were *that* exhausted—I have no idea."

"Sure, but *all* at the same time? Come on. That's weird. It was pure chaos before… and now it's as quiet as can be!"

"Well, let's be thankful for that. Maybe all our hard work has paid off. Time for them to get some rest. And same for us."

Adam went back to his security desk to try to calm down. It didn't make any sense. The loud noises. The patients not sleeping. The mud in the keyhole. It was all too much for any of the staff to grasp. They were all exhausted and confused. It all seemed like a bad nightmare, but it wasn't.

❧

In Wiesbaden, Joseph had no idea that any of these strange events were happening at Cottage Grove. The only thing on his mind was his grandfather's book. He barely slept during the night, tossing and turning, waiting for his sister wake up so he could give her a call. After a few hours of broken sleep, he decided to grab a coffee in the hotel lounge and replay the times he remembered reading his grandpa's book. It was all a bit fragmented and so long ago, but he could now grab on to a few times when he had shown his friends the book in his bedroom late at night during a sleepover—and at their ghost hunts at St. Elizabeth's Hospital. Looking around the lounge, he soaked up bits of memories he had of when the place was broken down and abandoned. He saw a figment of himself as a preteen, running through the halls with the book in hand and his friends running behind him because they thought they heard something. These long-forgotten memories were coming back for a reason. Joseph had been through a lot, and many of the tragedies life had tossed his way had polluted his mind and pushed much of the yesteryears into the background. And the older memories were slowly being lost to the elements of time and clutter. New memories being made were always tainted with a darkness so deep in him that it could never seem positive or good.

When the clock struck 7:00 a.m., Joseph gave his sister a call. After a few rings, Anna picked up.

"Hello?" Anna said groggily.

"Hey, Anna. Sorry to wake you up if I did. I need to get into Mom's place, and I realized I don't have a key. Can I swing by and grab it?"

"Sure. Is everything okay? You're up early."

"Yes, everything's fine," Joseph said. "Remember Mom talking about the box Grandpa Franz left for me? Do you know where it is?"

"I think she said it's in the basement. Why?"

"Oh, nothing. I just need to find it."

Anna sighed. "What's *really* going on? Why is this box so important?"

"I guess I had a very nostalgic meeting last night with Patrick. A trip down memory lane."

"Memories of you guys picking on your weak little sister?" Anna said. "Holding her down and tickling her to death? Jumping out and scaring her to death? Those kinds of memories? You guys were always so mean to me."

"Very funny. It was all out of love, trust me. Although those were great memories—ones I remember to this day—they were nothing we talked about. Do you remember when we used to go to that old hospital?"

"Not really."

"St. Elizabeth's. You probably were too young to remember, and we only took you with us once. It was far too scary for someone your age. Well, this hotel where I'm staying… *this* is the old hospital. My friends and I used to ghost hunt here. Patrick refreshed a memory in me that really stuck. One that involved a book Grandpa used to have, and I used to take from time to time. He'd leave it on a small bookcase, almost as if he wanted me to read it. I was always afraid to ask because it looked very important. It had these crazy ghost stories and myth-type things, and his handwritten notes were on all the pages. I had completely forgotten about that book. I have a feeling it might be in his belongings, the ones Mom wanted me to have."

"So you stole Grandpa's book and you just remembered it, and you think it has to be in the box he left for you? He had hundreds of books, Joseph. Why would he hold on to this particular one?"

"I don't exactly know. I just have a feeling. One I can't ignore. Something was always special about that one to me, and I think he knew that."

"Joe, if you need to relive your childhood, be my guest. I think it's probably a good thing. Maybe a trip through your childhood will get you back to your old self."

"I don't want to relive my childhood. I'm just starting to remember things that for whatever reason were long forgotten."

"Come get the key then," Anna said. "I'll meet up with you at the house later in the morning. You doing okay otherwise? When I asked you to stay a few extra days, I was worried how this would end up. I had a feeling you'd either tell me to screw off, or you'd be working, sitting with your laptop in your hotel room all day."

"You ready to be proud of me? I ignored several calls from the hospital last night!"

"You *what?* Well, then, hell has officially frozen over. No more Dr. Hoffmann! Say hello to Joseph, the man of ghost memories and childhood dreams. A man of family and friends. A true character of gratitude and—"

"Okay, okay. I get it. You don't need to rub it in. I knew you'd be proud of me."

"I am," Anna said. "I'm always proud of you. Now come get the key and find that box."

"On my way!"

Joseph quickly hung up and headed out the door to find the nearest cab.

◌◌

He arrived at his mother's house after getting the key from Anna. Walking up the driveway, he remembered all the times he had played basketball with his friends growing up. He remembered building racetracks for his bike, using chalk to draw the lines, and setting off fireworks by the street on New Year's Eve with his sister and friends from the neighborhood. He walked to the front door, put the key in to unlock it, then headed inside. It was like stepping into a time machine.

The house was clean, and most of the ground floor was packed up into boxes. It still smelled like the home Joseph remembered, just a much older one. A musty scent lingered, while fresh wipe marks of recently removed dust stained the shelves. The house had been left mostly untouched in recent years while their mother was at the nursing home. Joseph spotted the same green couch and chairs he had grown up with. Some family photos still hung on the walls, and Joseph remembered all the wonderful things about his mother and all the good times he had there while growing up. She always loved photos, and any time the family got together for holidays, she took so many photos it would cost her a fortune to develop them all. Family was the most important thing to her. Joseph always remembered this, even when he was away from home, which was something that was very dear to him. For many reasons though, it became harder as he grew older to return home and see where he had come from. He had a fantastic time growing up, but after Helen's death and the trauma that it had brought him, he felt he could never leave her, even long after she passed.

Much like his mother, he held on to memories. But in a different way. His memories were selective, and instead of hanging family photos on his walls, he'd leave rooms untouched with Helen's belongings or other pieces of his dark past locked behind closed doors. When he glanced around the living room, he saw similarities between his mother and himself. Pieces of his father's life were still there, as though they were the only bits left that she could hold on to. And Joseph's baseball trophies sat on the mantel. Even his old felt Alpine hat was still hanging inside a cracked-open closet. Around him were memories his mother never had wanted to part with. Now the time had come to have both his mother's and father's memories placed into boxes and stashed away for his own keeping. Joseph couldn't help seeing the irony in it all.

Memories that a person treasures so much that they keep them with them at all times, only to become a memory themselves, handed off to the next generation still alive and able to keep the memories going. It's like a domino effect of the living and nonliving, all coming full circle to who, or what, is to be remembered and handed down to the next person, only to wind up in a box in someone else's basement. Or, in the best case, sifted through and hung on a wall for new eyes to see. A gallery of memories, with only life as the artist, and the viewer appreciating it for all the wrong reasons—or for all the right reasons. Joseph could never decide.

There was only one stash of memories he was after at that moment, and it was downstairs, hidden somewhere among spider webs and dust.

When Joseph approached the storage area underneath the basement stairs, he realized none of the stuff sitting there had been moved for a long time. Some boxes were moldy, and others were damp with water that had dripped from the pipes in the ceiling. Not a big fan of grime, Joseph cautiously moved the boxes apart from one another to look for the one his mother had mentioned. After searching for a few minutes, he couldn't find anything but old clothes and some of his sister's toys. He worked his way a little farther back and noticed a box that was jammed underneath the bottom stair. Joseph turned on his phone's flashlight to get a better look. Crawling on all fours, he reached the box and gave it a hard tug to free it.

After pulling it out, he put his phone away and wiped the dirt off his hands before he opened it. Upon first glance, all he could see were a couple pictures of Grandpa Franz, some of himself as a kid, and a toy airplane his grandfather had given him when he was six. After putting the pictures and the airplane aside, he saw another picture of his grandpa, but this time he was in an unusual place. It seemed to be some kind of dig site, deep in a forest. There were shovels behind him, and tables with large pictures and maps sprawled out all over them. It looked like he was searching for something. Joseph flipped the photo over and saw a note: "Hoia Baciu Forest, Romania, 1952."

Underneath the photo was a box of jewelry that looked very old; it was filled with little trinkets and beads from some type of tribe. Then just below the wooden box was a book.

That's it! That's the book! I knew it!

Joseph picked it up as fast as he could and blew the dust off. It had the black leather casing he remembered, with torn edges and a copper lining on the spine. The book didn't look like a normal book, though; it had no title on the front and nothing written on the back or side. Joseph carefully opened it to find some loose pages barely hanging on to the spine. While flipping through, he quickly realized this wasn't really a book at all, but rather a notebook of compiled memos and typed stories. In the margins were a significant number of notes, all intertwined with certain parts that were typed into text and some that were underlined or circled.

This seems to be a notebook for studying something. Personal memoirs too. But what was it for? Why this fascination with historical stories and folklore?

Joseph turned a few more pages, and as he arrived at the middle of the book, a photo dropped out. It was Grandpa Franz in a lab uniform. On his shirt, Joseph made out a name badge: "Dr. Arthur Franz."

Doctor! No one ever told us he was a doctor. Did Mom even know?

As far as his family knew, Grandpa Franz had been a janitor at a medical building in a confidential laboratory. He told everyone he cleaned the facilities until he grew too old to do so, and then he retired before his dementia set in. Joseph turned the page and skimmed the book's stories and notes. There, between two worn pages was a fully typed story: "Catori's Curse."

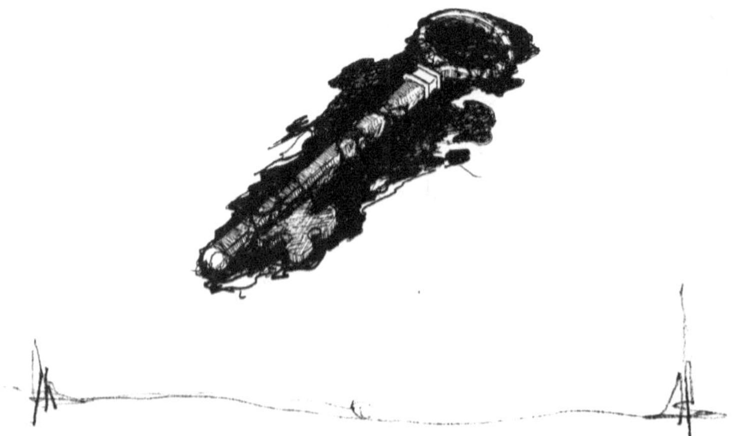

Chapter 12

Catori's Curse - 12/06/1958

Little was known about the Raven River Nishawka tribe, aside from what we've learned from some of their stories and folklore, which continued to resonate through the centuries. They were an extremely reclusive Native American tribe, living near Raven River in a forested valley in the American Northwest. The tribe leader, Picasha, known as the "The Thunder Prophet" to his people, was the brother of a medicine man, Powtacca. Picasha and Powtacca were thought to have had many years of rivalry, with Powtacca constantly trying to take over leadership of the tribe. The tribe's people weren't sure who they trusted or feared more. The Nishawka often turned to the worship of their natural surroundings to help make decisions and relied heavily on the elements of the earth for all their answers.

Powtacca's daughter, Catori, was believed to be cursed when she was born. Her mother died shortly after giving birth, and as Catori got older, she started to see things no one else could. But no one believed her.

The tribe blamed Catori's curse on her father Powtacca's use of dark medicines. His self-consuming vengeance against his own brother eventually took hold of his mind, and Picasha and the tribe banished him to the forest, to forever live alone. Picasha took Catori in as his own daughter and gave her trust and support from the tribe. As time went on, however, her visions grew stronger, and she eventually had a vision of Picasha dying a gruesome death. The tribe began to worry her curse was growing too strong and the visions would become reality. They lost trust in Picasha's decision to take her in and asked that she be banished to the forest, as her father had been. But Picasha resisted and said he could never do that to Catori after she had already lost her father.

One night, a scream came from Picasha's hut, and one of the tribesmen entered to see what had happened. Picasha lay dead on the ground in front of his bed. He had been covered in mud and ash, and his mouth was broken wide open, his eyes staring toward the hut's ceiling. The tribe blamed Catori, believing her vision had been a warning that she would kill him. Now, leaderless and under no control, they wanted her killed to rid the curse from the rest of the tribe.

Catori was tied to a wooden plank made from a broken tree and carried through the forest along muddy trails. After the tribe arrived at a deep ravine where they held their rituals and sacrifices, they propped up Catori and began to chant. A fire was raging, and the flare-ups grew bigger and bigger. Then, head first, they dipped her into the burning embers. After all the screaming stopped and the tribe was certain Catori had crossed over to the hands of their gods, they threw the burned, cracked body over the ravine's edge, chanting louder and louder while doing so.

Legend has it that Catori's father, Powtacca, was watching the entire ceremony, standing in the shadows of the forest. When they put Catori head-first into the fire pit, she looked up and the last thing she saw was her father lurking in the shadows, not coming to her aid. Before taking her last breath, inhaling the flames and breathing out in agonizing pain, she wished her soul would remain earthbound for eternity, to haunt anyone who had blamed the death of her uncle and her visions on a curse. And to haunt anyone who didn't believe those who could see. They say the only way she can reach those who don't believe is through the shadows and inside the minds of the weak.

Powtacca was found shortly after the ceremony, lying on the forest path, in the shadows of the trees. His eyes and mouth were frozen open, his neck bent, his eyes staring up at the sky. His body was disfigured beyond recognition. Catori was given the name "Shadow Licker," and her story would forever remain in the hearts and minds of the Raven River Nishawka tribe and other generations to come.

Some claim the forest knows where her spirit roams still to this day. The trees will always lead the way, pointing both the living and the dead in the direction of her restless soul.

❧

Surrounding the story were handwritten notes. Some were questions, such as "What other religions or cultures have seen this darkness and what did they call it?" or "Ancient civilizations seem to rely on their own beliefs to mold their societies, but what is to be believed and not believed?" Even though some of the notes didn't make much sense, one thing was certain: Grandpa Franz's life had just become one big mystery.

So many strong feelings poured over Joseph while he looked through the book; it was like walking through a snowstorm of emotions and confusion. He was sad because his grandpa was gone. He was sad because his mother was gone. But he was also angry that so much had been kept from him while he was growing up. As puzzled and hurt as Joseph was, he was determined to find the truth. He kept stirring in his thoughts while staring at the pages, sitting cross-legged like a giant kid with the book in his lap. The grandfather he had known growing up was a storyteller, so maybe everything he had been told was simply that—a story. A life of fiction laid out for the world to believe. A man who had made so many ridiculous claims that even Joseph's mother called him a phony and warned Joseph not to believe his stories.

So why were we told he was a janitor when he was actually a doctor? And what kind of doctor was he?

Those were the first questions that needed to be answered. With his mother now dead, it would be impossible to ask anyone else who knew him; Joseph and his sister were the last two surviving members of the family, so it all ended right there. He continued to look through the box, searching for clues. After he made it to the back of the book, he found a torn, open, empty envelope stuck to the back page. A stamp with butterflies was on the top right, with the words "United States Postal Service" and "5 cents" on the border. On the top left corner of the envelope was a return address, barely readable due the aging of the paper and smudges of water and dirt.

"Branson Center for Folkloristics and Mythology." Joseph read the degraded words out loud, revelation stiff on his tongue.

He knew what he had to do if he wanted to figure this out.

But first, he needed to speak with Anna about his discovery. She needed to know. After a quick call, Joseph waited impatiently for her to arrive at his mother's house. He took the box upstairs and placed it on the table in the living room, then paced back and forth. A car door shutting outside disrupted his anxious thoughts, and he raced to the window. Before Anna could even make it into the house, he rushed to the door and opened it.

"The box! And the book! It's all there! But Grandpa lied to us! So did mom! It's all a lie!"

"Joseph, what the hell are you—"

"Seriously! It's all a lie! I'm not even sure if he was actually sick either!"

"Okay, that's going too far. What in the world was in that box?"

Anna gave Joseph the same look their mother did when he got overly excited about something. A slightly raised eyebrow and a look of "yeah, right" spread over her face. In fact, many of Anna's mannerisms and looks were similar to their mother's. Same straight blonde hair. Same freckles on the cheeks. As much as Joseph took after their father, Anna was the spitting image of their mother.

"Answers, Anna! Answers! Well, actually more questions than answers—but it's all there. Did you know Grandpa Franz was a doctor?"

"He worked at a medical facility, but he was a janitor," Anna replied, half questioning what Joseph said and making a statement at the same time. "He definitely wasn't a doctor. Why do you think that?"

"The photos! Here *look*!"

Joseph handed the photos to Anna. Her forehead crinkled up, and her brow lowered.

"You see the name badge, don't you?"

"I see it all right. Dr. Arthur Franz. That *is* super weird."

"Yes, I know!" Joseph said. "And the stories, I think he typed them. He typed this entire thing. It was his memoirs, not a book. He even wrote notes in it. He was studying something. I have no clue what, but he was up to something."

"So was he an archeologist or something?" Anna replied.

Joseph shrugged. "I don't know. But whatever kind of doctor he was, he wore a name badge that said so. And he was in a lab coat."

"That's so strange, and Mom never said anything to you about this? Not even a hint?"

"No, but maybe she didn't even know."

"Surely she looked in that box when Grandpa gave it to her. She was always as curious as a cat."

"True," Joseph replied. "She must have known. So why did they keep it from us? And for our entire lives? Even as adults no one ever said anything. I don't know what this is all about, but I'm going to find out. Look at this."

Joseph handed his sister the aged envelope.

"There isn't anything inside," Anna replied, peering in.

"No, it's not what's inside. Look at the outside. The return address."

"Center for Folkloristics—is that even a word? We knew Grandpa was into all that folklore crap."

"Yes, but that must be a way to find out about him. If that place is still around, they must have known him. Another doctor sent him something, so maybe they have records about Grandpa there."

"That's a long shot, Joe. This place has probably long since shut down."

Joseph grabbed his phone to do a quick web search. After only a few seconds, he had a website open. "See! Look! Right here!"

On the screen was the website for the Branson Center for Folkloristics and Mythology.

"Well, email them. I'm curious now too," Anna said eagerly.

"But this isn't all. Look at this…"

Joseph handed her the photo of Grandpa Franz at the forest dig site.

"Is he hiking or something? What is this?" Anna said.

"It's a dig site—look at the shovels. What were they even digging up? Were they searching for something?"

"I think you should start by emailing the Branson Center," Anna replied. "I'd really like to know about all of this. It's so weird that he had a secret life we never knew about."

"And I read this really strange story in his book this morning."

"What's it about?" Anna held the book open and turned the pages.

"It's the tale of Native American girl who was put to death for a curse the tribe believed she carried. They called her the Shadow Licker."

"So she was cursed? Like a *witchy* curse type of thing?"

Joseph chuckled. "Not witchy—just cursed. At least they thought she was. She saw and knew things the rest of the tribe didn't. But no one believed her. After her uncle died, they blamed her for his death and burned her alive. Her father watched her get killed, but he didn't stop them."

"Man, that story is messed up! And what kind of asshole was her dad?"

"No worries," Joseph said with a half grin. "She got vengeance on him. And yes, this story is pretty messed up and gruesome. It was my favorite story when I was young, though."

"Wow, Mom let you read this kind of stuff? No offense if you do, but you sound like you actually believe this story happened. Surely you don't, right?"

Joseph waved a hand. "I don't believe this nonsense. Mom hated it when Grandpa told me these stories. She thought they were way too dark for a young kid. They didn't seem so bad when I was young, though. They actually seem much darker now that I'm older. That's kind of backwards, I guess."

Anna nodded. "Maybe because you never knew what darkness was as a kid, so you apply your experiences and what you know to your imagination. You have the boogeyman and monsters in the closet as a kid. That's about as far as it goes. But this story is descriptive. I mean… Shadow Licker? Even that name gives me chills!"

"Me too. It makes me even more intrigued about what Grandpa was really up to. Let's get the rest of the boxes inside packed up and finish tidying up. I'd call but it's night in Seattle right now. I'll send an email to that website tonight. It's worth a try."

Anna and Joseph packed up their parents' belongings and straightened up the house. While cleaning, they kept talking about Grandpa Franz's stories and other memories they had about him. As much as Joseph tried to ignore it all, the memories kept flooding back—as did the questions. He had to figure out what was going on. He had to figure out who his grandpa was.

Chapter 13

"The darkest mystery in life is one's self."
—anonymous (Corinth, Greece; 570 BC)

It was a long three days. Joseph kept himself preoccupied by going for jogs or walks and getting his mother's house cleaned up. His voicemail had been filling up with calls from Cottage Grove, but he was so focused on his thoughts of his mother's passing and his grandfather's secret life that he hadn't had a chance to listen. The night after he had found the box, he emailed the Branson Center to ask about his grandfather. Every time his email notification chimed, he rushed to his phone or quickly grabbed it from his pocket in hopes that it was a response from them. It wasn't until the morning of his flight back to the States that he received the response he'd been waiting for. The phone buzzed, and Joseph felt the tickle in his jacket pocket. *Probably just some spam,* he thought. He continued toward the gate for his flight.

Once he arrived at his gate, he sat down and placed his briefcase on top of his carry-on. He reached into the pocket and flipped the backlight on to view his phone's notifications.

FROM: Branson Center
SUBJECT: Dr. Arthur Franz

Joseph attempted to unlock his phone so fast that he fumbled and dropped it on the floor. A boy walking by picked it up and handed it to him. "Thanks," Joseph said, trying to play it cool, remembering he was in a public place.

Once he unlocked his phone, he opened the email and read it.

FROM: Branson Center
SUBJECT: Dr. Arthur Franz

Dear Joseph and Anna,

Thank you for your message. We're deeply sorry for the delay, as I'm certain you're eager to find the information you're looking for. We had to look through our records to find any mention of your grandfather. It didn't take long, actually, but the amount of information we found was extensive. Unfortunately, our records are not as complete as we would like. We do know that Dr. Franz was working closely with a branch of our center that was involved in relics and folkloristics, along with onsite surveyors. This was a team that went to archaeological sites when items of interest were found, to determine whether they were of any use to our folkloristics or mythology collections and studies.

We were surprised to find that many of the forms we had were left blank or redacted. They seem to be considered confidential—the term used was "high-security information"—held by the organization in Germany where he did his primary research. We do know he worked closely with our leading experts in relics and folklore, and it looks as though he did for a better part of a decade, up until the late 1950s at least. I'm sorry we don't have any more information than this. I hope this can at least help you in your pursuit to find out more about your grandfather and his work. Now that we're aware of his association with the Branson Center, we're as curious as you are. At any rate, it seems he was a man of great importance and vast knowledge. If there's anything else we can do to help, please don't hesitate to ask.

Sincerely,
Thomas Greensfield
Executive Director
The Branson Center for Folkloristics and Mythology

Joseph couldn't believe his eyes.

Great importance and vast knowledge? Great mysteries and vast lies is more like it. Who the hell was he?

He made a quick call to tell Anna and forwarded her the email. He had to hurry because the gate would be closing soon, and he still had to board his flight. With nearly a day of travel ahead of him, he would have plenty of time to mull this over. He got on the plane and found his seat. Looking out the window, he found it difficult to see much with the morning fog that hung over the runway.

He closed his eyes. *Why does all of this matter so much to me?*

Joseph couldn't tell if it was the longest or shortest trip of his life. He felt like he had just left yesterday for Germany, but so much had happened. So much had changed. The Joseph who had left the U.S. not long ago was stuck. He felt like he was hanging on by a thread, both regarding his sanity and his feelings of worth. And now he had something new hanging over his head, occupying his mind and making everything worse. The thoughts of his grandfather were so consuming that he hadn't even checked in on the hospital a single time. Joseph hadn't necessarily opened a new chapter, but he had definitely added a new weight to the already-existing problems he battled with each day. He was buried in lost memories and didn't know whether they were fact or fiction. Instead of finding a feeling of relief, he had found himself on the hunt for something more. Something that was causing him even more suffering.

❧

After driving home from the airport, Joseph dropped off his bags and headed straight to work with a feeling of guilt that he hadn't answered the hospital's calls or checked in yet. But he was confident that the night nurses and doctors had handled whatever was thrown at them. Driving through the forest, he noticed nothing had changed. Same trees. Same signs. He continued driving, winding around the curves and darting through the haze. He rolled down the window to feel the crisp morning breeze on his arm, then turned up the classical music on the radio. The melody was serenading him and helping calm his nerves. The thought of being back to work was taking him over the edge, so any small thing he could hold on to would help keep his mind at ease. The music was beautiful. After all, Chopin's *Nocturne in E Flat Major* was Joseph's most loved song, and he couldn't have asked for a better time for it to come over the radio. The piano seemed more vibrant than ever. It was almost as if the music were being played privately for him and was his own personal symphony. During each curve he hugged around the trees, the music swayed from side to side. Crescendos and diminuendos carried him along. It was elegant and the drive was smooth. The sun was coming up and thinning out the haze, making the road grow longer in front of him. The bursts of high notes and low tones pulsed and floated as he drove faster and farther down the forested road. He had his eyes half-closed, holding them open just enough to keep himself on the road. Each and every hair on his arm was moving to its own cadence from the wind coming through the window. He felt small drops of rain fall in, but he didn't mind. It was all part of the music's serenade. Joseph almost lost himself entirely by falling asleep at the wheel, but then something caught his attention— something that forced him to go wide eyed instantly.

It wasn't a tree. It wasn't even another car. It was Helen.

She stood still, looking lost in the middle of the road. Joseph was hurling toward her at a high rate of speed. Helen was alive and soaking wet, wearing her favorite blue silk dress.

When he put his foot on the brake, he felt like everything was moving in slow motion. His eyes met hers. He hadn't seen those eyes for years. His face was filled with fear, yet hers wasn't. She looked at him, knowing he couldn't stop in time, but she was still fully content, with a slight smile bending her lip on one side and a dimple on her cheek. Joseph swerved and tried his hardest to miss hitting her. Every muscle in his body locked up, and his teeth clenched as he waited for the impact. He tried to turn the steering wheel even further, but it was too late. He closed his eyes tighter than he thought possible. With his eyelids sealed, and a quick screech of the tires, the car came to rest off the side of the road. He jumped out and rushed to help Helen. He was certain she was dead.

Nearly tripping while getting out of the car, Joseph looked around. There was no Helen. There wasn't even a body. There was the smell of burned rubber and pine trees but not a single person in sight.

But... but she was right here.

He couldn't understand what he had just witnessed. Helen was alive and he had nearly killed her... again. He tried to collect his thoughts and get back into his car. Shaking, his hands gripped the steering wheel, and he dug his fingernails in. He knew all too well where this was coming from—it was his guilt eating him alive. He spun his wedding ring and took deep breaths, gathering his composure.

I really need to get back on my anxiety meds. I can't blame myself forever.

Joseph steered back onto the road and kept his eyes forward, self-diagnosing and trying to ease his mind.

It was nothing. Just guilt. Exhaustion. Helen wasn't there.

His focus on the road in front of him kept his eyes from seeing the reality that was behind him: a cold and rain-soaked Helen, standing in the middle of the road. All he needed to do was look in the rearview mirror, but he didn't. He kept his eyes forward, unaware of her presence. Helen was soaking wet, wearing a look of hope, begging him to turn around… but Joseph just sped away.

What lay behind him was not important, it was whatever was still to come that occupied his thoughts.

❧

The hospital parking lot was covered with puddles from the storm. He pulled his car into his personal parking place, then looked up to make sure his name was still on the wall: RESERVED FOR DR. JOSEPH HOFFMANN.

Of course, it's still there. Why wouldn't it be?

He knew it would be there, but something inside him felt like he was still a million miles away and perhaps someone more fit had filled his position. One week of ignoring hospital calls and pushing any thoughts of work from his mind had made him feel like he was neglecting his patients' needs and, as a result, was undeserving of his job.

He headed up the sidewalk to the front door, making his way around the puddles. When he opened the front door, Adam greeted him. But this time Adam looked more worn out than Joseph could recall, a little more on edge than usual too. And with dark circles under his eyes, Joseph knew something wasn't right. Aside from Adam's exhausted face, Joseph looked around and everything else seemed the same as it always had been. Joseph still had no idea about what had happened while he was away. The keyhole and mud, the screams from all the rooms, and the patients staying awake for days. Seeing how quiet and normal the ward seemed, Joseph harnessed a feeling of relief.

See? They didn't even notice I was gone.

"Dr. Hoffmann," Adam said. "Thank God you're here!"

"Thank God I'm here? Looks like everything is exactly as I left it."

"Yeah, now it is. But Doctor, it was absolute chaos while you were gone. We tried to call you. Well, I didn't. But the nurses tried. And all of us were so uncertain what to do. It was just… crazy, Doc."

Joseph lifted an eyebrow. "It was *chaos*? How so?"

He remembered the battle he'd had with himself when he'd ignored the phone calls from the hospital.

Adam heaved a sigh. "You won't believe half of it, even if I tried to explain. There was so much confusion, and none of the patients could sleep. The day after you left, things got complicated and stranger than anything I've ever experienced. Even the nurses couldn't keep up with it all. Night doctors and nurses running around like chickens with their heads cut off. Putting this one to sleep, next one down, up again—it was an endless cycle."

"*No one* was sleeping? Were they all keeping each other up?"

"No," Adam said. "It seemed like something else. It wasn't like one patient was being too loud and the others couldn't sleep because of it. This went on for *days*! The nurses have the papers and notes written for you. It's probably a book, I tell you. I overheard them talking that they were needing to be sure you got wind of what happened and they put the notes into the internal server. We had to go into full lockdown and put all them in their rooms. And then Matthew… Matthew somehow got mud into his room! And Diane was back off her meds; we don't know how. The nurses weren't sure why she was back to seeing and hearing things. We couldn't keep up with any of it!"

"Mud?"

"Yes! Mud! Stuck in the keyhole of the door to Matthew's room. I finally got the key in and the door opened. Then there was Matthew, being even weirder than usual, talking to me in his crazy way. It all creeped us out."

I need to get to my desk, Joseph thought.

Adam continued. "The nurses were handing out Thorazine like it was candy. But it seemed to only help for a short time. Then, out of nowhere, *boom*! Everyone went asleep or quiet. The meds weren't all administered at the same time or anything. We think they fell asleep from exhaustion."

"That definitely sounds strange. Very strange." Joseph paused, then added, "You messing with me, Adam? Is this some welcome back joke you guys planned?"

"No way! Check the files. I'm sure the nurses wrote it all down for you."

"All right, I'll go over them when I get to my office, but is everything okay now?"

Adam nodded. "Everything's fine. Everyone's back to normal, it seems."

Joseph said goodbye while walking toward the door of Hall 1. *This is exactly why I should have checked my messages.*

In his office, Joseph tossed his briefcase down and sat at his computer to dig into the notes from the events that had transpired while he was away. Out of habit, he started the coffee maker. He still had his doubts, but he also trusted Adam and knew there would be no reason for him to lie about such a thing. Joseph scanned through the documents that had been placed in his inbox.

July 1, 12:32 a.m.
Nurse: Janet Miller
Patient: Travis Ratcliffe
Hostile verbal altercations with other patients and doctors. Shouting and yelling. Travis kept waking up the neighboring rooms' patients. Aggression and anger observed. Assigned to PS unit for observation.
Update: 4:05 a.m.
Patient calmed down enough to discuss with us and apologize. He seemed to have come to terms with his episode earlier. We needed the PS rooms for two other patients who were having their own issues, so Travis was allowed back to his room with a watchful eye on him.

July 1, 7:55 a.m.
Nurse: Shawn Blakey
Patient: Matthew Quinn
Patient isn't responding to verbal warnings to stop interviewing other patients. None of the patients are sleeping due to the screams coming from all the rooms, and Matthew wouldn't stop with his preaching. I've never witnessed such anger from our patients as I have this morning. Matthew had always had his angry moments, but it was almost as if he projected this same emotion onto everyone else throughout the night. The screams coming from the rooms are at an all-time high. This all started shortly after sunup, right when I started my shift.
Update: 8:25 a.m.
Matthew has been put into his room, and the door has been locked. He seems to have quieted down. As for the rest of the ward, it's

just as loud as it was. We have to keep an eye on all the patients, and especially Matthew. It's all getting out of hand, but we aren't sure how to handle the situation yet.

July 1, 1:53 p.m.
Nurse: Shawn Blakey
Patient: Susan Eckwood

Patient seems excessively anxious. The entire ward does in fact. It hasn't quieted down even the slightest since early this morning, and we're trying to find a cause. Surely the patients haven't planned some kind of riot, have they? Susan is pacing back and forth when locked in her room. We let her out shortly before noon, but she'd just stand at the end of the hallway facing the window. We'd bring her to the rec room, and then she'd eventually make her way back to the hallway and stand looking toward the window at the end of the hall again. We're running out of luck with talking to the patients; verbal discussions don't seem to work. I have a feeling there will be a lot of meds administered tonight.

July 1, 4:11 p.m.
Nurse: Shawn Blakey
Patient: NA/Personal Filing for Staff Procedures

My shift is almost over. Everyone's still acting up. We're all exhausted and not sure how we'll prepare the night shift for this upheaval, which has lasted the entire day now. We've administered drugs to at least half the patients. This has helped for a short time, but some have little to no reactions, so we need to check the dosage charts again before readministering the drugs.

July 1, 8:27 p.m.
Nurse: Janet Miller
Patient: Diane Lynch

Patient has been having psychotic hallucinations again, claiming she has seen her son. We've talked with her about the hallucinations, and she seemed to understand. She remained silent on her bed. No drugs were administered. The rest of ward seems to have more problems than usual.

Update: 11:21 p.m.

Patient began to have psychotic episodes again. We only had time to come in and briefly check on her. The entire ward still hasn't slept, and no one is going to bed. We put the entire ward on lockdown. None of the patients are responding to the drugs as administered.

No one was responding to any medication? Joseph thought. *That doesn't sound right.* He flipped through to read more of the notes about the patients going without sleep, along with numerous personal staff notes highlighting what they tried to do to get the patients to calm down. All the chaos seemed to have led to the moment when Adam and the nurses rushed into Matthew's room the following night.

July 3, 2:30 a.m.

Nurse: Janet Miller

Patient: Matthew Quinn

Patient somehow got mud into his room and stuck it in his keyhole. We aren't sure how. The hospital has been on lockdown off and on for two days. We also didn't allow any visitors to drop by. The patients who had been unresponsive to medications the past couple days have finally fallen sleep. We're all very relieved and hope it will continue. But it still doesn't explain what happened.

July 3, 10:07 a.m.

Nurse: Shawn Blakey

Patient: Diane Lynch

After a complaint from the patient about a handprint being on her window, we sent a nurse to look into it and to wash it off. The handprint was made of mud and placed on the window of her room from the outside. Assuming it was from patient Matthew Quinn, who had mud in his room the same night, we have a feeling where he got the mud from—during his scheduled cafeteria visit. But we're still unsure how Matthew could have brought the mud into his room without us noticing it. The ward also had been on lockdown, and Matthew was observed staying in his room or the halls the entire time in the recent days. Adam and the rest of the security department have observed no breaches, and when reviewing the security footage, he saw that Matthew had never left the ward except to go to the cafeteria. And we can confirm the handprint somehow appearing last night, so none of this makes sense.

July 3, 1:13 p.m.
Nurse: Shawn Blakey
Patient: Jennifer Macklin
Over the past few days, we've been checking in on Jennifer. Overall she seems content, even with all the noise. She seems stable, even with everything going on, which is obviously much different than the rest of the patients in C Ward. I checked on her twice last night and once this afternoon and saw no changes in her demeanor.

Joseph was extremely perplexed by everything he'd just read. It was bad enough that he felt he was losing his mind lately, but now he had the entire ward dropping into what seemed to be something unexplainable from something unknown. *I need to connect the dots,* he thought.

And my goodness, there are a lot of dots to connect.

Chapter 14

"Red eyes gazed onto my weary soul, and I couldn't fight back.
The night grew longer, and the bed sank deeper,
until the ceiling turned black.
'Don't take him, please! For he is only a child!'
But the darkness grew in strength, and then it gave me a smile."
—anonymous (Lancaster, England; 1782)

Joseph felt Jennifer might be the perfect person to talk to about everything that had happened. She was keeping her cool while the other patients were experiencing extreme psychotic episodes. She might provide one of the missing pieces to the puzzle.

"Good morning, Jennifer," Joseph announced as he entered her room. "How have you been holding up? I heard C Ward got a little… over the top this past week."

Joseph tried to act like he wasn't as curious as he was.

Jennifer rubbed her eyes. "So many questions, Doctor. A bit early in the morning for this, isn't it?"

"Never too early to check in on the patients and see how they're doing." He took a seat and pulled it up to her bed as she sat up. "So while I was away—"

"You were away, weren't you? Next time take the crazy with you. It was pandemonium in here," Jennifer said, as if she were putting herself above the rest of the patients—as usual.

"We don't say the word 'crazy' around here. And yes, I understand it was a little… hectic."

"Hectic?" she scoffed. "Way to downplay the patients' disorders. It was turmoil. No one was sleeping, and it was just noise on top of noise."

"I heard. That's why I wanted to check in and see what you experienced. How did you handle it, and how are you holding up? From what I read in the staff notes, it seems you might have been the only patient not having any problems during everything that transpired."

"I handled it the same as anyone could," Jennifer said. "Pillow over the ears. Screaming for them all to shut the hell up. At night it was ten times worse. I managed though. You wouldn't believe…"

While she continued about her disgust regarding the noise and the "crazies the doctors locked me in here with," Joseph noticed something out of place.

"Jennifer, I see you moved your furniture around. Would you like to tell me why?"

"I didn't. I told you these crazies were messing with me, even when I tried to sleep. With the blanket over my eyes and a pillow over my ears, who knows how that happened."

"You remember the rules we spoke about when you came here, correct? One thing is certain: no patients should move their furniture around." Joseph got on his hands and knees to look at the bottom of the table for the fastening bolts. "And how exactly were you able to break these tables free from the bolts? We keep these fixed to the floor for a reason."

"I'm telling you, I didn't do it! It's those damn crazies!"

Joseph stood up, shaking his head, and walked over to a chair next to Jennifer. "This is one of your symptoms, I believe."

"You and the rest of them, I swear. One of my symptoms? *Pfff,* yeah right."

"Yes, part of your hallucinations. And have you ever been known to sleepwalk?"

"Sleep *talk.* Yeah, sure. I talk a lot. Even in my sleep. But sleepwalk? Not that I know of. Wait a second, Dr. Hoffmann. Are you suggesting that I got up out of my bed during the loud-as-hell nights and stayed asleep, then unbolted my tables and chairs from the floor without tools, then returned to bed, without remembering a thing?"

"I'm not saying you did this. I'm just asking a simple question. I'm trying to figure out why something that was a symptom of your hallucinations is now something you acted upon."

"I didn't do it!" Jennifer snapped.

"Now, now. No need to raise your voice."

Joseph fully realized what he'd said wasn't likely. It was just something that could ease his mind from yet another unknown.

"The nurses," he went on, "came and talked to you, and they told me you were fine. Why would you be acting up all of a sudden now? And why are you so angry about the noises? I have here in my notes that you were completely compliant and okay with everything that was going on at the time."

Jennifer shook her head. "I didn't talk to any nurses. No clue what you're talking about. They were busy running around the halls. It seems like you're the one who needs a checkup, Dr. Hoffmann. Maybe you and I should trade spots. What do ya say?"

Joseph smiled. He knew where he belonged in the doctor-patient relationship. Jennifer was suffering from delusions, and he knew he shouldn't make her problems his own, like he had a habit of doing.

"Very funny, Jennifer. I'm glad to see you haven't lost your sense of humor. I'm here to help you—and the entire ward—feel better. I've had a long week, and the last thing I need is to come back to a hospital full of patients who want to play games with me."

Jennifer stood and approached him. "I'm not being funny," she said, jabbing a finger at her chest. "And *some* of us don't want to be told things aren't how they actually are. Even when someone thinks they can see them in a different way, it's never the only way. Do you really think this is your reality? And you're certain this whole *game* thing isn't a clever way to fool yourself into believing your reality is the only way things can be, and the rest of the world lives inside it? We're *all* part of this. We're in this together. Every single one of us. But we each find our own way through it. You just haven't let yourself see it for what it is."

"What '*what*' is?" Joseph questioned.

"All of this…" She gestured around her. "It's your game, Dr. Hoffmann. You're making the rest of us pawns inside of it."

Joseph fought the urge to reflect too heavily on the events that had taken place this week. That would surely put him right next to Jennifer in his own room. His mind couldn't take much more of the unknown. It felt like his reality was beginning to fracture, and he had to find grip on it all, and fast.

He took a second to think of a response, then decided not to. It was unneeded right now. Once again, Jennifer had gotten the upper hand on him, and this time it had caught up with him. He closed his folder and walked to the door. Jennifer laughed as he exited the room—the kind of laugh that burns into a person's mind.

Joseph closed and locked Jennifer's door behind him.

Two can play at this game.

Anxiously he tapped his finger on his folder and headed down the corridor. He knew he wasn't the one who had lost his mind. He was helping others keep theirs. Jennifer was merely another patient and surely not one he should allow to come between him and his work.

Tapping more rapidly on the folder, he knew what he had to do. It was time to check the security cameras to catch Jennifer in the act of moving her furniture around.

He entered the security room and didn't see anyone around. Trying to remember how Reggie had worked the controls during their last viewing session, he sat down at the computer. There were four flat-panel monitor screens, each divided into a dozen smaller views. Looking at all the screens, feeling like he was in a Big Brother lookout tower, he searched for Jennifer's room. On the far-right bottom corner, next to an empty coffee mug, was the monitor for room 407, illuminated with gray letters and numbers in the bottom right-hand corner of the screen.

Looking at the live view of Jennifer's room, he noticed something strange: the room was exactly as it should be. No furniture moved, no table unbolted… not a single thing out of place. He was looking at a standard patient room, with Jennifer sitting at her desk, drawing on a piece of paper. He knew there was no possible way she could have already put everything back to how it was; he had been in there only a few minutes earlier.

Fumbling with the controls, he scrolled back and accidentally went too far, arriving at a previous night. He watched the monitor as a nurse walked into the room, sat on the bed and looked to her left. She was having a conversation, but Jennifer wasn't there. The nurse was talking to no one.

What the hell is going on? I must be losing my mind, Joseph thought. *Either that or this nurse has.*

He pushed the playback forward until he reached the point where he saw himself enter her room. He watched as he got on his hands and knees and looked under the table. But the table wasn't there. Her room was exactly as it should be, and the table was still across the room in its rightful place.

Someone's playing a horrible trick on me.

Joseph stood up and ran full speed out of the security room, through the middle lobby, and down to the end of Hall 4. The door in front of him was his moment of truth. He fumbled with his keys, then flung the door open and saw Jennifer sitting, drawing at her desk as she always did—exactly as he'd seen in the surveillance video.

"What is it, Doctor? Am I also not allowed to draw in here? Another one of your *rules*?"

Joseph didn't respond. Trying not to look embarrassed, he closed the door behind him and left the room. Then he rushed to the hospital's front door, with staff and nurses following him.

"Doctor! Doctor! Wait!"

"Are you okay, Doctor?"

"Dr. Hoffmann! Stop! What happened?"

Through the halls and through the swinging doors, straight to the front of the hospital, the word "Doctor" echoed in his head from all directions. Nurses, janitors, the guards—no one was going to stop him. He slammed through a tray of food that was being sent to a patient's room and pushed the guard aside. He had to get out!

"Doctor!"

"Someone help him!"

"*Doctor*!"

The words scrambled around his head, and he felt like he couldn't run fast enough.

Gasping, he had nothing but doors in front of him. The patients all watched as he made his way, stumbling with his keys and clipboard in hand. He frantically struggled to remember the right numbers and punch in his PIN to open the front doors. He felt like he was suffocating. The walls were closing in fast, and so were the nurses and staff trying to calm him.

Patients huddled around the windows and hallways near the lobby to watch Joseph's mad rush. He couldn't differentiate whether he was running to something or from something. He just knew he needed air, and the air was running out.

9

He punched in the first number and panicked about whether it was even the right one. Slamming his back against the wall, he tried to remember the next three numbers.

1

The second number was even harder to push than the first. He felt like he wasn't able to control his hand as he pushed the third number.

6

Feeling like he had lead for hands, he found it nearly impossible to pick up where the last number left off.

5

He did it. He was out of the hospital. But now, he had almost forgotten why he even wanted out so badly in the first place. He tried to control his breathing enough to make it to his BMW and get home. He found his way to his car and got in. Before getting the key into the ignition, he dropped it several times. He turned the car around and sped out of the parking lot with nurses and staff in his rearview mirror waving and yelling at him.

"Doctor! Where are you going?" they shouted.

Doctor. That was the last word he wanted to hear. The hospital was behind him as he wound back down the forest roads as quickly as he could. He needed a break to gather some peace of mind and figure out what was happening to him. Whatever was going on wasn't even allowing him to work anymore. He was in a world of confusion and disarray.

Panic attack. I'm having panic attacks again.

The doctor came back into the picture, and he self-diagnosed.

I must be tired from the flight, and something set me off today. I wasn't able to make sense of it, and then I got frightened and panicked. That's all.

A doctor's self-evaluation… or maybe just something to ease his mind… he wasn't even sure anymore. He wasn't sure about much at that moment.

The car kept winding around the trees. Only a couple of hours earlier, he had seen Helen in front of his car. Twenty minutes ago, he had seen Jennifer's furniture switch around. Only moments earlier, he had flipped out and run out of the hospital in front of the staff and patients.

Great. Not something a doctor needs to be doing. It'll be a wonder if I even have a job tomorrow.

Joseph pulled into his driveway, shut off the engine, and walked up to his house. Questionable things had led him here, and he needed to sleep and forget about all of it. He went up the damp steps to the front door and put his key in. The big wooden door swung open, and Joseph threw his white jacket on the floor. Looking up, expecting to see the comfort of his home, he found the room wasn't as he had left it that morning—the furniture had been moved. The coat rack was in the opposite corner, and the lamp was on its side on the table, which had been placed in the center of the room. The chair, which used to be against the left wall, was now on the right, and the pictures of Helen were all hung upside down.

He shook his head. Then he shook it even more forcefully.

No, no, no! This can't be happening!

He stood still, frozen with fright, before looking around again, trying to make sense of it all. Then a feeling of warmth took over his right hand, and he began to feel at ease. Slowly and carefully, he looked down, following his right arm, leading down to his hand. But when he saw his hand, someone else's was holding it. One he knew very well.

Helen.

As fast as it came, it went away.

He looked up to see his house put back in order, and then he fell to his knees and wept. He couldn't tell if they were the tears of exhaustion or because he was able to feel Helen's touch once again, something he had wanted for a very long time.

Chapter 15

"The children play at night near the deepest, darkest hole.
Inside is where she lives, surrounded by the shadows
and filled with the dread from lost souls looking in."
—anonymous (Nieu Bethesda, Karoo; 310 BC)

Joseph woke up from a hard-earned nap, wondering if it had all been a nightmare. After rolling over and looking at the thirteen missed calls from the hospital on his phone, he quickly realized it must have actually happened. He felt lost and unsure what to do. He could return to work, but they'd probably send him back home because he obviously wasn't well. Even worse, they could lock him up at his own hospital as a patient. He could stay home and bury himself in questioning what had happened, but that wouldn't do him any good either. As he was a man of habit and punctuality, missing work was a horrible feeling. And dashing out of the hospital while on the clock was unfathomable. He knew what he had done was extreme, but it was for the best. He had too much on his mind, and he needed to free himself from some of it.

He decided to call the hospital and face what had happened. He had an excuse after all; his mother had just passed away, and it had been a very heavy week for him. *After a long, sleepless, flight home, this could happen to anyone, right?* He called and broke the news to Dr. Riley that he needed to rest and apologized for rushing out earlier. Even though he could sense the tone of worry from him, Dr. Riley seemed to understand and told him Joseph should stay home and take care of himself, until he felt better. Now the question was how much could Joseph free himself from his own memories, his own curiosities, or in this case, his own past?

Joseph made himself a small glass of whiskey to calm his nerves, and sat down in his home office, looking out the window as a breeze pushed through the trees. He tried to keep what had happened out of his mind while remaining calm and considering all the options. He talked himself into believing it had all come from exhaustion, and he had gone back to work far too quickly. The death, the travel, the book. It was all so much at once, and he knew he had to get rid of some of the clutter in his mind. He glanced at the box from his grandfather, which stared back at him from the corner of the room, but he quickly reset his eyes out the window, into the forest again.

Since when could a box grow such a stare? No, I can't... It'll only add to my stress.

Joseph kept bouncing his focus back and forth between the box and the forest, each time fixing his gaze a little longer on the box. Curiosity always killed the cat, and he knew it was no good to dive back into one of his stressors.

But maybe it would be therapeutic if I could figure some of this out. It might free up some of these stresses. It's so bothersome that I don't have any answers.

Joseph couldn't let go—he had to keep himself occupied. Knowing what he was about to do was perhaps not the right choice, he stood up and walked over to the box. He then carried it to his desk and opened it. Pulling out the book, he felt like he was cheating himself of his sanity, but then he placed the book in front of him and grabbed a pencil and paper to take notes.

Maybe I shouldn't have gone back to work today after all.

Feeling like a kid in college again, he copied down what he could read and understand. He looked over the pages of the book and jotted down some of his grandfather's notes:

She found her way through the shadows. Where else can she travel?

The bodies are twisted and the mouths are always pried wide open. The eyes are facing upward toward the sky. Is she trying to tell us something through the body's disfigurement?

Joseph felt a little uneasy about how open-minded his grandpa was to these dark stories, with no care regarding whether they were fact or fiction. He had written his notes as if all of it were true.

What was Grandpa even doing with all of this? Joseph wondered. *Who was he anyway?*

Joseph tapped his pen on the back of the book while remaining deep in thought, but then he noticed a small tear on the last page. He peeled it back slightly and realized it was actually two pages stuck together. With ultimate finesse, he pulled the pages apart and discovered an entirely separate slip of paper with his grandfather's handwritten notes that wasn't attached to the book's seam:

She cared so much because no one believed her. She tried to explain, but they'd never listen. This must be why. This must be the missing connection.

It is the bond between her and her father. It is the difference between understanding the realities of the sane and insane. It is a darkness only grasped by those in need and those who can't see it. She finds her way through it to others weak enough to let her in.

Until we can fully grasp the concept of what it means to be sane or insane, we will never fully grasp what it means to be understood.

She was telling us all along, but I never could see it. The only way to rid us of darkness is by keeping those we love closer to our hearts than in our minds.

At the bottom of the page was something stamped in red ink, then signed underneath:

Dr. Arthur Franz, Doctor of Psychiatry/Anthropology
Memoir #53: October 1958
Project: Shadow Licker

Joseph couldn't believe his eyes. A doctor of psychiatry and anthropology. Right there, written in front of him, was a piece of the truth he was after. He and his grandfather shared a connection, even from beyond the grave. Franz had been a psychiatrist too. The irony overwhelmed him. To think he had gone into psychiatry because of his grandfather's disease and battle with Alzheimer's, and Grandpa Franz had been a psychiatrist the whole time. Some of it started to make sense now. But one thing was still uncertain: what was Grandpa Franz really up to with his studies? Joseph wondered why his grandfather had left the box for him in the first place.

Was it because he knew I enjoyed his stories so much as a child? Joseph shook his head and looked back at the book of notes and typed stories. *Or am I meant to finish his work?*

That thought stuck in his mind like mud on silk. Even if it wasn't what was meant of him, it was exactly what he was going to do. But before he could even finish the thought or bask in the satisfaction of what he might have figured out, he was startled by a sound that shook him to the bones. From the floor above him came short, quick, heavy steps, running briskly away, right above his head. They stomped in rapid motion to the other side of the upstairs room. After a brief pause, longer, louder, more exaggerated steps started at the end of the upstairs hall. Between the steps, Joseph heard several drawn-out moans.

Whoever it was walked steadily down the staircase, then stopped at his office door. Joseph's heart bundled up in his throat. The breaths and moans grew deeper and heavier, and he felt at any moment the door to his office would slam open, and he'd meet his maker once and for all. After a long gurgling sound, silence came, but he was unsure if he should continue to sit or approach whoever was on the other side. Before Joseph could move, a loud thump came from the hallway outside his door. It sounded like something had fallen to the floor, and Joseph was chilled with terror. After a few short moments, he couldn't hear any more noises, and felt it was safe enough to approach the door. He made his way toward it, cautiously, his heartbeat thumping in his chest.

While walking the old wooden floor creaked beneath his feet. "Hello? Who's there?" Joseph called out. He put his hand to the knob and opened the door, cracking it just enough to see what was on the other side.

No one.

Although he was slightly relieved, he was even more terrified now.

Even though no one was there, *something* was. He saw a diary on the floor in front of him. But not just any diary, it was one he remembered from years ago. Helen's. Ever since her death, it had been locked away with her other belongings, tucked away in a closet upstairs.

Surely someone's playing a trick on me, Joseph thought as he picked it up. He looked toward each end of the hallway, but no one was there. With Helen's diary in hand, he headed to the front door to look for signs of entry but found nothing. He looked at the forbidden door at the end of the hallway and pushed down the dark thoughts that had built up inside him. He then went to the floor above his office to check the other belongings in the closet. The door was tightly shut, the lock in place. The only key was hidden away in Joseph's desk. It looked as though nothing had been disturbed.

After returning to his office to get the key to the closet, he went back upstairs, opened it, and looked into the wooden chest. He found that only the diary was missing, with everything else in the same place it had been for years. Joseph sat down on the bed. Holding the diary, he once again questioned his sanity.

Who could have done this? This can't be happening to me again. It has to be the jetlag. Who the hell am I kidding? I must be going mad. I'm totally losing it.

To keep his sanity in check, he started to come up with his own conclusions as to how the book had gotten in the hallway in front of his office.

Maybe I'll open it to find a stupid letter saying it was one big joke from my friends at work.

But Joseph knew he wasn't nearly close enough to anyone there to be on the receiving end of such a cruel and senseless joke.

Or maybe I've been sleepwalking. I used to as a child. Maybe I put the diary there during my nap and didn't notice it before walking into my office.

He knew this was unlikely. He was reaching for answers, but none of them made sense. He always knew Helen had a diary, but he was never the type to go snooping through it. After debating whether he should open it, curiosity got the best of him. Someone must have left it there for a good reason. Most of the pages looked a little worn, with handwriting across them, dating up to the day before Helen died. On the next page with writing, he noticed something odd. Today's date was at the top of the page, and the ink was still fresh. He then began to read what was written:

I'm worried about him. He's working too much. He isn't talking to anyone, and he obviously needs help. He's feeding himself with lies, which is keeping him further from the truth. If he isn't more cautious, it'll get to him too. I can see it looking at me. Even while I write this. Those eyes are nothing but hatred, and I can see its blank gaze crawling down the back of my neck from the room behind me. It knows what I'm about to do, but I have to do it.

Joseph, the hospital is in danger. The force is stronger than you believe. You have to find the answer yourself. It's the only way you can see the truth.

With his eyes tearing up, Joseph placed the diary on the nightstand, then looked out the window. He knew Helen had come back to help him. As insane as it was, he knew it was true. He felt her presence. Over the tops of the trees, he saw the hill where the hospital stood. He walked downstairs and put on his jacket. He then got into his car and made the drive to the hospital, knowing the staff would be worried that he had run out earlier. It was time to go back. Instead of leading them to believe he had lost his mind, he decided to play everything off.

A lot of pressure and stress have been raining down on me, he thought. *The nurses and staff will understand I have a lot going on. I'll explain that working and keeping busy will help me cope. Help me cope with the loss of my mother. Help me cope with life and press on.*

He knew it would be hard to convince them, but it was what he had to do.

If I've lost my mind, so be it. And if all this is only a figment of my imagination, then fine. Either way I'll get to the bottom of this.

Joseph felt there was connection with everything he had been experiencing—and someone had to bring it together. All of the events kept rotating around in his mind like hard-edged fan blades, and each rotation of thought sliced through with another brisk slash, leaving holes in his sanity. Helen, the hospital, his grandfather, the book, even his childhood memories, they were all submersed in a world of mystery. But the one thing they all had in common was him. He knew they all had come back into his life for a certain reason—he called it destiny—and now they deserved his attention.

Joseph pulled into the parking lot. Taking a deep breath as he left the car, he noticed the guard and a nurse were looking out the window at him, concern written across their faces. He needed this to be the acting role of his life, and the hospital was the stage for his debut.

Here we go.

He put on a fake smile and walked toward the hospital, while also trying not to seem like everything was too perfect. He knew that would be far too conspicuous. Reggie met him at the front door.

"Dr. Hoffmann! What the hell happened earlier? We were all worried sick!"

"I'm sorry. I really am. I had a bit of a freak-out because of my mother's death and the long travels. I'm fine now. I just needed to take a rest before coming back. I'm okay. Trust me."

"You sure? You should be at home, shouldn't you?"

Joseph continued to walk while keeping up the conversation. "I'm fine. Like I said, there's been a lot going on lately. I have to keep myself occupied, and you and I both know it drives me crazy to be sitting at home when I should be at work."

Reggie nodded. "True. Well, you know best what you need to do, I guess. We were all very worried. The nurses said they called you a dozen times. No answer."

"I was taking a quick nap and had my phone on silent."

"Okay, I mean, I know I'm only a guard… What do I know? But I think—"

"You think I should stay home and be by myself, surrounded by my emotions and feelings, trying to sort out what happened at the hospital this past week? All while I grieve for my mother and what life has thrown at me, all by my lonesome self… dwelling… sitting alone, in silence, thinking about it all? Is that what you were about to say?"

Reggie smiled lightly. "When you put it that way, maybe it is good you're here with us. Sometimes being around other people is the best solution to keep the mind busy. Just know that we're here for you."

"Thank you for that, Reggie. It'll all be fine."

Joseph continued into the hospital and looked around, feeling proud of himself for the stunt he'd just pulled. He now had an entirely different outlook on the place he called work. He was looking for anything that could reveal a clue as to why Helen's diary had mentioned the hospital being in trouble. Any little details that seemed different. He was now an undercover sleuth, trying to piece everything together.

"Doctor! What are you doing back?"

"What happened? Are you okay?"

Several nurses flooded Joseph with questions, but he kept his cool. After telling them the same sob story he had told Reggie, they seemed to understand—except for Dr. Riley, who they'd called in to replace him after he ran out. Dr. Riley had different ideas altogether.

"Joseph," said Dr. Riley with a caring tone while pulling Joseph to the side of the hallway. "You need to talk to someone."

Joseph knew that if he disagreed Dr. Riley would find reasons he wasn't fit to be there. He was another psychiatrist after all, and would be much tougher to convince.

"Let's make a deal," continued Dr. Riley. "You talk to me so I can make sure you're okay, and then I'm sure everyone will agree you're fine to come back to work today."

"Sure. It's probably the best for me anyway."

"Great, then let's have a talk in your office."

The two made their way toward Joseph's office. They heard patients giggling behind them, and whispers and murmurs floated down the hallway. It felt like they were in high school, and the patients were exchanging rumors of what had happened earlier while pointing at them. Joseph stayed calm, and Dr. Riley ignored them. They continued down the hallway and into his office, closing the door behind them and blocking out all the chatter.

Chapter 16

"I stood in front of the door with a head full of fright.
Shapes cut into the floor from a timid moonlight.
Feeling the courage build up,
I tugged on the knob, but the door slammed shut.
Could this be the punishment for all of my sins?
God, give me forgiveness! For I am only a man!
After a moment of stillness, the room began to spin."
—anonymous (Bandera, Texas; 1891)

"So tell me, do I ask you to 'please have a seat,' or do you ask me?" Dr. Riley said. Joseph laughed a little, perhaps a bit nervously, and Dr. Riley went on. "Well yes of course you should sit at your own desk, Joseph. Neither of us are patients, are we?"

Joseph sat at his desk, trying to remember what it was even like to have his usual morning routine. He glanced at the coffee machine and back at his computer monitor, seeing his reflection in the screen. It was like a distant memory. Things had changed so much, and he craved a feeling of stability and everyday normality. He placed his hands on the desk and felt the hard, cold wood.

"Feels good to be back in the chair, doesn't it?"

Joseph was pulled out of his trance-like thoughts. "Yes, of course it does. This job is my life."

"I understand that feeling," Dr. Riley said. "But sometimes we have to help ourselves before we can help others. That's the case for everyone in times of crisis."

"I agree. I truly do. I just feel like I should be here so I can keep myself occupied."

"But what happened earlier? All I know is that I got a call from C Ward telling me you ran out in a huge panic. Did something trigger it?"

Joseph knew he had to lie. He couldn't let Dr. Riley know about anything he had seen or experienced. He was one response away from being locked up.

He shook his head. "Not anything to do with the hospital. I simply felt tired, and it triggered a bit of a panic attack, I think. I haven't experienced my normal routine for a while now, and I went straight from an international flight to come to work."

"May I ask about your mother? I was told you were away dealing with her death and funeral. That is, if you want to talk about it. I don't want to step over any lines."

"Yes, of course we can. My mother had been sick for quite a while, and we all saw it coming. She passed in her sleep about a week ago. Still, it doesn't make it any easier. But it did allow me to handle it differently than if it were sudden. I do miss her, but I know she's at peace now."

"I'm sure she is, Joseph. I'm certain she is. It seems you're taking it well then?"

"I am," Joseph said. "I have my sister Anna, too. We've always been very close, and she helped me with everything. So it wasn't like I was alone there."

"That's good to hear. With these kinds of crises, being alone can be the worse. That kind of brings up the reason for this whole conversation, doesn't it?"

Joseph nodded. "I just think it's best for me not to be alone at home all day. Sure, I let my anxieties get the better of me earlier.

Like I said, I was exhausted. I went home and took a long nap, but then I felt if I stayed home, I would only get upset again. I need to do something to keep myself busy, and work has always kept me occupied."

Dr. Riley took a long hard look at him, almost as if he were acknowledging that Joseph was lying. "I get it," he finally said. "I lost my father a couple years back. It's always hard to handle, but the worst is not being able to get back into your routine or familiar surroundings. We both love our jobs. I was in your same shoes. I couldn't even hit the golf course—something I love—but I sure as hell was okay back at work. Maybe it helps us when we know we're assisting others in times of our own need. Maybe that's the power of being a psychiatrist. But the most important thing is that we can take care of ourselves. It seems like you're doing exactly that, by figuring out what will enable you to cope and grieve in your own way."

Joseph felt confident he had fooled Dr. Riley. He definitely was sad about his mother and didn't think for a second that he was using it as an excuse. His mother had given him the box as one of her wishes, so he was certain she wanted him to figure out why all these strange things were happening.

"One last thing," Dr. Riley said. "Can you tell me why you were in the security room? What does that have to do with your mother dying or your grieving?"

"How did you know? I... I was—"

"Because the door was left open. The guard saw it as a breach of security and went to check on the cameras to see what had happened, and then he saw you walk in at a very fast pace, almost running. We saw you weren't with any of the security staff to view the footage. It looked like you were trying to find something. You know the protocol. We have to have security personnel with us."

Joseph knew this was it. They were going to lock him up and throw away the key. He hadn't realized he would end up at the tail end of his lie, and he didn't know what to say. He had to come up with something fast. As much as he knew he probably belonged in the hospital with the rest of the patients, he had to fight for his freedom.

He took a second then responded with as much confidence as he could muster. "It's a dark room. And a place that's quiet. I was so tired I had to find a place to relax my eyes for a minute. But then I remembered I had to check on Jennifer Macklin, and I dashed over there, but it was too much. I was too exhausted and my mind broke down once I arrived at her room. I couldn't even think straight, so I had to go. I'm pretty sure I had a panic attack."

"I get it. I often sneak off into the doctor's lounge when no one's in there and take a quick nap," Dr. Riley said with his hand to his mouth, as if he were revealing a deep dark secret. He then winked and stood up. "I guess you knew there was no camera in there to catch you sleeping on the clock. We all find those secret slumber chambers. Anyway, Joseph, it seems like you're going to be okay and you're okay to be here, but I'm sure you don't need me to tell you that. We have each other's backs, and I want you to know that. You and I, we come from the same mold. But we can't forget about our own sanity in times of stress. Please come talk to me if you ever need anything. Welcome back, Doctor. Hope it's an easy rest of the day for you."

Joseph hadn't felt that relieved after telling a mouthful of lies since the time in high school he had been caught sneaking out late at night—although he was certain his mother knew he actually hadn't been at the arcade at midnight with his friends.

The two said their goodbyes, and Joseph shut the door. He had to gather his composure again before he could push through the day.

He knew he couldn't focus on his grandfather's book the entire time. He had to focus on the diary and what it said about the hospital. This felt like an immediate threat. Deep in his heart, he believed Helen had left it there for him. He knew he couldn't lose himself to his own mind, but it all felt too real not to. He pulled out his agenda to figure out what he could do with the rest of his day.

After gathering his composure, Joseph walked out of his office. He was met with dozens of staring eyes and whispers coming from down the corridor. The patients who had seen him run out of the hospital seemed to have their own beliefs regarding whether he was sane. Joseph knew he'd have to keep up his act and keep it up well. It takes one to know one, after all. Joseph continued down the hall toward the peering eyes and chatting coming from behind the window of the hallway's door. He heard laughter, and patients pointed at him as he approached. Joseph took a deep breath and opened the door.

"I told you! I told you he'd come back!" one of the patients said.

"He's crazy just like us!" another said while laughing.

"He belongs in here with us!"

With his sanity on the line, addressing the gossip and banter from the patients would do no good for him, so he continued on, ignoring them. A nurse came into the hallway as he passed by and asked the patients to calm down and stop their misbehavior. Joseph stayed strong and kept walking. He was on a mission but wasn't even sure where to begin. Looking at his clipboard and agenda, he knew he needed to avoid Jennifer, not only because what had happened was embarrassing, but also because he felt she would be a trigger for him, especially because she always put herself above everyone else. She seemed to feed off his reactions. So instead, Joseph went to Travis's room, which was situated next to Jennifer's. He couldn't forget the feeling he'd had when Jennifer had spoken to him, or the panic of watching himself looking under a table that wasn't there. Expecting to see her standing at her door, watching him come down the hall, he was relieved that she was nowhere in sight. Instead he was met by a nurse helping a patient pack her belongings in a room next to Travis's.

"Where are you off to?" Joseph asked, confused why she would be moving her things. The patient looked like she hadn't slept in days. Black circles sat below her eyes, as dark as the pupils above them, and her face was as pale as a white linen sheet.

"Maria complained about feeling uncomfortable having her room next to Jennifer's and Travis's. So we're moving her to Hall 2 to see if that helps her," the nurse said as she and the patient left the room with the woman's belongings.

Before Joseph responded, he stopped in his tracks. He thought he remembered seeing a note about this from the nurses at some point, but it seemed like everyday drama that was common on the ward. He never looked into it further than that. He looked at the patient walking down the hall, then looked back at Jennifer's door. He tried to figure out what any of this could mean. As much as he wanted to tell Maria he knew exactly how she felt, he couldn't. He was the doctor after all, not the patient. He felt anxiety take over his body and mind merely knowing he had to walk past Jennifer's room. At that moment, he realized he wasn't even sure if it was fear of Jennifer or fear of what had happened. He couldn't figure out if he was scared of what she had done to the patient to make her move out, or if he was in denial of what he had done earlier by running out in front of her.

Joseph knocked twice before he opened the door to Travis's room. Unsure how Travis would react to his actions earlier, Joseph went in with a smile and a greeting.

"Travis, how are we?"

"How are *we*? I should ask 'How are you?'" Travis replied with a smirk.

"I know it looked rather strange earlier, with me running out and all. We all have our limits. I just needed some rest," Joseph replied.

"So why aren't you resting?"

"Because work is important. Helping my patients is important."

"Helping yourself is also important," Travis said.

"I *am* helping myself by being here. That's exactly it. I lost a family member, and my way to cope is to work with my patients."

Travis nodded somberly. "I'm sorry to hear that. Losing someone is a strange feeling. I remember when I was sixteen, and I first felt like I lost someone, but you know the weirdest part about it? The person I lost wasn't my mom. It wasn't even my dad. It was myself. I felt like I was falling apart. Other kids at school picked on me. Just because I had to live with my grandma and had no parents. Calling me bastard this and bastard that. It wasn't sad losing my parents. They never loved me anyway. It was sad when I felt like I was losing *me*. So I know how you feel, losing a loved one. I used to love myself too."

Joseph was curious why Travis seemed so… sympathetic and understanding. Maybe his opening up a little had allowed Travis to open up, too.

"Why don't you love yourself anymore, Travis?"

"Probably because I'm locked up in this mental ward with crazy people as far as the eye can see. One end of the building to the other, riddled with insanity and confusion. Wanna know the best part about it? It isn't just us patients who are the insane ones. We all are. The staff, the guards, even you."

Joseph knew that on any other day, he would keep himself in check, knowing he wasn't the crazy one but the one helping the mentally ill. But today was different. He knew he belonged here right next to Travis. Travis seemed to understand this. Joseph understood what it was like to lose someone, and had even started to understand what it was like to lose himself, but he wasn't going to let Travis know that.

Joseph leaned against the wall and crossed his arms, stepping back into the doctor role. "I think there's a difference. You did something to end up here. You tried to burn down your grandmother's house. And as far as progress, I think you're capable of trying that again. I wonder if you're even improving. We'd have to know you'd never do that again before we'd release you."

"And what about you running out of here? How sure are we that you'd never do that again?"

Joseph wanted to lash out as anger grew inside him, but he also knew Travis was right. He wasn't even sure he'd never do that again. In fact, he felt like doing it again right now. He wasn't sure what he was even capable of doing anymore. He was as brittle as glass and fragile to the core.

"I'm not sure actually. But I am certain that if I ran out of here, I wouldn't be doing harm to anyone."

"Except yourself," Travis completed Joseph's thought.

Joseph shrugged.

Travis laughed lightly. "So let me get this straight. If *you* harm *yourself*, it's okay? There is nothing 'insane' about harming yourself? Is that what you are getting at? Because as far as I can tell, half this hospital is full of people who harm themselves, and that's exactly why they're here. But then again, I guess it's okay when a doctor harms himself—"

Joseph put a hand up. "You can stop right there. That's not at all comparable to the harm these patients are trying to do to themselves. And I'm certain you know that."

"Maybe I do know that. I know all too well about the different levels of pain a person can endure, or what the pain can do to a person's mind. It toys with you. And pain and fear go hand in hand, Doctor."

"Are you fearful of something then, Travis?"

"I'm not, but by the looks of it, you are."

Joseph tried to grasp where Travis was going with this statement. Loss and pain were always the first things to come to his mind when he thought about his past—or his future for that matter. His life was centered around pain. But fear—fear was never a thing that came to mind when he observed his life's tragedies. He had to remind himself that he was talking to a patient who knew nothing about him. All Travis had seen was his doctor running out of the hospital in a panic.

Travis continued once he noticed Joseph was deep in thought. "And you don't need to be afraid of Jennifer—"

Joseph cut him off as fast as the word "Jennifer" left his mouth. "No, it's not Jennifer. I'm not afraid of her. I was tired and had a panic attack due to some of my recent stresses."

"You sure looked scared as hell when you tried to punch those numbers in to get out."

Joseph didn't realize so many patients had seen him do that, but of course they would have. The barrier between the patient halls and the front lobby was nothing but glass all the way to the main security entrance.

"I wasn't scared."

"She isn't all that bad, you know. She's probably the most normal person here," Travis said. "I mean, she doesn't do anything but sit there and draw. She doesn't do anything to the other patients but talk to us like we're normal people. Something none of you do—that's for sure."

"Jennifer is a patient too, Travis. Don't let her fool you."

"No, don't let her fool *you*, Doc. If you aren't scared of her, then what are you scared of?"

Joseph thought about what he was scared of. Perhaps he was scared of himself, scared of who he had become. Maybe he was scared of everything that had happened to him lately. He was fearful of a lot of things, but he was convinced Jennifer wasn't one of them.

"You know what I'm afraid of?" Joseph responded with utmost confidence. "I'm afraid you'll get out of this hospital someday and hurt yourself or someone else."

Travis looked at him as though he knew Joseph was saying this only to convince himself there wasn't more to his fears and to reassure him that he was the doctor talking to a patient. They both knew it was an easy way out of the conversation.

"If people start to finally listen to me, there won't be a need for any of it," Travis responded.

"Any of what?"

"Any of the fear. No one would need to be scared of me. Not even my grandma. I would never want to hurt her."

"I'm sure you'd never want to hurt anyone. But sometimes we do things we don't mean to because we're caught up in our own dilemmas. In our own fears and tragedies."

Travis and Joseph looked at each other in a moment of silence, knowing at this point they were speaking the same language. They understood each other and what it took to get a person there. Whether it was fear, sadness, or rage, the emotions that consume someone can lead them to do things they normally wouldn't. Joseph turned around and walked out of the room. Not another word needed to be said between them that day.

After Joseph left Travis's room, he realized he didn't feel nearly as anxious walking past Jennifer's door as before. His talk with Travis had eased his mind that she was, in fact, merely another patient. Joseph was still reaching to find himself again and put himself back up on level ground. It was becoming increasingly difficult, but he felt it must still be in him to feel that this was his hospital, his patients, and he was the doctor. He made his way back into his office to get a grasp again on why he had come back that day in the first place.

The diary.

The diary had told him to, but still unsure how the diary had even gotten there, he felt like he was losing his connection to reality even more.

Joseph sat down at his desk. After a couple hours of trying to continue with his work, he couldn't get the diary and its warning out of his head. He began to look through all his recent patients' files, thinking there must be something in there. He first looked over the case of Diane Lynch, the self-proclaimed mother who believed she had lost her son. Then he moved on to Travis, the boy who thought no one would listen to him no matter how hard he tried and was violent whenever he felt ignored. And then there was Jennifer, the college student who had slowly lost her mind to schizophrenia and was trying to come to terms with it. Before closing the folder, he arrived at Matthew, the preaching patient who never seemed to be quiet. Joseph tried to put it all together in his head, but nothing came of it.

Does any of this even matter?

Joseph thought long and hard while looking out the window toward the forest's edge. Now that he knew where to look, he saw the prayer tree he had found on the trail. Very faint and partially hidden by a massive boulder in front of it, it was tucked deep into the forest's dark gloomy overcast and pointing directly at the hospital. Joseph felt like it was peeking around the boulder just to show him it was still there. Like the memories of his grandpa, the tree stood there doing all it could to remind him of so many unknown parts of his past. Joseph put his hands on the back of his head and leaned back in his chair. He could barely see the dim light of the afternoon sun shining into the office window, inching over the treetops. It would be nighttime soon, and he should head home. He was proud that he had come back to work that day, even if he hadn't found what he was looking for. He was proud that he had proved to his patients and colleagues that he was still capable of being the doctor he had become. But one question was stuck firmly in his mind: *Am I really doing any of this for the right reasons anymore?*

Joseph couldn't find anything out of place at the hospital yet, but he knew it was only the beginning. Someone was there to help him, and he still believed it was Helen. He packed his briefcase and locked up the office before heading home, so many questions riddling his mind.

Chapter 17

"Believing what is there that we can't see isn't hard to do.
Knowing why you believe is."
—anonymous (Majuli, India; 1644)

When Joseph entered his house, it was much colder than it should be for a summer evening. He made his way to the thermostat, and it seemed to be working fine. After checking his face and forehead with his hand, thinking maybe he was coming down with the flu, he realized he felt fine. He checked the air conditioner, and it was running. He didn't see anything out of the ordinary, but decided it would be best to call the company that had installed the air conditioner and have them come out and check it. However, they were closed for the day and he only got the automated messaging system.

Joseph threw on a sweater then made his way to the kitchen to make himself dinner. Just a couple steps before making it into the kitchen, he was stopped in midstride by an unknown force, and he looked up as if he had hit a wall.

What's going on? It feels like my feet are glued to the floor, Joseph thought while trying to move forward.

Eyes wide, he felt a cold breeze come over the side of his face, moving slowly down his neck, and stopping on top of his shoulder. The shock of uncertainty and helplessness came over him like a cold rain. He felt a slight tug on his right shoulder as though he should turn around and look behind him. Since he didn't know who was there, he stood motionless. As he kept his focus forward, a kitchen light turned on dimly then flickered back off. A bright glowing ball of light moved from the opposite side of the kitchen and floated toward the sink before centering back to the middle of the room above the table. Another hard tug pulled his shoulder, trying to force him to turn around. The coldness ran deeper into his skin, arriving at his hands and feet. Whoever or whatever was behind him wanted him to turn around, but the glowing ball of light in front of him kept him facing forward. In denial that any of this was happening, he spoke through shaky breaths.

"None of this is real. None of this is real. *None of this is real,*" Joseph repeated, giving himself a mantra to try to keep calm. While he continued talking to himself, the golden ropes holding the dark blood-red silk window curtains together began to unwind and the curtains started to unravel. The curtains slowly pulled together, closing off any of the moonlight that was seeping in. The light over the stove flickered twice before shutting off, and the ball of light fluctuated in brilliance over a few long seconds. Joseph remained still, but panting with fear. Another tug on his shoulder, and deeper the cold went into his body, taking over his stomach.

Joseph shook as frost came over the room. The ball of light grew, and the tugs on his shoulder became more forceful. The sound of a light switching on came from behind him in the hall, and then the lights turned on from both sides of the hallway.

The ball of light doubled in size, and the tugs on his shoulder became twice as hard. He felt like the bright ball was battling for his attention to keep his focus away from whatever was behind him. He saw his own shadow take form on the kitchen floor, and standing over his right shoulder was a massive form.

Closing his eyes in fear, he repeated his mantra. "None of this is real. None of this is real. Please, please, please don't be real."

Feeling a pulse come from directly in front of him, he peeked out from tightly closed eyes to find the ball of light racing toward his face. He ducked as fast as he could, and then everything stopped. He opened his eyes to find that the shadow and ball of light had vanished, with only his own shadow cast on the floor. The only light still glowing came from behind him in the hallway. Shaking heavily, he finally turned and faced the other direction. At the end of the hall, a door was cracked open. It was everything Joseph feared: the forbidden room.

There was one thing no one knew about him or his past, and the one thing he kept pushed the furthest away. He and Helen had been trying to have a child before her death. After many years of trying, they finally found out she was pregnant. Over the moon with excitement, they decided to build a nursery. Helen died only a couple weeks later, and so did Joseph's dreams of having a family. This was the one room he always kept locked and had avoided ever since that horrible day. While he was trying to collect his thoughts about what he was seeing, the door creaked open even farther, just enough for him to make out the corner of the crib. As quiet and cold as the rest of the house was, warmth came from the room. A rocking chair was squeaking, back and forth, back and forth again, and a musical nursery rhyme played. A female voice he had never heard before sang in a minor key:

A tall man once came to me,
all dressed in glory,
from his head to his feet.
Asking for love,
with a bag full of ash,
his body was twisted,
and a head full of wrath.

Terrified, Joseph stayed as quiet as possible while watching the door, praying it wouldn't open any farther and reveal whatever wretched thing was behind it singing. The voice continued with the nuance and melody of an eerie bedtime story.

"Face first," they said,
and into the pit I went,
coming out a monster,
with a neck that was bent.
Now I lurk in the darkness,
where the ground is all wet,
with mud-covered feet
and the ash on my head.
The shadows of truth
will start to come out
and you'll end up like Father,
with your body turned inside out.

Everything grew silent except for a slight breeze moving in and out of the nursery, as if the space were breathing on its own. Joseph felt like whatever or whoever was in there was fully aware of his presence. The breeze grew in strength, and a silhouette took shape near the edge of the door, stretching into the floor of the nursery's glowing light. A long slender arm attached to a petite body took over the small gap he could see. And then an ash-covered hand wrapped around the doorknob before slamming the door shut, the sound echoing throughout the house. Above him, he heard the sounds of footsteps, and then the sound of crying took over. He heard mournful shrieks along with the footsteps moving slowly toward his office from above. With the slam of the office door, the sounds of crying and footfalls stopped. He didn't feel cold any longer, and the lights came back on. Everything was back to the way it should be. Whatever weight was hanging over the house had somehow been lifted.

"I can't do this anymore!" Joseph cried out, and then he fell against the wall and wept. He pounded the floor with his fists before screaming out to whatever it was to leave him alone and let him be. Anger quickly replaced his tears. He wanted to feel normal again, but he wasn't even sure what that was anymore. With tears in his eyes and shaking from what had happened, Joseph cautiously made his way to his office. He still wanted to know where the footfalls were coming from. The last time he heard steps, he had found Helen's diary.

Maybe she's here with me.

After climbing the stairs to the second floor, he opened the office door. He saw Grandpa Franz's book still on the desk, but all the objects that had been inside the box were scattered across the floor. The book was the only thing left untouched. He walked around the childhood toys, pictures, and other objects and made his way to his desk. Looking back up at him was a page he'd never seen before. A loose piece of paper with a single note written on the middle of the page: "It is in all of us. It is here."

Joseph stared down at the note. As fatigued as his mind and body were, he somehow felt strength come from its words—strength to allow him to understand more and possibly add a missing piece of the puzzle as to what this could all mean. He abandoned the notion that he was crazy. He was certain he wasn't, because all of this was real. It seemed that he was living among a world of spirits, breaking into the present from his haunted past. He felt like all these things were happening for a reason, and he'd have to figure it out once and for all. Whatever had just happened downstairs had its purpose. Joseph was being pulled in two directions, and he felt something was helping him by keeping him from looking back. He needed to face his demons, even if it meant he had to enter the room he had sworn never to return to. Something wanted to show him those dark memories, and something else was telling him why. After looking at his grandfather's note for a few minutes, trying to decipher its meaning, he decided to go back downstairs and into the nursery.

Knowing it wouldn't be easy, Joseph still felt compelled to go in there. Whatever, or whoever, was behind that door was giving him a glimpse of something he needed to see. A past that was tormented but still entirely his own. He had to try to view himself from another angle, and he felt like maybe someone was there to help him by showing him the way. Dizzy with thoughts of opening the forbidden door, he grabbed the dusty skeleton key hanging by the dining room and walked down the hall toward the nursery. He was very concerned that the person on the other side was still there, but that wouldn't stop him from going in. He wiped the tears from his eyes and took a deep breath.

Trying to forget the creepy nursery rhyme and the ash-covered hand, Joseph inserted the key and jiggled the door open. No shadowy figure in sight. Not even a light on. Just a dark room, with dust and cobwebs hugging everything like a blanket of soot. Joseph flipped on the light and saw a room that hadn't been touched in years. The once bright-pink baby blanket was now a chalky gray from years of being left to dust. The mobile that hung over the crib was covered in rust and grime. Joseph knew the room would look aged but found it hard to believe it could have aged this much. As he walked a little farther in, he noticed a corner of damp wood and carpet that gave off a musty smell. Joseph put his hand onto the rocking horse and knelt. The sound of laughter came back to him as a memory poured back in.

"Joseph! Get off that rocking horse! You'll break it!" Helen burst into laughter as she entered the nursery with a box of toys.

"I was just testing it out! Have to make sure it's safe for the baby!"

Helen beamed. "Oh, Joe, you'll be a great father."

The voice faded from his mind, and Joseph was back in the dark, cold, dusty room. He pulled his hand away from the rocking horse, then stepped a little farther, rubbing his finger along the rim of the crib. Then another memory came.

"How long does a baby stay in the crib until they move to a bigger bed?" he had asked Helen. "Will she climb out and hurt herself? Should we put her bed next to ours until then?"

"Joe, you've asked twenty questions about this kind of stuff today. If you don't stop worrying about the future, none of this will be any fun. We'll have to take it day by day. And, according to the mothering book I have, no later than two years old."

"See! You were wondering too! I'm not the only one scared about what's to come. It's good to be prepared."

"I think it's best you read the book when I'm done," Helen said. "It'll put your mind to rest about some of your questions and save me from having to answer them."

"How long do we—oh, here I go again. Ignore me. Go ahead. Give me the book."

Both Helen and Joseph laughed, and then the memory disappeared as fast as it had come when Joseph took his finger off the crib.

I worry far too much. I worry about so many things I can't change.

He looked toward the corner where the rocking chair was—the same rocking chair he could have sworn something evil was sitting in earlier. Joseph walked up and gave it a good push. It squeaked as it rocked, exactly the same sound he had heard earlier. A memory flooded his head, but Helen wasn't there this time.

"Come on. You have to take it easier. It might break otherwise."

A young man, dressed in a doctor's coat, was straddling a chair. A patient looked up with glassy eyes toward the doctor, his mouth sewn shut by thread.

"You can't put it on too tight. You have to be gentle."

Joseph knew this memory wasn't his. He felt like he had been thrust inside someone else's past. There was a flash of light, and then he was in the chair, looking up at the doctor and nurse.

"Yes, just like that. There you go. Now slowly—slowly put it in."

A strong shock came over his body, and then his mind went blank and everything around him whited out. The white slowly dissipated, and his blurry vision became clear again. Now he could recognize the doctor. It was his grandfather.

"Grandpa? What are you doing to me?" Joseph mumbled the best he could behind a mouth sewn shut. But his grandfather continued working as though he couldn't hear any of it.

"You'll feel better soon. We only have to do this a couple more times."

A warmth took over Joseph's body, and then his vision went blurry again. He felt his fingernails digging into the chair he was in and the cold metal pressing into his back and arms. Once the warmth went away, and the vision came back enough, Grandpa was turned around, talking to a nurse at the door. Joseph couldn't make out what was being said.

After the conversation ended, the doctor turned around. Through his foggy vision, Joseph saw the doctor walking back toward him. Once the face came back into view, he realized it wasn't his grandpa anymore… the man had become himself.

"I'm here to make you better, but you have to trust me. You can't give up until you can see the end and what it's for." The voice was his own when he had started speaking, but then it changed into a female's voice halfway between. "You have to believe me. You have to save them." The voice morphed even further into a voice Joseph recognized: Helen's.

"You have to save us."

With Helen's voice fading, Joseph found himself back in the nursery. He was sitting in the chair, rocking back and forth. He knew he wouldn't sleep very well that night. Not after everything that had happened and what he had seen. But he had to return to Cottage Grove the next morning and try to keep all this a secret and continue with what felt like a ghost chase. The visions were getting stronger and more revealing, but he wasn't sure why. But he *was* starting to accept what was going on with him. He was done trying to fight it. He did question, however, whether these phenomena were there to help him or to drive him further into the darkness of his past. It felt like someone was tapping into his mind, but why?

Chapter 18

"Without the darkness, you can never see the light.
And without the light, you can never find your way out."
—anonymous (Medan, Indonesia; 1413)

The ward was quiet. Most of the patients were fast asleep, but Travis was awake. Staring at the ceiling, he was breathing heavily with his eyes wide open. It was as though he was seeing something hanging above his bed and it was scaring him. The moaning began the second the heavy breathing stopped, and his eyes closed shut and his body jolted, bouncing up and down in the bed before violently shaking. It looked as if he was suffering from a seizure, but it was something far more sinister than that. The shaking grew more intense and then stopped. He sat up in bed with his eyes still shut, his legs tucked halfway under the gray blanket.

"I… d-don't… know," he said.

The words came out jumbled, falling from his lips as though they were having a hard time getting out of his mouth.

"They never listen… to… me."

His head was facing forward, his eyes closed. After a moment of silence, he turned, pulled his legs out from under the blanket, and placed his feet on the cold tile floor.

"Grandma would know. You should know that."

He talked as though he were half asleep. His head flinched every once in a while, and then he'd speak again.

"On top of the door to room 304."

Whoever was talking to him seemed to need to know something.

"They'll see me," Travis said. "They'll know what I'm doing."

His voice lifted at the end, as though he were concerned about getting in trouble.

"Only if you say so."

Travis remained motionless, his eyes still closed, and after he gasped for air, they opened wide. But he still wasn't there; it was like no one was home inside him. He was an empty shell, with despair in his expression. He walked with a slight shuffle and made his way to the shelf with his clothes and pulled out a key that he had stashed. It was a master key to all the doors in the hospital. He then moved towards the door and put the key in before unlocking it.

His head jerked rapidly again, then the door opened. Travis stumbled out. A nurse doing her nightly rounds was coming from the lobby toward Travis's location, but even without seeing her coming, he stopped and waited. It seemed like he could see around the corner without looking, or something unseen was helping him to see. The nurse quietly opened a door to check in on a resident, and the second her attention was on the sleeping patient, Travis moved forward before she could turn around and spot him.

Walking jaggedly, like a dangling puppet on strings, he continued to Hall 3, then stopped in front of room 304. With a heavy arm, he threw his hand above the door's metal holding mechanism and felt around. He frantically searched until he found what he was looking for: a small black lighter. Before heading back to his room, he unlocked the medical room's door and cracked it open. Again, it seemed like he knew without looking that no one was on the other side of the door. He found a bottle of rubbing alcohol near the cushioned medical chair where patients had their blood taken. He then slipped back down the hall and into his room as quickly as his staggering body could allow, shambling around like he was partially paralyzed. The conversation started again as soon as he entered his room. He whispered to make sure no one heard him.

"You're the only person who listens to me…"

"Yes, of course I tried."

"But… I don't think I should."

Tears rolled down his freckled cheeks, but his face was still emotionless. The smell of the rubbing alcohol took over the room as he poured it over his face and chest, then rubbed it into his skin like it was lotion. Keeping his eyes forward as they turned red from the alcohol fumes, he grabbed the lighter next to him on the bed.

Flick. Flick. Pfff.

After a couple quick tries, the lighter lit up with a bright orange-and-blue flame. Travis held it in front of his face, then slowly pulled the flame toward his head and pushed it up to his hair. The room, which had been as dark as night, ignited with an orange glow as bright as the sun. There was no scream, only the putrid smell of burning hair and flesh. The stench made its way to the hallway, where the nurse was still doing her rounds. Right at the moment she got a whiff of something burning, the fire alarms triggered and the entire ward woke up. The sprinklers sprayed water into the rooms and halls and put out the fire. The staff ran chaotically from room to room to get the patients out and into an organized line and bring to them to the safety of the grounds between the ward and the cafeteria.

Outside, many of the patients tried to look in, wondering where the fire had come from. A few minutes later, two fire trucks roared into the parking lot. The patients heard the walkie-talkies of the firemen as they made their way into the hospital with Adam's help. After a quick check of the halls and rooms, they couldn't find the location of the fire until they arrived at Travis's room. They opened the door to find his burned body face down on the floor, with a blackened neck and scalp. The firemen and Adam raced in to check on him. He was still breathing but barely alive.

"How the hell did this happen?" Adam yelled, then noticed the bottle of rubbing alcohol.

"Please, sir. Step away and exit the room. We need to get this boy to the hospital," a fireman said while two EMTs picked up Travis's body and put him on a gurney. A loud grunt came from Travis as they put him down, and the EMTs and firemen rushed him outside to the ambulance. Adam returned to the main yard to tell the nurses what had happened, all while speaking quietly to make sure the patients didn't hear him.

"Travis is burned really badly. I saw an empty bottle of rubbing alcohol next to him."

"How did he get that? Wasn't the medical room locked?" a nurse responded.

Adam shrugged. "He was always stashing things. Maybe he had it stashed somewhere."

Patients were running to the fence to try to get a look at who was being wheeled out to the ambulance, but it was impossible to see around the corner of the building to the parking lot. The questions began, and the nurses could only lie.

"Everything's fine, everyone. Please stay calm."

The staff knew things would only get worse if the residents found out what had happened. And they'd be blamed for it.

Moments later, several police officers came out the back door and toward Adam and the nurses, then waved them over to the entrance.

One of the officers held up a baggie with the burned bottle of alcohol and the lighter. "Here are the culprits," he said.

"I don't know how this happened," Adam responded, his voice quivering.

"We need to review the surveillance footage to find out."

Adam and the policemen went back inside while the nurses and patients waited in the yard. The patients were growing impatient, and the nurses had to act fast.

"Okay, everyone," one of the nurses said. "As you know, we had a fire. We're all okay. Please remain calm. We'll let you back in once they say we can."

"Where's Travis?" Matthew called out. "I don't see him anywhere."

"He was hurt in an accident, but he'll be all right. Everyone, please remain calm."

The nurses continued trying to assure the patients everything was okay. Thirty minutes later, Adam and the policeman came back to the central grounds.

"It looks like he had the lighter stashed in Hall 3 on top of a door," Adam said, "and then he slipped into the medical room and grabbed the rubbing alcohol. He was walking like he was drugged out, like he wasn't all there... Maybe his medications were too strong."

A nurse shook her head. "That's horrible!"

"Let's just hope he'll be okay. The police officer said he's in critical condition but stable. Go ahead and get the other patients back into the building. No one could have seen this coming.

Travis's room will be locked for further investigation, and we'll move the patients in adjacent rooms to another hall for tonight."

Adam and the nurses had their hands full getting all the patients back into the rooms and into bed, while trying to check the computers for water damage and get everything dry. The ward had become a cesspool of turmoil and confusion. It was only a couple hours before Joseph would return to work, once again none the wiser regarding what had happened. It was becoming obvious that whenever he was gone, something malevolent was taking control of the ward.

❧

Joseph pulled up to the hospital and parked his car. While walking up the sidewalk, he noticed two mops and some buckets by the front door. Maintenance was usually a little more careful about leaving their equipment around. Even with all of the weird things going on in his life, something felt off. Ordinarily Adam would buzz him through the door, but he was nowhere to be seen. Joseph punched the keypad and let himself in through the front security doors, arriving in the lobby. Towels and blankets were hanging to dry over the chairs. Patient gowns were piled high, soaking wet, being wheeled down the hall in a gigantic laundry hamper by one of the janitors. The facility's laundry, usually closed tight, was bustling with activity.

"What's this all about?" Joseph asked.

"Dr. Hoffmann!" Jocelyn seemed greatly relieved to see him. She hurried around the front desk. Taking Joseph by the elbow, she led him to a quiet corner.

"Jocelyn? What's the matter?"

"It's Travis. They took him to the ICU!"

"Why? What happened?"

"As far as we know he's alive, but he tried to burn himself."

"He tried? Or he did?"

"He did burn himself. I mean, he obviously tried to kill himself, though. He stole rubbing alcohol from the medical room and had a lighter stashed. Then he lit himself on fire!"

Joseph replayed the last conversation he'd had with Travis just the day before. His final words to him rang into his ears: *Sometimes we do things we don't mean to because we're caught up in our own dilemmas.*

Joseph knew Travis was capable of anything, but he never would have guessed he would do something like this.

"Where is he now?" he asked.

"Central Memorial Hospital."

"Thanks, Jocelyn," Joseph said before turning around and heading to the front door.

"Where are you going?"

"To check on Travis."

Joseph stormed out of the ward with a million thoughts running through his head, slamming the front doors as he left. He knew this must be part of the big picture, but he was also angry it had happened and he couldn't have predicted it. He felt like he was to blame but wasn't sure why.

The diary warned me. I could have saved him.

Travis was the key to this. He would have the answers Joseph was looking for, and Joseph was going to find out.

❧

Joseph arrived at the intensive care unit at Central Memorial, which was only a couple miles outside Cottage Grove. He asked the receptionist at the front desk which room Travis was in. She gave him a pass, and he went directly to the nurse's station. He presented his credentials and asked to see the attending physician. Dr. Witkowsky was a short, cheerful woman, and she informed him that Travis was badly hurt, but stable. Joseph found relief in that, not only for the sake of Travis's life, but also because he could ask him why he had burned himself.

When Joseph entered the room, he saw a body on a hospital bed wrapped in white gauze and bandages, looking like a mummy. His memories of his grandpa's mummy and scroll story briefly came to mind, but he let the thought pass and walked closer. A nurse who was checking Travis's vitals glared at Joseph when he entered, but when she saw he was a doctor, she went back to writing down some numbers before leaving the room. Joseph took a seat next to Travis's bed. Mumbles of pain leaked from Travis's bandage-wrapped face.

"Travis… it's me, Dr. Hoffmann."

Travis didn't respond with words. He only moaned.

"Travis, I know it hurts, but you're going to be okay."

After a few more seconds of weeping and groans, Travis finally spoke, his words muffled by the gauze that covered his mouth and face.

"It wasn't me. I couldn't control it."

"What couldn't you control?"

"The pressure and pain. There was something there with me. I was asleep, and then I felt something come into my room. Then I lost touch with everything I knew that was real."

"Who, Travis? Who was it?" Joseph said forcefully, standing up and hunching over him. "Who made you do it?"

Travis was still dazed. "I couldn't feel anything but pain after that. Even more pain than now. They didn't tell me who they were. I just felt pure dread and hatred the whole time until I woke up here. 'I am in control now' is what it said, and then I totally lost myself."

"What *it* said? It is… an *it*? Not a someone?"

Joseph knew that if he had heard one of his patients saying this a few weeks earlier, he wouldn't have questioned whether or not it was real. "The mentally ill patient didn't see any of that," he would have written in his notes, and then he'd continue his diagnosis and analysis. But not anymore. Now Joseph knew this incident was related to everything he'd been experiencing. This was why he had been warned. He believed Travis. They had a mutual understanding and had both experienced something that wanted to rob them of their sanity.

"I don't know," Travis said. "It didn't feel like a person had walked into my room. It felt like something much... stronger. Something much bigger than any of us. It felt like it knew everything long before we could ever think of it. Something that knows everything that's going to happen. Almost like a god."

"You think a god walked into your room?"

Travis gently shook his head. "No, not a god. But that's the only word I can think of to describe how much power this thing had over me. It's like it came from another place. A place of pure hatred, darkness, and torture."

"So... Hell?"

"Whatever took me over has seen something much worse than Hell."

"What's the last thing you remember?" Joseph asked.

"I remember feeling something hold me down on my bed, and then I woke up. Then something took over my whole body except my eyes. I couldn't see it, as hard as I tried. I could only feel it. But it could see me. It told me it's been watching me for a long time."

"And then what? You blacked out?"

"No," Travis said. "I was taken to a dark, terrible place. Somewhere far away from here, deep in the woods. The shadows surrounded me, and moved back and forth, and then the trees started to bend toward me."

Joseph sat in the chair next to the bed, finally starting to grasp how all these worlds collided. The bent trees were something he was very familiar with. They were part of his childhood memories, and they were part of his grandfather's stories. He even had found one on his walk the other day. Pointing directly to the hospital, it stood in the forest, lurking in the shadows, standing as a reminder of everything Joseph had endured and everything he had seen. Being logical always had been one of Joseph's strengths, and logic told him that Travis's room at Cottage Grove was on the same side of the building as his office, so maybe Travis had seen the strange tree from his window too and had had a bad sleepwalking episode. But logic no longer had a place in Joseph's world; trying to reason with any of this would only drive him further into madness.

He believed Travis. But he couldn't quite make the connection.

"Thank you, Travis," he said. "I'm so sorry," he added.

"You think I'm crazy. I know it. I'll get out of here and go right back into Cottage Grove and be locked away forever, if I don't die first."

"You won't die. And Travis… I believe you."

Joseph couldn't see it, but he could sense it. Travis was smiling underneath his bandages. No one ever listened to him. No one ever believed him. But now, out of anyone, Joseph did. Whether he was falling into insanity himself, he was unsure. Or maybe the insanity was becoming the reality Joseph had never seen before or been able to acknowledge. Either way, he could now see why he had been warned. This was why his memories had come back to him and why his grandfather had left the book for him. It was his destiny to pick up where Grandpa Franz had left off. There was truth in all of it, and now maybe he could find it hidden deep in the shadows once and for all.

Chapter 19

"Fire, fire, burning bright,
take my soul, light up the night.
The flames of truth, both big and small.
Inhale the fumes, brimstone and all."
—anonymous (Centralia, Pennsylvania; 1962)

After his talk with Travis, Joseph felt he was a step closer to understanding. A step closer to figuring out where all this was coming from. He returned to work to do his daily routines, all while keeping the other staff and patients believing he was back to his old self. It was far from the truth, but it was what he had to do to keep moving forward. Nothing suspicious came to mind while at the ward. However, every time he was in his office or in Hall 4, he felt he was being watched. As he peered outside, the tree felt closer than it had before. Either that, or Joseph felt its presence much more.

Joseph finished the day and went home, eager to look at his grandfather's book again. He knew the connection had to be made, and it would be waiting for him there. Once he settled into his home office, he opened the book, scanning it to try to find where the connection was. He read and reread, trying to better understand what his grandfather had been doing with all this, but he came up empty. His eyes grew heavy, so he laid his head on the book and fell fast asleep.

"The misery, damn it! It's the damn agony you put us through!" A patient strapped to a wall was having a discussion with two nurses in black gowns. "You keep letting us beat our heads against the wall until it's time to take us to the cellar again."

The man apparently was angry about something, but Joseph was unsure why he was even there to witness this. It wasn't a ward he was familiar with. Cottage Grove had white walls with wooden trim, but these walls were cracked and gray, with splatters of rust thrown onto their dull surfaces like abstract paintings made of nightmares. Screams came from every direction in the halls.

"What are you doing to him?" Joseph asked the nurses.

The nurses didn't respond and instead reached over to a metal rolling tray with medical tools scattered on it.

"Where am I and who are you?" His voice echoed as though he were in a deep cave.

"Come here and look for yourself!" one of the nurses said.

He was certain she was talking to him and had responded to his question, but then a man who looked like a doctor came into view, holding a clipboard, reading it thoroughly.

"Is he responding to the treatment yet?" the doctor asked. "Or do we have another crippled soul to deal with?"

"The only response he's giving is loudmouth excuses."

"Then take him to the red room. We'll try again."

The doctor turned around, leaving the nurses to untie the patient and walk him out the door. Joseph felt like he was being pulled further into the darkness of the room, until he heard taps come from behind him. After turning around, he was met with another room, one he recognized: Diane Lynch's. She was holding a baby in her arms, but she was turned away from him and singing a nursery rhyme he remembered hearing her sing before.

"There was an old lady who swallowed a fly.
I don't know why she swallowed a fly. Perhaps she'll die.
There was an old lady who swallowed a spider
that wriggled and jiggled and tickled inside her.
She swallowed the spider to catch the fly.
I don't know why she swallowed a fly. Perhaps she'll—"

She stopped singing, as though she noticed Joseph standing behind her. She slowly turned around and looked straight into his eyes. Her hair was wirier and bushier than usual, and her eyes seemed to peer far back into Joseph's mind. She placed the baby in its crib then walked toward him. A bony, white, fragile arm was held up, her index finger pointed at him, almost as if it had been taken straight from a corpse. Cautiously, she moved farther into the darkness in which Joseph stood.

"You took him away! You took him away from me! You took Jean-Paul!"

"Diane, stop! I didn't take your son!" he yelled back, feeling extremely uneasy with her tone of voice and the tension in the air. She crept further into the darkness of the room in his direction. When each foot went down on the tile floor, it left a muddy footprint behind her.

"Diane, it's me! Dr. Hoffmann! Can you see me?"

"You took him from me! You killed my son!"

"Diane, please. Please stop!"

Diane came closer, until she nearly touched his face, her eyes filled with rage. He scurried to the left, expecting her to turn in his direction, but she kept pointing and walking straight ahead.

"It was you! I know it was you! Admit it!"

She continued pointing and blaming whoever was in front of her until she disappeared into the darkness of the room, and her voice faded. Joseph was in the darkness without a single sound around him. He was trying to figure out where he was—and what any of this meant. The room became directionless. He was blinded by darkness. It was the blackest of black, and he could only hear himself breathe. Stepping forward, he noticed the sound of water splashing and that he wasn't wearing shoes; he felt cold water run over his toes. Looking down at his feet, he realized he couldn't see them. It was far too dark. He took another step, and the sound of water came again.

Am I standing in a puddle? he wondered before taking another step.

He held out his hand, feeling in front of him, waving it back and forth, making sure he wouldn't run into a wall. After a couple more steps and splashes, he felt his hand hit something. It felt hard, but not like a wall. He rubbed his palm down it, trying to feel the texture. It felt like leather and fabric, but then it moved back and forth when he pushed it, as though it were hanging from the ceiling. Joseph gave it another push, and the sound of a chain creaked above him before swinging back and tapping him enough to give him a small nudge. He kept feeling up and down, trying to figure out what it was hanging in front of him, but he couldn't make out what it was.

"Don't trust her."

A voice came from behind him, one he had never heard before.

"I said, don't trust her. She's going to mislead you."

It was a man's voice, but he didn't know whose. Then the sound of a TV flipped on, and the room lit up in front of him. He saw Adam watching a TV show, eating chips and laughing.

"Adam! Man, it is so good to see you!"

"Oh, my! That's, like, my favorite drink too! Wow! We're twins!" said a female voice on the TV. Adam continued watching the show and munching his chips. Quickly, Joseph walked toward him, but as fast and far as he could walk, he couldn't make it to him.

"Adam! Please, can you hear me? I don't know where I am. I think I'm lost—"

When Joseph said "lost," the room spun. Adam and the TV began to age rapidly, like time set on fast forward. The chips rotted. The skin fell from Adam's bones. His skeleton showed through old rags of clothing. The TV became decrepit and rusted, and the screen fractured until it was in a thousand pieces. Cobwebs and grime took over the desk. Startled, Joseph backed up until he hit whatever was hanging from the ceiling behind him. He turned around, but the glow from Adam's desk light wasn't strong enough to let him see.

"Joe, are you still working? It's almost lunch. I thought we were going to meet today."

Joseph knew this voice, and he remembered the conversation—the last conversation he'd had with Helen before she'd gone for the run that ended her life. When he turned back around, Adam was no longer sitting there. It was him, Joseph, sitting at his desk, on the phone with Helen, saying he couldn't have lunch with her because he had to work. The conversation continued, and he could recite every one of their last words to each other. He could see himself talking and looking down at his desk, while getting angrier and angrier at her for blaming him for not having time for her that day.

"Go meet her, you idiot! You have to meet her!" Joseph yelled, as if he could change the past. "You have to. You'll lose her forever. Stop working and go! You're making a huge mistake!"

His voice echoed through the water-soaked room, but it didn't change a thing. Then a shape took form behind his other self while it was sitting at his desk. It was a light. The same light he had seen in his kitchen. It grew in size until it took form. It was Helen, but she was translucent and cloudy. The apparition put her hand on his shoulder. He watched his past self, on the phone, snapping at Helen, while her hand rested on his shoulder in the present, trying to give him a sign of comfort. Helen's warm embrace took over his body as he stood in the dark room observing his past.

"I said, don't trust her." The voice came from behind him, but it wasn't Helen's; it was a man's deep, brain-tingling voice. "Don't let her fool you, Joseph. She isn't here for you anymore. You killed her."

Joseph turned around to find out who was speaking to him, but he placed his eyes on something much worse. It wasn't someone who could be talking at all. It was a body, hung from a rafter, swinging back and forth as though he had just jumped from a chair with a noose around his neck. The dim glow from the office shone onto the body's legs, but Joseph couldn't make out the face, or who it was. Struck with fear and shock, he gasped for air.

Feeling something wet come over his right cheek, he realized he had fallen asleep, and apparently had been drooling. He opened his eyes then locked his vision on something he had been searching for, there at the bottom of the story of "Catori's Curse."

"Some claim the forest knows where her spirit roams still to this day. The trees will always lead the way, pointing both the living and the dead in the direction of her restless soul."

Travis, Joseph's memories of his grandfather, "Catori's Curse"— it all involved these strange trees. Joseph shut his grandpa's book and looked at the clock to see how long he had been asleep. It was nearing 5:00 a.m. *These nightmares are getting worse,* he thought while gathering his things for work. He had to go back, because he knew someone didn't belong there. But the question was who.

❧

Another return to the ward with another piece of what he'd been searching for. At least Joseph believed he had a new clue to bring everything into view. The diary had warned him about the ward, and now he felt he knew why. It wasn't just coincidence that the memory of his walk with grandpa in the forest and their discovery of the bent trees had flooded back shortly before he had found his grandpa's book. Travis had solidified this by nearly burning himself alive and mentioning the trees. As hard as it was to believe, Joseph didn't feel like he had lost his mind. In fact, he felt saner than ever. He was starting to see how everything was coming together, even as dark and inexplicable as it all was. He'd need to look further into what his grandfather had found out in his work as a psychiatrist. He must have known something no one else did. And he must have figured it all out during the process of losing his mind to dementia, so no one believed him anymore. But Joseph did. He had always believed his grandpa and his stories. All this tumbled around in his brain as though it were an overloaded washing machine. Each dirty sheet and pillowcase that rolled by was another thought or memory he tried to absorb.

When he pulled into the parking lot, an ambulance sat out front with the back doors open. A nurse was crying and talking to one of the medics, and Adam was not at his usual spot waiting for him. The morning sun crept over the forest, barely producing enough light to shine onto the hospital's roof. Joseph felt something very bad must have happened. After speeding up just enough to get to his parking stall a few seconds faster, he grabbed his belongings and raced up the path. Stopping a medic who was walking back from the ambulance, he asked what was going on. The man told him to remain calm, and then a police officer grabbed him.

"I'm a doctor here!" Joseph exclaimed. "What happened? Is everyone okay?"

None of the staff responded. They were all too distraught. The officer holding him back replied instead. "Sir, we've had an emergency. All the other patients and staff are fine. We need you to remain calm and stay here."

All the other patients are fine? Who isn't fine then?

Joseph spotted Adam coming out from the lobby. After Joseph called out his name, Adam rushed up to him.

"He's dead. He's freaking dead," Adam said with tears in his eyes.

"Who? Who's dead?"

"Matthew Quinn. He hanged himself."

"How? Where? How could that have happened?"

"The chapel. He did it in the chapel. He tied himself to the rafters with a shower curtain."

Joseph knew Matthew loved to spend time in the chapel. Everyone at Cottage Grove could sense something wasn't quite right after what had happened with Travis, but now... now Matthew was dead. At that moment, no one knew something wasn't right at the hospital as clearly as Joseph did. While Joseph was trying to make sense of it all, Matthew was wheeled out on a gurney with a white sheet over his body. Joseph knew whatever Matthew had seen before he died must have been exactly what Joseph was searching for. Joseph knew it had to have gotten the upper hand on Matthew's mind and controlled his actions. Just like Travis, Matthew probably didn't even realize what he had done. He was in another place, in another time, experiencing pure terror, while his body and mind made a decision that ultimately would keep him there forever.

Instead of asking Adam more questions, Joseph headed inside. He was going to find something that he knew could help him better understand what had happened.

The tapes of Matthew's preaching.

Chapter 20

"The pain will stop once the shadows are let in, and a dying light
on my journey will be the only fear I know."
—anonymous (Leptis Magna, Libya; 755 BC)

Trying to ignore the nurses' concerns when they walked up to him, Joseph told them he'd deal with the situation with Matthew later. They could tell he was angry... and on a mission. He stormed into the records room and looked through Matthew's files. Eventually he found the box of tapes, each with a date on them. He had heard all of them except one, the one dated the previous day... the day before Matthew's death. Picking up the tape, Joseph knew the only place he could listen without interruption would be in his office with headphones. He put the tape into his bag, along with the tape player.

Faces filled with grief and worry were sprinkled throughout the ward. He could see it, but he didn't acknowledge it. He knew something the rest of them didn't—he knew Matthew hadn't done this to himself. At least it wasn't entirely him. After closing and locking the door behind him, Joseph put the tape player on the desk and put the tape in. The tape reeled back. Once it was at the start, Joseph put on his headphones and pushed the "play" button.

Matthew spoke with a shaken, sorrowful voice. "Ahem. I'm doing this one because I know it's my last one. I've tried to tell everyone, and I've tried to warn them that it's here. Its presence is all around us. It's like nothing we've ever experienced, but at the same time, we all know it very well. As I have lost my mind more and more each day, the darkness became all that I knew, and it took me further down with it because it knew it could. It knew I was weak. I was weak of mind."

Joseph kept listening, trying to hold back the tears that welled in his eyes.

"Look, I know… I know I could keep going and keep trying. But it's gotten a hold of me. It has a grip on everything I stand for. I can't tell if I'm dreaming or awake, and I can't tell if I'm doing any of this because it told me to, or if I'm doing it because I want to. Travis tried to show how. We all will try if it ever gets its way. If I'm the one keeping it here, I have to end this by taking my life. That way it won't keep growing inside us. I can see the past and future tallies of darkness. I can see where it's taking its believers. It wants what we all have. It wants our darkest moments. Our broken minds and broken hearts. Our broken pasts and broken memories. It thrives on that."

A knock on a door was heard on the tape, and Matthew responded to the nurse by saying he was "fine" and would be "going to the group meeting shortly." The nurse let him continue with his recording.

"I know you're going to listen to this, Dr. Hoffmann. You're the only one who can understand. It has a hold on you too. You and I aren't much different. We're made from the same mold.

We just have different ways of expressing it and different ways of understanding it. It has different ways to consume us too. I think my sacrifice will rid it. At least it will rid it for myself and my own pain. Travis understood this. Diane also has what you need to know. It's all about the order of things now. Predictable things in this unpredictable reality."

There was a short pause, and then the sound of white noise took over the speaker. The same white noise Joseph had heard before on the tapes and in the surveillance room. Matthew's voice became lost in it and fractured and glitched out, to the point where Joseph couldn't understand anything he was saying. Then another voice that was much deeper—not Matthew's—was heard. It was the same strange language Joseph had heard before.

"Ohanzee... Wayo... Kapi... Kokipa..."

Then the tape stopped. Someone had been there with Matthew when he had recorded this. Everything Matthew had said shook Joseph's soul. It wasn't a suicide note as much as an explanation. Joseph knew he had to take Matthew's words to heart and take the situation seriously. Everything Matthew said wasn't insanity, but instead clarity regarding what was going on. Whatever "it" was, it was something much bigger than anyone could imagine, and Matthew had understood this. Joseph rewound the tape and listened again to the strange voice at the end. Then he took a pen and paper and wrote down what he thought it had said. He also wrote "Diane" below it, knowing he needed to talk to her. Matthew had said she had what he needed to know, and it was time to figure out what that was.

☙

Room 302

A big black-lettered sign hung in the hallway, as he had seen many times before while entering Diane's room. Diane was sitting with her back to the window, reading a children's book. When Joseph walked in, she didn't even look up. She just continued reading, letting out slight giggles from time to time. Joseph couldn't resist the edgy feeling he'd had from his nightmare from the night before. Looking down at her fingers to see if they were as bony and corpselike as he remembered from the dream, Joseph saw they really were. The hair, maybe not as wiry as in the nightmare, was still spread everywhere on top of her head, with a makeshift bow put in, made from pajama pants. She seemed jittery, but otherwise she was as he always knew her to be.

Joseph pushed his nightmare aside and took a seat on her bed. "Good morning, Diane."

Diane remained silent, reading the book. Joseph looked at the cover and saw a picture of a frog and a forest, with dark shapes of houses in the distance.

"What are you reading?"

Her gaze remained fix on the book. It was obvious she didn't care that he was there, as if she were a child ignoring her father. Joseph wondered if she'd start talking. She always had so much to say, so he wasn't sure why she wasn't talking now.

Maybe she's in shock from everything going on around here lately, he thought.

He was wondering what he could say to open her up. Then it dawned on him that it might be best to flat out say why he was there. There was no longer a divider between him and the patients anyway. It was time to take down the wall he had built.

"Matthew told me you know something I need to know," he said.

Diane looked up from the book and locked eyes with him. Still unsettled from the nightmare and remembering her rage-filled eyes, Joseph tried to maintain eye contact.

"Matthew killed himself," Diane said, her French accent in full effect.

"I know. That's why I'm here."

"You think it was me? I didn't do it."

"No, I'm here because Matthew… Well, let's just say he understood something maybe you do too. Maybe we both do."

"He understood how far it can take you."

Joseph realized she knew all too well what had happened.

"Tell me, Diane. What do you have for me?"

She shrugged. "I don't have anything for you. I don't tell you anything because you're the doctor. The big bad doctor who gives me more medication then takes everything away. My son and my mind."

Joseph realized he had built the wall so tall it would be hard to tear it down. He had to make Diane realize he wasn't the person he once was. Not the person she thought he once was, at least. Even if he told her everything, he knew the nurses wouldn't believe her if she told them.

"Diane, I'm not 'just the doctor' anymore. I *was* the doctor. I was the doctor before all these unfortunate events started to happen. I know I never believed you. I never believed any of it. I never believed the patients and always reached for prescriptions rather than conversations. I know that. But it's something I had to see for myself. I need to know what's going on here, and I need to know what I can do to stop it. I need to know how to save you and all the other patients."

"You don't understand. Any doctor would say that to get me to be 'crazy' in their eyes again. But you don't get it."

"I saw things, Diane. Things I can't explain. Things from my past. I even saw you. I saw you in a dream last night."

Diane's eyes widened, and she began to cry. Rocking back and forth, she shook her head. Joseph knew what he said must have triggered something in her.

"No, no, no, no! You didn't see me. You didn't see any of it. Tell yourself that, please. You didn't see it."

"But I did. I did see it," Joseph said. "You were in my dream. But I saw more in my waking life too."

As Diane continued to cry and rock back and forth, Joseph decided to dig deeper.

"In my dream, you had a baby too. I think it might have been your son."

"My son is dead! How dare you say you saw my son!"

Anger overtook her sadness, and he realized Diane had never said this before. She always believed her son was coming back; he would return to her, and she would be forever happy. Something had changed.

"Why is your son dead? How did he die? Talk to me, Diane!"

He noticed he was speaking the same way someone would about a real person who had died, even though he always believed this to be part of her mental illness. Something had changed not only within her but also within himself.

"Because the man told me so. The whole time, it was just the man. The man told me Jean-Paul was gone, and she took him."

"Who took him?"

"His daughter, the chosen one. The man knew everything."

"Tell me about this man, Diane. Tell me more."

She stopped crying when it became obvious that Joseph believed her now. He wasn't just a doctor anymore and wanted to understand more.

"I had a nightmare," she said. "It was the same one I've had for a long time, but I could remember more about it each time I woke up. And every time I woke up from the nightmare, I'd see Jean-Paul at the window. I'd try to get him in my room, and I'd try so hard that the nurses would come in and give me more medicine. I always could feel his presence, and I'd try to see him one last time. But the medicine kept me numb. It kept me away from him. Then last night it changed. A man came to my window, and I thought it was my son, so I invited him in, but by then it was too late. It wasn't my son. It was a man I'd seen a while ago, but that time he was outside my window looking in. It was dark, but I could see his face. He had paintings covering it, and gray ash on his forehead and cheeks. It was the same man who came to me another time during a storm, but this time he was closer than he'd ever been. I begged for him to come to me, thinking it was my son. But I invited in a stranger who told me things he said I needed to know. I thought he was there to hurt me, but instead he began to calm me. I sat on my bed, and he put his ash-covered hand on my head. He spoke to me in a language I didn't understand, but once the ash was put on my head, I began to understand what he was trying to tell me."

After a brief pause, Joseph urged her to go on, and she continued.

"The man showed me things. Things I thought weren't real. He showed me Matthew and Travis. He told me she wouldn't die unless the darkness died too. He said she's cursed, and we'll all be taken to eternal darkness if we can't rid her of everything she seeks. He watched her die and didn't stop it because he thought it could finally rid us all of the darkness. But it only made things worse."

"Who is she?" Joseph said. "Did he tell you who she is? Or who *he* is?"

"He's the father and she's the daughter. He said it was much like my son and me, but my son is gone forever. His daughter is still alive in the hearts of many. But she's only a vessel for others who came before her. It moved on through her. He said her name was Catori."

Joseph couldn't believe what he'd just heard. His grandpa's stories were true—the truth was there the entire time in the book.

"Where is Catori? Where is she?" He stood up and walked toward Diane in such a demanding way that it scared her.

"I don't know! I don't know where she is!"

"I'm sorry." Joseph lowered his voice. "I don't mean to be so intense. It's… It's been a lot to handle. All of this is a lot to handle. I need to know where she is."

"He only told me she was among us and we need to believe it to see it."

"Thank you, Diane. Thank you for all this."

"Doctor," she said, "you have the darkness. She's already inside you."

Knowing what Diane said was true, Joseph started to walk out of the room before turning around to tell her one last thing. "I promise you're going to be okay, Diane. We're all going to be okay."

Not even sure of those words himself, he made his way out of her room and into the corridor. Still feeling the concern of the rest of the staff and patients regarding Matthew's suicide, Joseph felt like he had to find way to ease it all. The only way he knew how was to keep pushing for what he believed. After walking down Hall 3 and into his office, he looked out the window and saw the bent tree peering at him from the forest.

She's here. She's here at the ward with us. The tree is pointing the way. But where is she? Who is she?

He knew he had to do further research into his grandfather's work. To know what she looked like and how she took form. He had to know how she got into his patients' heads. He was concerned about Diane and the other patients, especially after what had happened with Matthew and Travis. Catori had to be stopped.

Joseph locked his office door before opening his briefcase, pulling out his grandfather's book, and setting it on his desk. He didn't want someone walking in and seeing such a strange book. It was best that he still kept this a secret.

It must be in his notes somewhere.

Joseph felt like he was able to keep the truth from the staff and the patients, but surely Catori knew that he was on to her. That he knew her presence was there. If he kept on that train of thought, he knew it would make him too paranoid to stay at the hospital, so he had to maintain his focus. Expecting his office door to slam open with some huge scary monster at any moment, Joseph kept his head down and pushed his anxieties away. It wouldn't help him to dwell on his fears. Every so often, he glanced up at the tree in the forest then put his eyes back on the notes. Searching from top to bottom for any details he might have missed, he copied his grandpa's notes down and tried to piece everything together.

"It comes in many forms. It isn't always what you expect it to be."

Joseph pondered this for a moment, wondering who, or what, she would be coming into the hospital as, thinking maybe he couldn't see her at all.

Could it be some kind of dark energy? Or some kind of ghost?

"She was the daughter of a man of black magic. The tribe blamed him for her curse since her birth."

Recalling everything Diane had said, he knew her visions had a purpose. *Was Catori's father really there in the room with Diane? Was he a ghost or spirit?*

"Was this the same source for different stories coming from all religions and cultures? Has it always been there with us since the beginning"?

Joseph couldn't help wonder if his grandfather was on to something. *Did grandpa find other stories like this one?*

"They didn't react, even when I tried the red room. I always kept it clean. I always kept within the legal boundaries of the organization. But the darkness was still there. I couldn't find where it came from."

What's he talking about? Were my dreams true? Would he make patients suffer to find out their darkest thoughts and memories? That sounds nothing like the man I remember. But I obviously had no idea who he was anyway.

As Joseph sat back in his chair, it dawned on him how crazy any of this would sound to anyone else. Joseph never could imagine he would believe the things he did now. But he also knew what he had seen, and he knew there was a truth in all of it. He looked back down at the notes.

"A darkness is in all of us. She feeds off it. But how do we rid ourselves of this evil"?

Grandpa seemed to know something no one else did, and no one believed him. No one… believed him.

That last part stuck in his mind.

No one believed him—that's it! She finds her way into those who are misunderstood. She finds her way into those who are never believed. But why would she find her way into me? Or has she? Diane must have known somehow. Why did I see the things I did? The nursery. The light. The dark voice in the nursery. Was that Catori? Was she in my house or in my mind? Or was she something even darker than Catori's ghost? Whatever it is, it's here. But what do I have to make me believe? There must be something else.

He got to the bottom of the notes and read the last one.

"The only way to rid us of darkness is by keeping those we love closer to our hearts than in our minds."

Grandpa must have felt like this is the way it could all end, Joseph thought. *He must have seen a separation of love and hatred, and of things we feel and what we think. But this doesn't make sense for the mentally ill. Even Travis has love for his grandma; he merely acted out of frustration and rebellion. And Matthew loved God. His heart was filled with love. And Diane, all she has is love for her son, whether he existed or not. So why would this evil spirit settle here? Why this ward?*

Joseph felt like his ideas were getting him nowhere. He was starting to give up when a thought replayed through him as though it were on a loop.

Whether she existed or not... Whether she exists...

A lot of what used to be misunderstood and shrugged off as insanity had now become Joseph's reality. He knew he had new eyes and a new understanding, and looking through the patients' files might open up something he needed to know. After logging in and opening the E.M.R. patient files program on his computer, he started with Matthew and began reading. Many of Matthew's symptoms were easily put off as schizophrenia. The voices, the false beliefs, the unclear thoughts. And Travis's rebellion filled pages of his file. There was nothing of note that he could see.

And Diane's son—no one could figure out if he existed beyond her imagination. The files they had for her didn't date far enough back to show whether she ever had been pregnant or had had a miscarriage. She had a standard case of schizophrenia and delusions of pregnancy. Joseph knew all too well what losing a child could do to a person. Having everything planned out, only for it to be taken from you. He understood more about these patients than he ever had allowed himself to realize, and now it had come full circle. He searched other patients' documents and kept coming up short. He looked through Susan's file, the shy girl from room 202. She never said much but was constantly on suicide watch. Nothing in her records stood out. He began to search Jennifer's records. As he looked over her files, she also seemed to have schizophrenia, presenting itself in the usual late teen years. Nothing seemed out of place until he reached the bottom of the signature page that had been turned in when her parents had brought her to Cottage Grove.

There isn't a signature. Didn't we have them sign her over to our care? I'm certain we did.

Looking further into Jennifer's admission forms, he noticed none of the sections were filled out. He grabbed his phone and called the nurses' station.

"This is Dr. Hoffmann. Can you please check the filing cabinets for Jennifer Macklin? I need to see her admission forms. Mine aren't updated on the computer system."

"Sure. One moment."

After a couple of minutes, the nurse returned to the phone. "We don't seem to have any admission forms for Jennifer Macklin. She's the patient in room 407, correct?"

"Yes. You don't have any admission forms at all?"

"None. All I see here are doctors' notes and checkups. We must have had the forms, because she's been here for a while. We should have noticed that kind of thing."

Joseph's heart sank, and a knot the size of a boulder settled in his stomach. He hung up and looked back at the admission form on the computer. No signature, and the only information filled in was from himself and his notes.

But Mr. and Mrs. Macklin sat right in front of me and filled these out. I watched them do it. Did they even exist? Was I talking to ghosts the entire time?

He searched for next of kin, where her contact was supposed to be her mother. There was no family listed. It was as though she never had any parents at all.

It was time to talk to Jennifer.

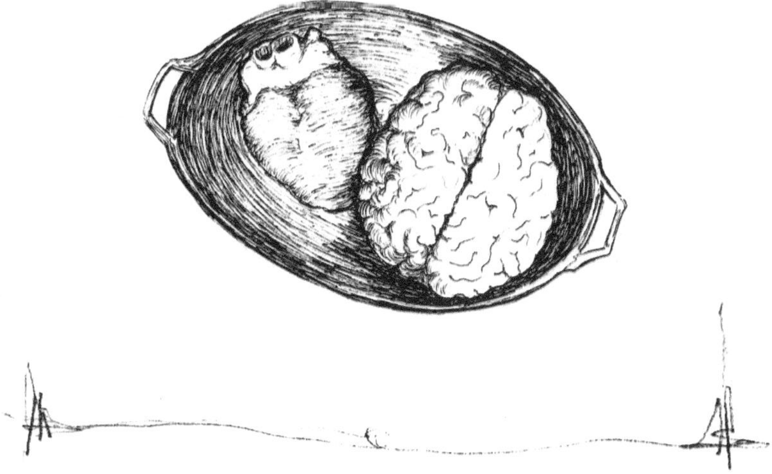

Chapter 21

"The shadow grew into a grisly apparition, and then it held me
down on my bed.
I begged for god to come save me;
She told me he was already dead."
—anonymous (Plymouth, England; 1619)

Walking toward someone—or something—had never been so hard. As Joseph headed to Jennifer's room, fear consumed him. Each step grew harder. Mulling over all the ideas of what it would be like to confront her only made it worse. His love for watching horror films growing up played out in every situation that passed through his mind. Expecting to walk into a room with a demon hanging from the ceiling, he prepared himself for the worst. He first assumed it was Jennifer holding him back from reaching her, but then he realized it was because of the dread of what lay ahead.

He turned into Hall 4. Jennifer's room was situated at the end. With each step came a memory. He wondered why he hadn't seen it earlier. All their talks, the furniture switching around, the neighboring patient asking to move to a different room—it was all coming back to him and made him realize he should have seen her for what she was much earlier. *Maybe Matthew would still be alive if I saw all this sooner,* he mused, then quickly tamed the thought that it wouldn't have changed anything. He was certain she still would have gotten to him if she wanted to. Jennifer must have been made up of everything that was evil in the world; Catori must have consumed her. Overwhelmed by deep anger and a feeling of power, he walked faster toward her room, each stride getting longer. *She probably knows I'm coming. She knows everything.*

His heart beat harder with each step. *I'm doing this for Travis! I'm doing this for Matthew!*

He slammed open the door to her room. Expecting to see some creature, or a demonically possessed human with her head on backward, he was greeted with something entirely normal. Jennifer sat at her desk, doing what she loved most: drawing and minding her own business. She turned around when Joseph entered the room, startled at how forcefully he had thrown open the door. He noticed she could see the strange look in his eyes as she stared at him from across the room.

"Doctor?"

Joseph battled himself, then began to give up.

That's it. I've lost my mind. I've finally done it. I've gone too far. First, I run out of the hospital. Then I start researching all my mentally ill grandpa's stories as if they mean something. I come up with farfetched stories to ease my own pains. I think I see the ghost of Helen. I think some type of demonic energy has taken over my house. No wonder I feel like I understand my patients more. I've become one myself. I believe their insanity because I've gone insane.

Jennifer stared at him, and he could tell she sensed he was about to cry. Joseph was happy the door was closed, and no one seemed to have heard him come in with so much anger. He felt like he needed to talk. He needed to talk with someone, anyone, who might be willing to listen. Jennifer always seemed to be well-spoken, smart, and had a good ear. Joseph decided now was as good a time as any.

With a caring voice, Jennifer stood and helped him sit down on the bed before taking a seat across from him at her desk. He put his hands to his face. He was weak, and the exhaustion of everything he had been going through for the past weeks had finally broken him. And now, here he was, sitting across from a patient, about to ask for help, like she was the doctor and he was the one who should be locked away in the room.

"Dr. Hoffmann, are you okay? You don't seem to be doing very good…"

"I'm fine. I'm fine. I have to be fine."

"It's okay. You don't have to be fine. None of us has to be fine. We just have to look inside sometimes. See what's bothering us and take care of it."

"I'm sorry. I'm sorry I ran in here like this. I'm sorry for everything."

"Don't be sorry, Doctor. You haven't done anything to me to be sorry for."

"I never meant to hurt you. I never meant to shrug you off that day."

"What are you talking about?" Jennifer asked.

"You died because of me. I killed you!"

Jennifer looked alarmed. "You didn't kill anyone. What are you talking about?"

The feeling of Helen's presence was overwhelming. Holding himself deep in his darkness, Joseph let out all the pain and grief he had kept inside him over the years. The part that knew he was talking to a patient was slowly overtaken by the part that thought Helen was sitting in front of him.

"I miss you so much. I want you here. I want you back. It's all I've ever wanted since that terrible day. I want our dreams of having a family to come back. I want our baby."

"Okay... I think I should call the nurses in here if you keep being weird like this, Dr. Hoffmann."

Joseph looked up with eyes filled with an ocean of regrets and realized he wasn't talking to Helen. He was talking to Jennifer. Extremely embarrassed, he stood up.

"I'm so sorry. Oh, my God, I didn't mean to... I didn't realize... I was just..."

"It's fine. We all have something inside us that keeps us somewhere else."

"What... what do you mean by that?"

"We're nothing but empty shells of our past, aren't we?" Jennifer said. "And some people, like you, are just empty shells. Empty with nothing to live for anymore."

Joseph's heart shuddered. He remembered Jennifer liked to take the lead in conversations, but it felt different this time. He felt her hatred. He felt her anger. He stood up, ashamed beyond all belief, and decided to leave the room. It felt very uncomfortable to stay there.

"Where are you going? You aren't going back to work, are you?"

"I need to keep on my rounds. I'm sorry you had to see any of this."

"Joe, if you keep working like that, you're going to die of a heart attack."

He knew only one other person who'd ever said those words to him: Helen. He turned around and looked at Jennifer, who was now standing up and facing him with a smile.

"What? Cat got your tongue again?"

Jennifer laughed, and Joseph noticed a reflection in the mirror behind her. He saw blonde curly hair, even though Jennifer had long, black hair. The person in the mirror was Helen.

"She isn't coming back for you. You don't have anything she wants. Trust me—you only have what I need."

He knew what he was seeing was the truth, finally laid out perfectly in front of him like an open book. Jennifer *was* evil. Feeling hopeless, he started to run for the door, but the door handle clicked and locked before he could open it. Joseph turned around, terrified of what he might see.

"Why did you kill me, Joseph?" Helen's voice came from Jennifer. "Why didn't you give me just a minute of your time?"

"You aren't Helen! You aren't Helen! Stop!"

Joseph covered his eyes, afraid he might see Helen instead of Jennifer standing there. He didn't want to believe Helen would blame him when he already blamed himself. A knock came at the door, and a nurse on the other side tried to open it, but she couldn't get in. "Dr. Hoffmann, is everything okay in there? Unlock this door!"

When the nurse tried to get her key in the door, mud blocked the keyhole and she couldn't get it in. The sound of white static took over all the TVs and walkie-talkies in the hospital, growing louder and louder until the ear-piercing sound was unbearable. Jennifer's laughter grew deeper, and an unknown force danced vigorously around Joseph's body.

"It's time for lockdown, Dr. Hoffmann," Jennifer said, her voice bouncing off the walls like a whimper coming straight from Hell.

☙

The day had turned to night, and the ward was locked down by Jennifer's darkness. The entire hospital was blacked out, and the only time Joseph could see anything was between the strobes of the emergency lights flashing from the hallway. He knew he was locked up with something malevolent. A darkness had seeped deeper into the ward's cracks than anyone ever realized it could. The halls were silent except for a sound from the end of the hall, where a klaxon was buzzing from the fire alarm box. Joseph was afraid Jennifer had killed everyone except him. Between the flashes, he tried to make his way to the door and get out, but his vision became blurry, making it increasingly hard to see as he tried to move toward the door. He fell to his hands and knees, then crawled toward the door, dizziness taking over his mind and numbness taking over his limbs. He felt like he was drugged, but he wasn't sure how or with what.

A voice came spinning around him, weaving in and out of the alarms. "Feels good, doesn't it? Oh, that's right—you can't feel anything right now. I hope the little prick of the needle didn't hurt, Doc. It'll make you feel better."

He couldn't tell which direction the voice was coming from. But he was certain it was Jennifer toying with his mind.

Joseph tried to gather his senses enough to focus on the door. After a couple of staggering slides on his knees and hands, he got his grip around the door handle. To his surprise, it was now unlocked. He budged it open. The strobing lights were still coming from the hallway, and the windows had been covered with rusty iron plates, making it impossible for any other light to seep in. He was locked in a building with nowhere to go. The ward had turned into something from a nightmare, and he was buried alive inside it. The walls were stained brown, and the tile floor had become brittle and warped, with cracks and fractures throughout. The smell of death lingered everywhere.

Joseph locked eyes onto the far side of the darkly lit corridor's wall. Strapped against a rusted chain link fence and pipes protruding out from the wall wrapped in hospital bandages was his sister, Anna.

"Anna! Oh my god!" Joseph screamed while trying to find enough balance to come pry her from the wall.

Between the strobes, the bandages began to unravel, and Anna began to contort in unsettling ways. Her arm bent behind her head, and the bandages fell to the floor as if they were being dropped in slow motion. Then between another flash of the strobe, she was gone. When the light flickered out from down the hall, a crackle of laughter spilled out between the darkness and the light. It had become obvious to Joseph that Jennifer had altered his reality and everything he believed to be true. She was there to take his sanity.

As the laughter faded, another voice came over the intercom, heavily distorted, speaking as though the hospital were under normal operations. "Paging Dr. Hoffmann to the nearest telephone. Paging Dr. Hoffmann."

He tried to get up. The drugs were stronger than he could take, and he couldn't stand for long as he held himself against the wall and tried to make his way to the lobby. After a few more unsteady steps, moans and cries came from Travis's room.

"Travis… are you in there?"

"Yes, please help me. Please! I'm stuck in here!"

Through his drugged haze, Joseph was unsure if this was actually happening. He felt around and eventually grabbed hold of the door handle and tried to open it.

"Please, please get me out of here!"

"The door—it's locked."

"Please, Doctor! I don't have much time!"

The door handle became so hot that it burned his hand. Smoke came from underneath the door, and screams took over the room. The screams quickly died out, and then the smell of burned flesh overtook the hallway. Joseph knew he had to get out of the hospital, and fast. As he stumbled down the hallway, the white noise started again, and a deep voice reverberated from the lobby.

"Ohanzee."

He kept as steady as he could and moved farther down until another voice came from behind him.

"Wayo. Kapi."

Feeling like someone was following him, almost right behind him, Joseph ran the best he could, eventually falling into a patient's room at the end of the hall. The second Joseph closed the door, another word was whispered over his left shoulder.

"Kokipa."

He fell against the door, trying to catch his breath and gather his senses while keeping out whatever might be trying to get in. The drugs were starting to wear off, and Joseph's vision wasn't as blurry as before. The room was pitch-black, with no strobing lights. Pure darkness surrounded him. An organ played, but the room was so dark he couldn't see where it was coming from.

Where am I?

With a click that sounded like it came from a tape player, someone started to speak. "We are gathered here today to talk about our Heavenly Father. The one true king and our one true glory. The man who knows how to take care of us all and truly take care of his children. Can I get an amen?"

A crowd responded with a boisterous "Amen."

"Thank you. We talk today, of course, about our one true Lord and savior, Dr. Joseph Hoffmann."

Joseph heard the group respond with a couple more "amens" and some chatter, but the room was so dark he still couldn't see anything but the dim glow of the red recording light in the corner.

"Wait. What's this? What do we have here? It… it couldn't be…"

The voice came closer to Joseph, so close that he felt the presence of someone standing over him and breathing onto his face.

"It's him and our prophecies are true! They have been fulfilled at last! He is here with us! Oh, praise the Lord! Our savior has arrived!"

The tape player stopped, as did the organ music and the preaching. Knowing it must have been Matthew's voice, Joseph tried to remind himself it couldn't be. Matthew was dead. Trying to find the slightest bit of light to help him see, he stumbled back, feeling for the door behind him.

Click.

Once the door opened, Joseph found himself face down on all fours. Still finding it hard to hold his head up, he could only see the floor in front of him between the strobes in the hallway. When he gathered his focus, Joseph was met with two feet covered in mud. He slowly moved his eyes along the feet and up to the legs, noticing they were wet and half-covered with a dirty patient gown. The farther up the gown his eyes traveled, the wetter and dirtier the cloth became, until he saw hands dangling down on each side of the gown, covered in mud and gray ash. A loud gurgling and choking sound came from above. Cautiously, with blistering fear, Joseph moved his eyes even higher. On top of a pale wrinkled body with a broken neck, was a head leaning sideways and forward, bearing the face of Matthew and looking directly at him. His eyes were white, with no pupils, his mouth pried open with fluid coming from it. Matthew tried to say "Dr. Hoffmann," but with no jaw or tongue, it sounded like choking fluids were stuck between the letters. As fast as Joseph laid eyes on Matthew's mutilated face, Matthew was pulled by a rope into the ceiling's tiles. Joseph was being tormented, and there was no way to stop it. Hopelessness couldn't even touch the surface of how he felt.

The flashes. The misery. Why won't it all stop?

Joseph built up enough courage and energy to make it to the end of the hall, where he opened the door to the lobby. He could see the rec room, where a TV was affixed in the corner. White static consumed the screen, with a male and female voice coming in and out from a program on the television. The flicker of the TV was faster than the strobing of the hallway lights, and the room was becoming bright white. Joseph held himself up long enough to make it behind the reception desk and tried once again to gather his composure. But there was no hope for making sense of any of this.

Whatever was here was far too strong for him. It had a hold on his existence and was taking over his mind one second at a time. This time it wasn't a nightmare. It was really happening, and he was stuck inside his own misery and a hospital from hell.

After a brief pause, Joseph moved toward the front door but heard a voice at the security desk. "Hey, Doc. Why are you here so late?"

It was Adam, but he was nowhere in sight. Only his voice remained, coming from where he usually sat each night.

"Hey, Doc," Adam repeated. "Why are you here so late?"

The voice came yet again, repeating like it was on a recorded loop.

"Hey, Doc. Why… arrre… youuuuuu…"

The voice came back again for another loop, then slowed down into a low-pitched rumble, eventually coming to a stop. Joseph moved past the front desk and made his way to the front door, trying to get out as fast as he could. After pulling himself up the wall with his limp body, he was able to punch his PIN into the keypad.

9-1-6-5

Nothing happened. The door's access system was dead. The electronic keypad wasn't illuminated, and he had to find a way to get power back to it. Joseph remembered the generator was in the security office. He would have to throw the breakers to get the power back on from there. The drugs were coming in waves and hitting him in the head like a train full of pain and confusion, but he kept fighting it, knowing if he gave Catori any more power she might consume him entirely. He moved as quickly as possible to the security room, then jolted open the door before shutting it behind him. None of the screens were on, and it was too dark to see, so he cracked open the door just enough to see where the breaker box was by using the light from the strobing alarm.

There it is.

Across the dark room was a gray box with all the breaker switches. He finally felt like he had some hope. Still fighting the drugs buzzing in his head, he moved toward the box. After opening up the panel, he flipped the switches that were pulled down. This was the moment of truth.

Click. Click. Click.

With a sizzle of electricity, the TVs in the surveillance room switched on behind him, lighting up the room. He turned around, praying for all this to end, but he knew deep down it wouldn't be that easy. Looking at the screens, Joseph saw that each monitor showed something different. And none of them were showing the rooms at Cottage Grove. Each screen showed a memory of Joseph's. One was with Helen, when they had visited Rome. The next one was in the nursery, when they had put the crib together. Another screen showed him sitting with Grandpa Franz, listening to his stories in the living room of his parents' house. And another display was filled with the memory of his mother getting him a brand-new red bicycle when he was a child. The visions kept rotating and switching around. Looking at them, Joseph began to break down even more. His past was right there in front of him. His whole existence flashed back and forth with memories of better times. Wiping the tears from his eyes, he tried to resist the urge to look any longer, but it was too tempting for him. Drenched in a world of nostalgia, he looked even closer, but then he noticed something wasn't right. In each of the screens, there was something out of place, something he never had seen at the time. A shadowy figure was lurking behind him, hanging over him in every memory. The shadow grew each time the video rotated back through, until it took over the entire set of screens. Then a shadow took over the wall in front of him between each strobe of light that came from the hallway. The shadow was now directly behind him, and Joseph felt its presence stronger than ever. Knowing he had nowhere to run, he was about to give up, but then something came to his mind.

"You always had something I never had. You had drive and passion. Ambitions. That's something many people lack. That's why you got the hell out of here!"

His talk with Patrick had come back to him at just the right time. He heard his friend's voice as plain as day, saying those words. It gave him the last bit of courage he needed to face whatever was standing behind him. Fortified with a second wind, Joseph turned around, ready to face the looming shadow.

But when he turned around, nothing was there. Nothing but the wall across the hall. It was time to run for it.

"Ohanzee."

The voice blared from Hall 4, and the white noise became so deafening that Joseph could barely stand up straight while trying to run for the door.

"Wayo."

Another voice came from Hall 3. Joseph felt it deep in his body, but kept pushing for the door. Between each strobe he saw figures take shape, coming from each of the halls. He was being surrounded by shadows of all different shapes and sizes.

"*Kapi.*"

The figures rushed him, and he ran even faster for the door, hearing their footsteps getting louder and faster, coming toward him. Still fighting the dizzy spells, Joseph knew he had to make it. He had to get to the door and punch in his numbers.

"*Kokipa.*"

The voice grew so loud he knew it was right behind him. He felt someone tug his body, trying to pull him back. He began to punch the numbers into the keypad.

9-1

The hand he was using was pulled back down, so he raised his other hand and continued.

6-5

Both hands were forced down, and screams and moans emanated from all the hallways as the shadows grabbed him from behind. He was being held down, but the door was opening. Yelling as loud as he could and putting all the strength he had left into breaking free from the shadow's grip, Joseph fell through the doorway and found himself outside. The shadows stopped holding him, as though there was something keeping them from leaving the hospital, and with a crash of lightning it began to rain. Joseph landed on the sidewalk in tears.

"Joseph."

A voice came from the wet field in front of him. "Joseph, it isn't done. It's still here."

Expecting another shadow or dark entity in front of him, he was surprised to see Helen. She stood in the middle of the field in front of the hospital, her hair spread outward as if she were underwater. She was as beautiful as he remembered, and he noticed all the trees around the edge of the forest were bent toward her. Crying in exhaustion, he stood up and walked forward.

"Joseph, you have to do what your grandpa asked of you. You have to."

"I don't know anymore. I don't even know what's real. I don't even remember what he wrote."

"You have to remember. You have to remember his words."

"I believe, okay? I believe all my patients! But believing hasn't saved me. It hasn't saved any of them. They're dying one by one."

The storm grew stronger and the lightning brighter, with rain pouring down. Joseph saw the strobes flashing and the shadows still growing behind the door of the hospital.

"You have to, Joseph. You have to remember… It can only come from within you."

Joseph was trying to think of what his grandpa had written, but with a foggy mind and exhaustion taking over, it was nearly impossible to gather a coherent thought. Looking back up at Helen, he walked into the field. More shadows were coming from the outskirts of the forest, following the direction of the bent trees. The shadows slowly became bodily figures that looked like tribal corpses raised from the dead. They walked toward him with skin that was burned and covered with mud, as though they'd been left in the forest to rot after a fire. He knew they were there for him.

"I can't… I can't remember."

Just then, he looked up and noticed the darkness around him. The darkness in front of him. The darkness of his memories. The note from his grandfather came into his mind: "The only way to rid us of darkness is by keeping those we love closer to our hearts than to our minds."

Joseph remembered now, but it didn't seem to change any of this.

The shadows in the ward were still growing, and the disfigured bodies behind Helen were still walking toward them. He repeated the line to himself over and over, hoping it would stop them.

The only way to rid us of darkness is by keeping those we love closer to our hearts than to our minds… The only way to rid us of darkness is… by keeping those we love… closer to our hearts… than to our minds.

The truth was right there. Deep in his heart, Joseph knew this would be the last time he would ever see Helen. They were coming for him, but he realized she was there to save him. He had to rid himself of the darkness that had held him for so long.

"You've found the truth," Helen said. "The darkness lives in all of us. It has since the beginning of time. We have to step out from the darkness before we can live. I love you with all my heart. I always have. And now you have to keep me in yours. Keep your memories forever in your heart and free your mind from the past. If you don't, the darkness will consume you and everyone here. You're the reason she's here. You have to let me go so you can save yourself."

Joseph knew what he had to do. He had always lived his life thinking. Thinking what could be or what could have been. He never believed for a second that there was another way to live. Now he knew he had to learn to feel with his heart and live for what was to come, not what could have been. The moment he realized this and felt it deep inside himself, the heaviness over the ward began to lift. When he felt the pain and agony of his own dark past, the darkness would come back. The ward had become an extension of his own existence, and Helen was there to ask him to let her go. If he held on to his regrets any longer, he could never heal and she would never rest. He kept his focus on his love for Helen and all they'd had. He remembered the good times and remembered her for who she was. As he knelt in the middle of the drenched field, he kept his eyes forward, watching her body slowly dissipate. The people coming from the forest fell one by one, face first into the field, then turned to ash to be consumed by the earth. The shadows filling the ward began to disappear. Joseph's love for Helen moved from his head to deep in his heart. His mind felt at ease for the first time in many years, and the darkness began to subside within him. When the clouds broke apart, the rain started to let up. The sun began to inch over the treetops, and the trees retook their normal shape.

The ground was damp and the frost melted into the air, creating a shimmering fog that seeped into the sunlight.

Joseph's grieving had begun.

Chapter 22

Precisely at 7:30 a.m. on the dot, Joseph arrived at work. A long day lay ahead of him. A few new patients had checked in over the weekend, and he had to get to know them to start their diagnosis. It had been a week since the nightmare had happened. It had been a week since the staff believed Jennifer had run away. Joseph dealt with the phone calls and police reports for five days straight. But he knew deep down that the reality was not as obvious as it seemed. Jennifer hadn't run away. She just had no more pain or grief to keep her there. After Joseph punched in his code, he spotted Adam at the security desk.

"Adam, you're finally back. How was your vacation?"

"It was good, nice and relaxing, right on the beach. My fiancée couldn't get enough sun, though, so my poor pale skin ended up a little more on the pink side than tan."

"I can tell, lobster boy."

"Hey, at least no more farmer's tan! So, Doc, I heard a huge storm happened while I was gone last week. Power knocked out and even the security cameras went down."

"Yeah, it was a big one. Lots of rain and thunder. The hospital's power grid was knocked offline for a while."

Joseph knew it would be too much to run through those feelings again, and Adam wouldn't understand anyway. Joseph continued through the lobby, looking down Hall 4. He saw Jennifer's room at the end of the hall through the big square windows on the swinging doors. Stopping for a second to appreciate that the walls weren't stained and the windows weren't covered with iron plates, he saw a new patient moving into Jennifer's old room, her blankets and pillows in hand and a nurse helping her in. Continuing toward his office, he saw Susan being her shy self, sitting on the floor. She reminded Joseph of Jennifer, sitting quietly with colored pencils in hand, drawing on a big sheet of paper and singing to herself. He recognized the melody of the song she was humming. It was a nursery rhyme he'd heard, but couldn't remember where.

"Good morning, Susan," he said to her along the way.

She gave him a little smile and went about her drawing, humming the nursery rhyme's melody. Joseph felt a little unease and wasn't sure why, but he continued on. When he arrived at his office, he placed his briefcase on the floor next to his desk. It felt good to be back to his normal routine.

Flip on the coffee machine.

Pour coffee.

Turn on the computer.

Wait for the screen to load.

Before the computer fully turned on, he caught his reflection in the screen. He realized he had a piece of his breakfast on the corner of his lip and quickly wiped it off with a tissue, knowing Adam must have been staring at it the entire time Joseph was talking to him.

Once the computer turned on, he looked through his files for the day and to see who the new arrivals were. Seeing Matthew's files wasn't easy. Knowing they were backed up on the hospital's server, he decided to put them in the trash. With one hard click of the mouse, the folder was gone, making a little crushed-paper sound as the trash emptied. Joseph knew it would be easier to let it go if he wasn't looking at those files every day. Realizing his coffee was getting cold, he took a few last sips and placed the mug down. A light on the office phone flashed, reminding him of the strobing lights during the storm. A few seconds later, a ring came and he picked up the phone.

"This is Dr. Hoffmann."

"Doctor, we have a couple of gentlemen here to talk to you."

He wasn't expecting anyone that day. "Who are they?"

Jocelyn pulled the phone away from her mouth just long enough to ask the men their names. She then continued, sounding a bit confused. "Dr. Theodore Tugman and Thomas Greenfield. They said they're from the Branson Center in Seattle."

Joseph's heart sank, and his mouth dried up, feeling like sandpaper making its way down his throat. "Oh… okay. Please send them back."

"Are you sure you're okay to talk with them?" Jocelyn asked, seeming to know the men shouldn't be there. "Should I tell them you can't take any visitors right now?"

This had to do with his grandfather. Another secret that needed to be exposed. The anxiety began to build again, and he felt like it would never stop. He wanted to forget about everything that had happened. Forget about all the memories and all the lies. He knew his willingness to forget would never be enough, so he decided to talk to these men and find out why they were there.

"Everything's okay. Please bring them to my office."

When he hung up, he knew it would be only a few short minutes until they arrived at his door. Joseph felt his heart pound in his chest—a feeling he remembered well. He stood up and straightened his jacket, trying to look and act as normal as possible. He brushed off his chest along each side and fixed the pens in his front pocket. He heard the door at the end of the hall open and two men talking.

What do they want with me? Just act normal. Just act normal. They don't know about any of it. They couldn't. No one does.

He spun the ring on his finger until it felt like it was turning into lava and getting too tight. With a deep breath, he took it off and put it in his desk drawer. The steps were getting closer, and he knew they would arrive at any moment. The door started to open, and with another deep breath, Joseph put on the best fake smile he could.

"Hello, gentlemen," he said. "How can I help you today?"

*"The darkness goes by many names,
and I've seen it take all that I love, including myself."*
—Dr. Joseph Hoffmann (Cottage Grove, Oregon; 2019)

Patient Medical Records
www.cottagegrovehospital.com/login
Login: DrHoffmann
Password: Helen1993

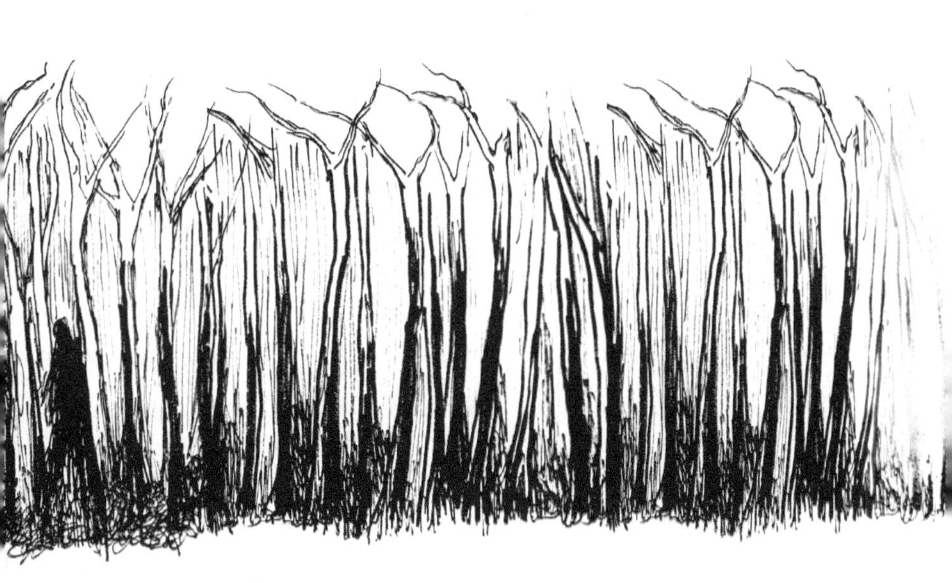

Acknowledgments

A very special thanks to Sarah for all that she has done, both within these pages and beyond. Thanks to my mom, dad, friends, and family; you have always stood by me. Special thanks to my sister Annie, for her extra insight and help. Thanks to Fabio for his illustrations and ongoing art concepts, Basil for the dirty font, Angela Brown for the great feedback and developmental edits, and to Matt and Tommy for their web skills on the medical records server. Thanks to Aaron for being the voice of Matthew. Thank you to Nat for the cover design.

Thanks to those who read this with the same sparkle in their eye that I had while writing it.

It keeps me moving forward.

Thank you to Steven and Leya from Genius Books/New Galleon for taking this book to new heights, with the same passion that I had while working on it.

You are all loved.

About the Author

Slade Templeton is a Switzerland-based, American-born musician, record producer, and author, living and working in Bern. Since a very young age, he has had a passion for anything dark, including art, music, and film. As he often produced piano concerts and recitals for his family at the age of five, titling the pieces "The Storm" and "Nighttime Fairytale," to name a few, it was destined that his world of music and storytelling eventually intertwined. Having written stories with grandiose plots and twists since a young age, he planned to write novels one day.

Truth of the Shadows became his first.

For more information visit: www.sladetempleton.com